HEART
QUEST.

*More to Love*

HeartQuest brings you romantic fiction

with a foundation of biblical truth.

A........ ystery, intrigue, and suspense

....ese heartwarming stories of

....nen of faith striving to build

....at will last a lifetime.


....Quest books sweep you

....f God, who longs for you

....rsues you always.

# Like a River Glorious
## LAWANA
# BLACKWELL

HEART
QUEST

*Romance fiction from*
Tyndale House Publishers, Inc., Wheaton, Illinois

**www.heartquest.com**

Visit Tyndale's exciting Web site at www.tyndale.com

Check out the latest about HeartQuest Books at www.heartquest.com

**Library of Congress Cataloging-in-Publication Data**

Blackwell, Lawana, date

   Like a river glorious / Lawana Blackwell.
      p.   cm. — (Victorian serenade)
    ISBN 0-8423-7954-1 (alk. paper)
    1. Man-woman relationships—England—Fiction.   2. Swindlers and swindling—England—Fiction.   I. Title.   II. Series: Blackwell, Lawana, 1952- Victorian serenade ; 1.
PS3552.L3429L54   1995
813'.54—dc20                                  95-14548

Printed in the United States of America

10   09   08   07   06   05   04
 9    8    7    6    5    4    3    2    1

*To Buddy, my husband and best friend—*
*and a godly example to our children.*
*Your constant, loving encouragement*
*has given all of us the confidence to pursue our dreams.*

*With special appreciation to Gilbert Morris,*
*my writing mentor and friend.*

Like a river glorious is God's perfect peace,
Over all victorious in its bright increase.
Perfect, yet it floweth
Fuller every day;
Perfect, yet it groweth
Deeper all the way.

—*Frances R. Havergal*

# 1

## 8 April 1863

Rachel Jones set the globe upon the lamp she had just trimmed and looked again at yesterday's *London Times* lying folded upon the end of the sofa. Dare she? *He's still away,* she reminded herself. And Mrs. Hammond would not wake for at least another hour. Still, she went to the parlor doorway and held her breath. Faintly through the open window behind her drifted the ringing of horse hooves against cobbled stones, the *sweet-sweet-sweet!* of a sparrow in the mimosa tree. But in the corridor, silence. Silence was good.

Still, she had to be careful. She carried the newspaper to the gateleg table where Mr. Moore and Mrs. Hammond took most meals, and positioned herself between table and empty fireplace so that she could watch the door.

The front page gave an account of riots going on in poor neighborhoods of New York, because a recently-passed military conscription act allowed a man to avoid service by paying a fee or hiring a substitute. With limited access to newspapers, nineteen-year-old Rachel possessed only scant knowledge of the progress of the war going on across the Atlantic. And so the prayer she sent up was vague, but she trusted God knew the details.

1

*May it end soon, Father, and may right prevail.*
With trembling fingers she turned to the last pages.

*Scullery maid required, 5 pounds per annum plus room and board, 17 Holland Street Kensingston, letter of reference required.*

The last statement may as well have read *personal introduction from Queen Victoria required* for all the encouragement it gave her. She ran a finger slowly down the column. The locations and positions varied, but every listing demanded a character reference. Until her finger stopped at one on Russell Square.

"'Parlormaid needed, clean and industrious,'" she murmured.

"Thinking of hiring one, Rachel?"

Rachel's heart lurched in her chest. She jerked her hand away from the newspaper. Gerald Moore stood so close to the other side of the table that his shadow lay across the page. How had she not noticed? "I'm sorry, sir. I was just . . ."

"Looking for another position," he finished. There was an almost feminine beauty in the thick lashes sprouting from his heavy-lidded eyes, but the irises were as pale blue and cold as chips of ice, and the aristocratic lines of his face were marred by lips much too thin. He shook his head, clucked his tongue at her. "And after all we've done for you. That really hurts, Rachel."

Cheeks burning, she could not meet his stare but trained her eyes upon his chin.

"But do tell me," he went on. "How will you manage that without a letter of character?"

"They don't all require one," she murmured, ignoring the warning in her mind.

"Indeed?" He sighed and nodded toward the newspaper. "Your naiveté is quite alarming. If you'll turn over to the 'situations wanted' page, you'll notice at least four times more postings, meaning four applicants for every position advertised. Whether or not references are mentioned, why would anyone hire a servant without them, with a labor market so bloated?"

*It's worth taking a chance,* she thought but did not dare say. Pain shot through her jaw. She realized she was clenching her teeth and eased the pressure.

"And besides, Mrs. Hammond and I can read those same advertisements," Mr. Moore went on, folding his arms. "You leave us, and I'll track you down, inform your new employer that we discharged you because you're a thief."

He was bluffing. After all, he spent most of every evening playing cards, and did that not require some deception? Gathering up every ounce of whatever inner fortitude had not been browbeaten out of her in over six years, Rachel raised her chin, forced herself to meet his eyes. "And I'll inform the police about you and Mrs. Hammond."

"Indeed?" His chuckle shattered Rachel's tenuous hold on courage. Leaning forward to rest his hands upon the open newspaper, he said gently, "You may just possibly convince the police to arrest us, but *holding* us is another matter. And while, yes, I'm obviously estranged from my family, my father would still use his vast resources and connections in a pinch. Did I ever tell you that a couple of the London magistrates were his Oxford cronies?"

He could read the uncertainty in her eyes, for the pale eyes narrowed, even as his voice softened. "And when the police let us go—which they'll be forced to do—I'll find you. And it won't be pretty."

This was no idle threat, Rachel knew. He was just vindictive enough. Tears stung her eyes and blurred the smug image before her. "Why me, Mr. Moore? You could hire someone else. I'll keep your secrets."

"Yes, you will," he said agreeably, as if she had just commented on the weather. "And to answer your question, there are three reasons we're obliged to keep you on. First and foremost, you know too much. Secondly, you're a diligent worker."

He was staring at her in such a familiar manner that Rachel was forced to look away.

"And thirdly, we're far too fond of you."

"What's going on?"

Mr. Moore turned. Mrs. Hammond had just stepped through the doorway, raven black hair spilling over the shoulders of her lavender satin dressing gown. For once, Rachel was relieved to see her.

"We were just discussing the news of the world, my love," Mr. Moore said smoothly, crossing the carpet in her direction. Over his shoulder he said to Rachel, "Run along and fetch us some breakfast."

~

"Well, how do I look?"

Turning in front of the long cheval mirror five days later, Corrine Hammond lowered her lashes and curved her lips into a prim little smile.

"Why, as if you just stepped out of a Gainsborough canvas," Gerald mocked, leaning against the wall with arms folded. "Her Royal Highness herself would be proud of you.

Where on earth did you get such a . . . hideously modest frock?"

Corrine laughed, slender hands fingering the lace at the severe collar of her turquoise-colored chambray gown. She nodded toward the four gowns lying across her bed. "Madame Beaufort went pale when I described the designs I wanted. When I insisted, she finally gave the job to one of her assistants." She inflected her voice with a heavy accent. *"Je ne sais quoi!* Zee woman's body is to be displayed, like a magnificent painting. Why do you wish to dress like a nun?"

Gerald gave her a knowing smile. "Yet you still couldn't resist having it tight around your little waist, could you?"

"Lord Burke may be a philanthropist, but he's still a man—at least I *assume* he is." She turned to the mirror again and piled her dark hair to the top of her head, angling her face to study the contours of her delicately cleft chin. "While I'm appealing to his more noble instincts, why not capture the attention of his baser ones as well?"

"The poor fellow hasn't a chance. May as well send for the engravers to start on your engagement announcements."

"That might be rushing things a bit, wouldn't you say?" She released her hair to tumble about her shoulders and moved over to sit at her dressing table. Picking up a brush, she said, "I haven't even made his acquaintance yet."

"A detail that will soon be taken care of, I presume? After all, we've been here three weeks now."

"You should know by now that these things take time."

"Of course they do." His voice took on an impatient edge. "But never *this* much time. After all the research I did to choose this poor devil, I should have thought you would have played your hand by now."

Corrine frowned and pulled the brush through her hair. "You have the patience of a gnat, Gerald. The problem is, you didn't choose a poor *devil* this time, did you? I had to order a complete new wardrobe . . . unless you prefer I call on him in my green silk. Or perhaps that red sateen you're so fond of?"

She heard his sigh, his footsteps. His reflection loomed over her in the mirror as her shoulders felt the weight of his hands.

"I have it on good authority that Lord Burke owns three thousand acres in Gloucester," he said softly, tersely. "He's the biggest fish we've gone after so far."

"Yes, but the fact that he's not married worries me," Corrine admitted. "There is nothing to stop him from going to the police after we've bled him dry."

Gerald shook his head. "The man's a hermit. He wouldn't want the publicity, wife or no wife. So I'll thank you not to question my discernment."

His know-it-all attitude could be so infuriating. Corrine smirked at his reflection. "Then, I'll thank *you* not to question my timing. A woman has an instinct about such things."

"Yes, yes. And your instinct serves us well. But we're very close to being broke again, and we can't keep up the rent on this place for much longer if nothing happens."

"Indeed?" She allowed just a bit of acid into her tone. "I'm glad to hear you're concerned enough over our finances to give up *gambling*."

Pain shot through her shoulders. She dropped the brush and reached up to push at his hands. "Gerald, that hurts!"

The grip loosened. He crouched down upon one knee behind her, chin resting upon her shoulder. "Just remember who you were before *I* found you and taught you how to get what you want," he said. "Would you rather be back milking cows in Leawick again, keeping house in a broken-down hut with a whining brat and that sot of a husband?"

~

The mention of her former life was enough to send a faint wave of queasiness through Corrine. The daughter of a farm laborer and eldest of nine siblings, she had shared a straw mattress with two sisters in a crumbling stone cottage, where there never seemed to be enough room to breathe—leave alone any privacy. At fifteen she married Thomas Hammond, a railway navvy . . . and the first man to ask her. How he had managed even to muster enough courage to propose was beyond her comprehension, for he could barely speak to her without stuttering—even after they were wed.

The privacy Corrine had left her father's house to find was at last realized. The Great Western Railway was stretching an iron arm out toward Shrewsbury, several miles away, and Thomas was absent for days at a time, boarding in company housing. On his rare homecomings he soon realized that his beautiful wife had no interest in anything he had to say, stutter or not. By the time their child was born a year later, he had discovered that a numbing solace could be found in pints of strong black English stout.

The infant, a girl, was a disappointment. Born with her father's sparse, fawn-colored hair and evidence of what could someday be the same weak chin, she was scrawny from the beginning and cried incessantly to be fed. Corrine resented these demands for nourishment, for they intruded upon her newfound solitude. The child was only a year old when Corrine turned her over to a younger sister during the day and found employment at a neighboring dairy farm.

She met Gerald Moore in the spring of 1856. In those days

he still lived off the legacy from his grandfather, and had sought out a secluded setting in order to start penning the novel he had yet to complete. An acquaintance had advised White Hart Inn, an old coaching inn three miles from Leawick. He was out in the garden with pen and paper when Corrine passed him with a delivery of cheese and butter.

"I was hoping the muse would visit," he had said, pale eyes appreciative as he rose to offer assistance with the heavy basket over her arm. "But you'll do very nicely, little milkmaid."

"And you can rot, sir," she had replied, already in a sour mood because Thomas had been home for two days now.

His chuckle had grated in her ears as she continued to the kitchen door, but when she came back outside, he assumed a more humble attitude. "I must beg your pardon for my forwardness, miss. Do say you'll forgive me."

"I don't like fancy gentlemen who make sport of common folk," she had said with chin raised to show him he could not dent her pride.

"Common folk?" His thin lips had curled into an appreciative smile. "*Common* would be the last adjective I would apply to you, miss."

"It's not 'miss,'" she had said.

"Indeed?" He gave a *tsk* of disappointment. "Lucky fellow, your husband."

The following morning she returned, but with no deliveries. They left together that day.

That was ten years ago. He had taught her how to dress, how to speak, and how to carry herself around genteel people with a self-confidence just short of arrogance. She owed Gerald everything. And *he* was aware of that as well.

8

~

Gerald watched her lips tighten in the mirror.

"I'll *never* go back, Gerald," she said. "Even if I have to go it without you."

"Without me?" He got to his feet. "Then perhaps you should, dear. Your sense of gratitude has been sadly lacking of late."

"Gratitude? I believe you owe some to me as well." She twisted upon the bench to glare up at him. "You've gambled away every penny of your settlement. I happen to be the only barrier between you and debtor's prison."

"You know, Corrine . . . you can be quite the bore," he said, and turned away.

"Then why don't you leave if my company bores you so much?"

"Excellent idea." He started for the door, one step, two, three. He could hear the swishing of the brush through her hair.

"You'll be back before nightfall," she said as he turned the knob.

"Not a chance, Corrine." He pulled open the door.

"Gerald . . ."

"I've had enough of waiting upon Your Majesty."

Stepping out into the corridor, he smiled at the sharp rap of the brush hitting the table, the dull thud of the bench toppling to carpet.

"Please don't go!"

He was fully out into the corridor now. Her footsteps padded behind him, and suddenly her arms were about his waist. "Don't leave me, Gerald!" she cried, pressing herself into his back. "I didn't mean that!"

9

"I believe you did," he said, taking hold of her wrists and turning as he unwrapped her arms. "A man has his pride, Corrine. I believe it's time to go our separate—"

"No! I love you, Gerald. . . . I'll *die* if you leave me!"

He released her arms and allowed her to put them about his neck, to lean her head against his shoulder. "There, there," he soothed, stroking her dark hair. He heard a sound and looked up. Rachel stood near the servants' staircase landing holding a tray.

"Take it back," he said.

She made a helpless little motion with her shoulders. "But Mrs. Hammond ordered . . ."

"And *now* I'm ordering you to carry it back downstairs."

~

Rachel's whole face burned as she knelt to polish the scrolls carved into the walnut sideboard in the dining room. A half hour after she had poured the tea down the drain, Mrs. Hammond had rung for another pot. It was awful when they fought—and worse when they made up!

She wondered about the man who was to be their next target. Lord Adam Burke, she had overheard them say, a viscount from Gloucester. Was he married, like Squire Nowells and the others before him? Squire Nowells had been a pleasant man, who tipped her sixpence almost every time he called on Mrs. Hammond. Until he hanged himself, and they had to leave Treybrook in a hurry.

Setting the wool cloth on the carpet for a moment, she reached up to tuck the stray honey brown curls tickling the back of her neck into the lace cap on her head. Poor Mrs. Nowells. And her family. Even though the children were all grown and married, it still had to hurt, losing their father like that. And the scandal it must have caused!

If only Mrs. Hammond and Mr. Moore had never appeared at Saint Luke's Foundling Home in Kingston, south of Canterbury, Rachel's home since infancy. Posing as a married couple over six years ago, the two had offered employment to an older girl. They could not pay much, they had explained in Rachel's presence to Reverend Stockbridge, but they could provide a decent Christian home and adequate meals.

They seemed like angels from heaven that day, for Rachel was on the threshold of her thirteenth birthday, when her stay at the overcrowded institution would have been terminated. Where would she have gone? To the workhouse? Conditions at the orphanage were sometimes harsh, but many a horror story about the workhouses had entered her ears.

*I don't mind the hard work, Father,* she prayed beneath her breath, lest God think she was lazy and did not deserve his help. After all, even at the orphanage, she had spent the better part of her childhood scrubbing and polishing. Physical labor was as natural to her as breathing. *And I do realize our Lord Jesus had a much worse time of it down here. But it's so painful to see them going about hurting people for money's sake! And I hate my part in it!*

A shiver snaked down her back as she thought of another, more compelling reason for desiring to leave. Since their little talk in the parlor five days ago, Mr. Moore did not pass her in the corridor without touching her arm or patting her shoulder—if Mrs. Hammond was not with him. Thankfully, he spent most of his days in bed, and left after supper most evenings.

She sought her reflection in the gilt-framed mirror above the sideboard. A pair of somber green eyes stared back at her.

In her whole nineteen years, no person had ever told her whether she was plain or pretty. But she had good posture, she thought, grateful that Mrs. Stockbridge had admonished her girls to carry themselves erect. In market, Rachel had seen too many servants with rounded shoulders from bending and scrubbing.

Sometimes as she worked, she daydreamed about some decent, kind man coming to her rescue. Like some hero from a fairy tale, he would spirit her away on his horse, tell her she was beautiful. But she wanted no such admiration from Gerald Moore. And she had started locking her door every night.

She had no illusions over his being in love with her. For years she had watched married men succumb to Mrs. Hammond's charms, and had concluded that certain types of men could not be faithful to just one woman. How any woman could settle for a man like that was a mystery to her. *If I ever fall in love,* she thought, *it'll be because the man is faithful and kind, and for no other reasons.* But falling in love was hardly a possibility as long as she lived in this household.

# 2

*Let's see . . . parsnips, bacon, celery, flour . . .*
Rachel took the basket from a hook above the
kitchen worktable on Tuesday morning. *Perhaps
a flounder, if I can get a good price . . .*

She sensed a presence and turned. Mrs. Hammond stood in
the doorway in her wrapper, cobalt blue eyes bleary. "What
have we to eat?"

Rachel set her basket on the table and pulled out a chair,
the legs scraping against the stone-flagged floor. "Here,
missus."

When Mrs. Hammond had taken a seat, Rachel glanced
helplessly back at the open cupboard. Seldom did her mistress
appear before noon, and the marketing had yet to be done.
"The bread's stale and we're out of cheese, but I could cook
up some eggs."

Mrs. Hammond's second yawn emphasized the fine creases
at the corners of her eyes. "Never mind, just tea. Bring back
some macaroons. And some peppermint sticks."

That was a secret the two shared—Mrs. Hammond's fond-
ness for sweets. Mr. Moore disapproved of her indulging in
any foods which might alter her figure, and thus their
income. As tiny as she was, she had a tendency to gain

weight, so he kept watch over her plate at every meal. The pastries and sweetmeats Rachel brought back from market were slipped into a covered crock in the cupboard and spoken of no more.

Rachel pumped water into the copper kettle at the sink, then carried it to the cast-iron range. Behind her, Mrs. Hammond said, "You're not to dillydally at market. I've an important errand for you."

Pressing fingers against her temples Rachel leaned against the range. It was starting again!

"Rachel?"

She turned. "Yes, missus?"

Mrs. Hammond blew out an impatient breath. "I said, I'll want you to deliver a message for me when you return."

*She says it so easily,* Rachel thought. She stepped back a bit, struck a match, and lit the jet. Flames circled the underside of the kettle. *As if she actually believes she's just being sociable by asking that poor man over. As if she did not even recall Rachel being in the same room when she and Mr. Moore discussed him!*

"Rachel!" Mrs. Hammond said irritably. "Did you hear a word I said?"

"Oh . . ." Turning, she gave the woman at the table a reluctant nod. "Yes, missus."

"And don't forget the macaroons."

~

April morning breezes pressed chill and dampness through the weave of Rachel's black broadcloth uniform and stirred the fringes of her grey wool wrap as she left the service staircase. As in most English houses, the kitchen was belowground. Mrs.

14

Hammond, a stickler for tradition, required her to use that entrance exclusively, as befitting her station.

Setting out northward up Charles Street with a basket in the crook of her arm, she sent a fond look back toward the house. It was the smallest they had ever leased, for Mrs. Hammond and Mr. Moore had not received as much money from Squire Nowells as they had hoped. Four white sash windows graced the narrow two-story redbrick exterior, and two dormer attic windows were set in a high-pitched slate roof. A trellised front porch, also white, lent a quaint look to the front.

Inside, walls were papered in subdued colors, greens and blues and browns. The oak floors were a burden to polish, but so beautiful. Chimneys rose from either side, and even Rachel's attic room had a fireplace.

As special as the house was, the location was even more attractive. Charles Street was a pleasant, leafy vista in northwest London, lined with similar terrace houses with cast-iron fences. One had only to walk a block south to come upon the rolling acres of Regent's Park and its delightful Zoological Gardens.

But she could not allow herself to become too attached to the place, for in all probability they would leave London within a year—two at the most. Mr. Moore was probably already researching his and Mrs. Hammond's next mark. That was how he justified his gaming, even when he lost. A winning hand, combined with gin's mellowing of the mind, and people were inclined to chat about what and whom they knew.

She walked a block north, turned west on Acacia Road, and continued two blocks. Housekeepers and kitchen maids returning home with laden baskets nodded sociably or smiled. A girl ceased sweeping the steps of a house long enough to bid her good morning. Rachel returned all greetings in kind, as if she were simply one of their rank with no taint of extortion upon her conscience. The pretense was more for her own benefit than for the sake of those she happened upon. The truth about oneself was a heavy burden to carry about.

The open-air market just south of Marlborough Road Station was thronged with carts of all sorts, from heavy lumbering wagons with teams of four horses, to jingling costermongers' carts with donkeys in harness. The pavement was already strewn with decaying cabbage leaves and other litter. Men were shouting, horses neighing, basket women talking, pie men singing the accolades of their wares, servants gossiping, and donkeys braying.

"Got some fine Kieffer pears here, too, miss," said the young man from whose cart Rachel had purchased produce a couple of times before. His teeth were as crooked as old headstones, and his fingernails grimy from the soil he brushed from his merchandise, but the grey eyes were friendly. "Six for a penny, and perfect for tarts."

He blushed and winced. "Not saying that *you're* . . . well, you know."

"No pears today." She smiled to show that she had not taken offense. "But I'll take four of the medium-sized parsnips and a head of broccoli."

When she had paid him the twopence for the produce in her basket, he cleared his throat and said, "My brother, Tim, rents rowboats at Regent's Park. He'd let us have one for free, if you'd care for an outing of a Sunday."

For a second she felt a bit of panic, as if Mr. Moore and Mrs. Hammond were standing there, privy to their conversation. "I work Sundays."

"Even the afternoons?" he pressed.

"Sorry, it's not possible."

But it was at least nice to have been asked, she thought as she walked away from his cart. From two other carts she purchased a flounder wrapped in brown paper and a half circle of Cheshire cheese. Her basket almost filled, she left the open-air market and hastened past shops standing cheek to jowl on Grove End Road. For once she was the only patron in Nellford Bakery, where she purchased a loaf of bread and a dozen macaroons. The bells from All Saints' Church were striking nine as she stepped out onto the pavement again. Rachel sent a longing look at the shop front three doors down. *Ivan Solomon Gallery* was etched in gilt letters onto the signboard.

*"Don't dillydally about,"* Mrs. Hammond had ordered. Yet Rachel had completed the shopping in less time than usual. *Ten minutes won't matter,* she told herself.

The interior of Solomon's was as cool as the morning air outside. A portly man with lined face and wire spectacles advanced from an arched doorway in the back wall.

"Ah, my good friend Miss Jones," he said. "How are you keeping?"

Rachel returned his smile. "Very well, thank you." A falsehood for which she would repent during her evening prayers, but what was the use in saying otherwise? The truth would only sadden a kind old man. "And you?"

He patted his chest and smiled. "As long as the heart is ticking, I shall not complain. I haff some new paintings. You have time for a look about?"

"Yes, thank you," she replied.

She set her basket out of the way just inside the door. From felt-covered walls hung framed canvases of landscapes and

17

seascapes, cottages and bowls of fruit, gardens and portraits, in oils, watercolors, and charcoals. Mr. Solomon dealt chiefly in estate sales, though he sometimes displayed the work of artists yet to be famous. The portraits interested Rachel the most. She paused at an empty space.

"Did you sell the one of the Welsh princess?"

*"Princess Charlotte Augusta* by Mr. George Dawe. It went to an Italian count." Mr. Solomon gave Rachel a sage smile. "For full price too. But come and see; you will find another just as interesting."

He motioned her to the wall facing east, to a portrait in oil on canvas. "By Sir Thomas Lawrence," Mr. Solomon said proudly.

While the painting was well done, there seemed nothing remarkable in the subject's face—a man appearing to be in the area of forty to fifty years old. Still, Mr. Solomon was beaming like a doting grandfather, so Rachel smiled and said, "Very nice."

He chuckled, folding his arms across his wide girth. "Very nice, you say? Do you not recognize the man?"

She studied the canvas and shook her head. "I'm sorry . . ."

"That is no matter. Stand here for a moment, Miss Jones. What do you see in him?"

She obeyed, focusing her eyes on the pair seeming to stare back. At length she was drawn up into what they seemed to be saying.

"He's a very kind man," she guessed. But that one was easy. "Yes, go on."

"And he's suffered bitter disappointment."

When Mr. Solomon did not confirm that, Rachel turned to

him. He gave her a gentle smile. "Have you heard of William Wilberforce, child?"

"No, sir."

"He devoted all his energy toward ending slavery in Britain, but did not see it happen in his lifetime. Hence, the disappointment. By painting Mr. Wilberforce's portrait, Sir Thomas allowed us to see not only the noble gentleman's face, but also a glimpse into his mind. And now do you understand the power of art?"

"Yes," Rachel murmured as goose prickles raised on her arms. She studied the portrait with a new respect. *If only* . . .

The quarter-past chiming of All Saints' bells brought her back sharply to the present.

"I have to leave now, Mr. Solomon," she said. "But thank you."

He inclined his head graciously, grey eyes crinkling behind the spectacles. "It is my pleasure, Miss Jones."

The smile Rachel gave him was half gratitude, half apology. "And thank you for not minding . . . that I never buy anything."

"Ah, but it is a compliment to my collection when an artist visits."

"I'm not—"

"Not an artist?" He shook his head. "That would surprise me greatly. I am seldom wrong about people, Miss Jones."

She opened her mouth, closed it. Since leaving the orphanage she had not allowed anyone a look into that aspect of her life. It was the one part over which she had a measure of control, and by keeping it private, she could keep it safe. From what, she was not certain.

Mr. Solomon was regarding her with infinite patience. And

he was not the sort of person who would destroy someone's dreams, she reminded herself. *He'll keep your secret.*

"I'm not an artist," she insisted first. To declare otherwise when surrounded by the fruits of true artists would seem almost a sacrilege. "But I'm fond of sketching people."

"Indeed? And for how long have you done this?"

She had to think about that one. "Starting when I was eight or nine, whenever I could lay my hands on a scrap of paper and pencil or bit of coal. Now I use charcoal pencils."

"But haff you never worked with paints?"

"No, sir." She could neither afford them nor lessons to learn to use them, but she could not say this without making Mr. Solomon pity her, or worse, assume she was asking for charity.

"You haff people sit for you?"

"Oh, no, sir. From memory."

Whenever she happened upon a face which captured her interest, she stored it in her mind until she could commit it to pencil and paper. Most belonged to those commonly looked down upon as the dregs of society—chimney sweeps, rag and bone collectors, careworn fishwives and the like. They had much more interesting faces than those whose paths were easier.

"You will show me some of your sketches, yes?"

"I couldn't, Mr. Solomon." She shook her head. "They're not very good."

"And who has told you this?"

"Well . . . no one else ever sees them."

He wagged a finger at her, but with an understanding smile. "No good thing can happen to you without some risk, Miss Jones. When I bring my family from Kiev forty years ago, I did not sleep for days for fear that it was not the right decision.

20

Even when we came to London, life was difficult, and so still those thoughts would not leave my mind."

Suddenly Rachel's sufferings seemed insignificant by comparison. "I'm so sorry."

"Sorry?" Mr. Solomon's brow creased above his spectacles. "Shame on me for making you sad! My family has a good life here, Miss Jones . . . the best life. Had I listened to my fears, I shudder to think where we would be today. And so one day you will tell *your* fears to go away, and will bring some of your work here for an old man's opinion."

~

*Oh where, oh where is my little dog gone . . .*
*Oh where, oh where can he be?*
*With his ears cut short and his tail cut long,*
*Oh where, oh where can he be . . . ?*

Rachel sang softly as she put away the food. Until now she was not even aware her mind had memorized the words and tune once heard from an organ grinder, for seldom was her heart light enough to prompt her to sing.

The goodwill from visiting Mr. Solomon had accompanied her all the way home, fortifying her like a bracing wind against the back. But the tinkling of the bell marked *parlor* brought her back to unpleasant reality.

She hurried up the service staircase, down the corridor and into the room. Mrs. Hammond sat upon the sofa; Mr. Moore stood upon the carpet casually juggling five walnuts. He was quite good, and once in a rare genial mood informed Rachel he had won many a wager in his Oxford years for juggling raw eggs a certain length of time without breaking them.

"Ah, there you are," he said, hands not breaking their circular rhythm. "I'm engaging a hansom to carry you to Lord Burke's house."

"A hansom, Gerald?" Mrs. Hammond said, and sighed. "Will you *stop* that?"

"From what I've learned, the man is quite democratic toward his servants." Mr. Moore caught the walnuts, one by one, and replaced them in their bowl on an occasional table. Sitting down beside Mrs. Hammond, he said, "We cannot afford to have him think you would send your maid walking two miles and back on an errand, or have only the means to put her on an omnibus."

Rachel stood before her employers with hands clasped behind her back and face ironed of expression, while memory served up scenes of herself being sent on four-mile walks to Mrs. Hammond's favorite bakery in Manchester, after Mr. Moore lost the horses and carriage in a game of faro.

Mr. Moore turned again to Rachel. "Of course, we don't expect that you'll actually be invited to *speak* with Lord Burke directly. But servants are notorious gossips, and word usually gets around to their masters. So you must appear grateful for Mrs. Hammond's thoughtfulness no matter who is about."

"Your livelihood depends on this, too, Rachel," Mrs. Hammond added. "So take our instructions to heart."

Crossing his legs, Mr. Moore sank back into the sofa cushions. "Now, what are you to do after delivering the message to the housekeeper?"

"I'm to say that Mrs. Hammond requests the favor of an immediate reply, if at all possible."

"Very good. We're expecting you to come back with an answer, so don't fail us."

22

The weight of their scrutiny added to Rachel's discomfort, and she longed for the solitude of the kitchen. But she had to make certain she clearly understood the instructions, for Mr. Moore had once struck her when she had failed to obey him to the letter. Now more than ever, she did not want his hands on her.

"What shall I do if Lord Burke is away?"

"He'll be there. The man's a virtual recluse." Mr. Moore shot Mrs. Hammond a self-congratulatory grin. "You'll see that I did my research well this time. He even sends his charitable donations by messenger or post—never in person. If he ventures out at all, it's in the confines of his walled garden. I gather none of his neighbors has even seen him."

Nervously, Rachel twined her fingers behind her back. "Then why is Mrs. Hammond asking him over for tea, if you please?"

Mrs. Hammond let out another great sigh, as if instructing such a simpleton had become a wearisome task. "I'm not supposed to *know* that he never makes calls, Rachel. We're counting on his reputation as a gentleman. When he reads the urgency in my letter, he'll simply be compelled to invite me to visit *him*. That is, if you've performed your duty correctly."

"Yes, missus."

"Now," Mrs. Hammond continued, "is your good uniform starched and pressed?" While lavish with purchases for themselves—when they had money—the two expected Rachel to provide her own clothing on the two shillings they grudgingly doled out to her most weeks. Their only contribution to her wardrobe was a crisp black poplin gown with a ruffled white organdy apron, and a lace cap with ribbon streamers. It was

23

only a tool to be used when appearances mattered, however, and not to be worn while scrubbing floors or laying fires.

Her lips pushed out another "Yes, missus," while her mind said *I'll go to the workhouse. I'll pack my bag and slip out.* But even as she resolved to do so, she recalled Mr. Moore once reading aloud a newspaper account of how some poor wretch had gotten an earlobe bitten off by a rat in one of those places on the East End. Perhaps Mr. Moore had only pretended the words were on the page, but then again, what if it were true?

Shuddering at the memory, she focused her eyes on the chintz-draped windows across the room and forced herself to block out the argument that was going on in front of her. She made a mental picture of Mr. Solomon. *Was my father like him? Kind to everyone he met?*

She realized Mr. Moore was speaking to her.

"Did you hear me?" he asked, looking at her expectantly.

"Ah . . . I'm sorry, sir."

"I said, nip upstairs and change your clothes."

# 3

Too soon the hansom cab was moving northward up
Abbey Road. The neighborhood of Saint John's
Wood had an atmosphere of quaint tranquillity,
with its shaded cobbled streets and mansions with vast gardens
behind stone walls and cast-iron gates. On Clifton Hill, the
cabby reined the team of red Cleveland bays to a halt outside
the gates of a Georgian home of mellow greystone with a
pillared portico.

The seat creaked as she rose a couple of inches to see more
of the well-tended lawn, adorned with flower beds and stud-
ded with elms and beeches and a silver maple. No sign of
life. That, she hoped, was a good sign. *If Lord Burke is such a
recluse, perhaps even his gardener isn't allowed to talk with visitors.*
Perhaps they would even refuse to allow her to deliver Mrs.
Hammond's note! She reached into her pocket, hating the
very texture of the crisp linen paper envelope against her
fingers.

"Miss?" The cabby, a lanky, weathered man with slumped
shoulders, was at the side of the carriage, holding his hand
toward her.

A horse snorted and stamped a hoof. Rachel blinked at the

cabby. "I beg your pardon," she said, taking his hand and rising.

"Shall I wait 'ere for you?" he asked as he helped her to the pavement.

"Please," she said, and mustered a smile. After all, she could not fault him for the part he was unwittingly playing in this evil drama. She paused at the tall gates, the back of her neck breaking out into a cold sweat.

"Miss?"

She turned to the cabby. He eyed her servant's uniform and said gently, "Perhaps we should go 'round to the mews."

Of course! What was she thinking, that she could boldly push her way through the gates and stroll up the carriage drive? "Thank you, yes."

He helped her back into the seat, and presently the hansom was turning down a gravel lane of stables and carriage houses and paddocks running between Clifton Hill and the street behind it. When helped to the ground again, Rachel thanked the cabby again and, steadying her nerves, pushed open the less-intimidating tradesman's gate behind Lord Burke's house.

If the front lawn was impressive, the garden was a paradise of cool greenery. She looked up into the branches and wide leaves of a tall fig tree at the center, caught a whiff of its musky aroma. *You could hide up there for days,* she told herself wistfully. Or at least until nature called. She sighed and started up a flagstone path, expecting any minute someone to pop out and demand she leave. But still, no sign of life, at least human life. The path meandered past flower beds and arbors, benches and fruit trees, stopping at a covered terrace. To the left was an iron-railed staircase, apparently leading down to the kitchen. Holding the rail, Rachel descended the stone steps and knocked at the oak door.

A second, two, and it swung open. A young red-haired maid smiled at her. "Yes, miss?"

"My name is Rachel Jones," she managed to push out past the lump in her throat. She drew breath to explain the reason for her appearance, but swallowed the wrong way and was seized by a fit of coughing. "E-excuse . . . me," she stammered between coughs.

The girl took her by the elbow, beckoning for her inside. Rachel stepped through the doorway into a lofty kitchen. Baskets and copper pots swung from overhead beams, and cupboards lined one wall. A vast fireplace took up another wall, and an open range squatted beside a bricked oven. A ruddy-faced woman with the same flaming red hair as the girl's looked up from rolling dough at a worktable.

"You just sit right here," the girl said, nodding toward a stool.

"But my throat's—"

"Sit, child," said the woman at the table, while the girl went over to the sink. "May as well rest your feet while you can."

Rachel obeyed. "Thank you," she said when the pewter beaker was pressed into her hand.

"I'm Lucy Taylor," said the girl, who couldn't have been more than fifteen. She watched with curious green eyes as Rachel emptied the beaker. "And this is my mother, Mrs. Taylor."

To her mother she said, "Her name is Rachel Jones."

"Thank you," Rachel said, handing the girl the empty beaker. "You've been most kind."

"Oh, we don't get many visitors," the cook said. "Just delivery men. Lucy gets excited when she sees someone closer to her own age than the lot of us old folks 'round here." The

27

woman began pressing a circular pie press into the crust for meat pies. "Now, what is it we may do for you, Miss Jones?"

For a few minutes, she had been just a young lady enjoying the company of new acquaintances. Heart sinking, Rachel showed the cook the envelope with the spidery script. "I've a message for Lord Burke from Mrs. Hammond, my missus."

"Very well," Mrs. Taylor said, as Rachel handed the envelope to her daughter. "Lucy, put it on the cupboard shelf so's it doesn't get flour on it, and we'll give it to his lordship after supper."

Rachel bit her lip. "And she asks for the favor of a reply, if possible."

"Today?" Mrs. Taylor pursed her lips. "Lord Burke hasn't a butler, and Mrs. Fowler isn't here. She's the housekeeper, and receives all the messages."

Lucy nodded, her young face grim. "She left yesterday—gone to Thruxton in Hereford for the month. Her mother's funeral and all that."

Relief washed over Rachel like a cool breeze, and she had to remind herself that it was the tragedy of a death which brought her some reprieve. "I'm sorry."

Mrs. Taylor nodded. "At least her suffering's over."

"I'm sure his lordship's in his study," Lucy volunteered. She looked at her mother. "I can carry it over to him if it's that important."

"Well, I suppose it's all right." Mrs. Taylor shrugged. "If he's too busy, he'll just say so."

Rachel watched the girl carry the envelope toward a door that apparently led to a service staircase. *Why must everybody in this world be so trusting?* An impulse seized her. "Wait, please."

"Yes?" Lucy turned, raised her eyebrows.

"If it's Lord Burke's custom to receive messages from his housekeeper, perhaps I really should wait until she returns."

To her employers, she would leave out the part where Lucy was so obliging. This would essentially turn her account into a lie, but she would rather have to repent of a lie tonight than a more damaging sin.

Mother and daughter exchanged looks, and Mrs. Taylor said, "But you just said your missus . . ."

"Forgive me for wasting your time," Rachel said, getting down from the stool. "You've been most kind, and I can't explain this, but I have to go."

"Oh!" Lucy jumped back as the door hit her. A gentleman in shirtsleeves and waistcoat bounded into the kitchen, holding one of his palms clasped in the other.

"Sorry, Lucy. Did I hurt you?"

"No, m'lord."

Rachel froze at the sight of the mass of scars on the right side of the man's face, reddish brown and shriveled and as stiff looking as shoe leather. She tried not to stare, but he was taking no notice of her anyway.

"Bernice, I've gouged my hand with the letter opener like a clumsy oaf. Will you tie something around it?"

"Let's wash the blood away first, m'lord," the cook said. With the two servants fluttering at either side, the man obeyed and went over to the basin. Mrs. Taylor washed the flour from her own hands, then washed his, as she instructed Lucy to tear a towel into strips.

"Ouch!" he exclaimed when the cook wound a strip about his hand. "Have a heart, Bernice!"

"You've got to tie it tight for the blood to stop," she said.

The man turned his head in Rachel's direction, as if just now really noticing the stranger in his kitchen. Rachel lowered her eyes quickly.

"This is Rachel Jones, m'lord," Lucy said as the man flexed the fingers of his bandaged hand. "She brought this for you from her missus." Then as if remembering what had happened just seconds ago, she gave Rachel an anxious look.

Before Rachel could respond, Lord Burke took the envelope from Lucy with his good hand and slipped it into his waistcoat pocket.

"Her missus asks for a reply," Mrs. Taylor said.

"Do you need for me to look at it now?" Lord Burke asked Rachel.

*Tell him you made a mistake . . . that you'd like to have it back.* But a picture of herself facing Mrs. Hammond and Mr. Moore chased away all courage.

*Besides, what if he demands to know why I changed my mind?* What reason could she give? That she had changed her mind and no longer wished to be party to a crime? *What if he sends for the police?*

Before she could make up her mind, Lord Burke motioned with his bandaged hand to the kitchen door. "Well, come along then. I'll read this in my study."

Woodenly, Rachel followed him through the door Lucy held. They walked up a staircase, down a paneled corridor and into a room furnished with a cluttered mahogany desk, a small brick fireplace, and three leather chairs.

"Please have a seat," he said, moving a thick book from a chair facing the desk. She obliged, while he seated himself behind the desk and broke the envelope's seal.

Rachel's face heated as she watched the man pull out

Mrs. Hammond's letter—unwittingly holding poison in his
hands. She knew the contents, had heard Mr. Moore and Mrs.
Hammond discuss the most effective wording. It had been
Mr. Moore's idea to include the fictitious cook and her poor
relation.

> *Dear Lord Burke,*
>
> *I am a young widow just recently relocated to London to
> escape the memories of my sainted husband, lost at sea two years
> ago. A sale is pending for our estate in Nottinghamshire, and
> I expect to have such business cleared up very shortly. On
> Friday past I happened to be delivering soup and clothing to a
> relative of my cook in the Seven Dials area, and was distressed
> to witness the severe poverty all about me. I am anxious to learn
> which charities provide for the destitute of such neighborhoods
> most effectively, so that when the funds from the sale arrive I can
> put them to immediate good use.*
>
> *I have learned of your generous philanthropy, and wonder if
> you would kindly advise me of such organizations?*
>
> *Time weighs heavily on my hands, Lord Burke, and grief is
> a frequent visitor. The thought of being able to give of myself to
> others again is the only thing which keeps me from giving in to
> despair. Will you consider joining me for tea one afternoon this
> week at your convenience, to discuss such matters?*
>
> *Respectfully yours,*
> *Mrs. Thomas Hammond*

When he had finished, Lord Burke steepled his fingers and
stared just above Rachel's right shoulder. His eyes were the
color of nutmeg, introspective, thoughtful. The brow
appeared to have been singed from above his right eye, but

both sets of lashes were thick. The lamplight caught streaks of gold in his brown hair. *He must have been a handsome man,* Rachel thought.

He blinked at her as if suddenly aware again that she was present. The left corner of his mouth turned up into a crooked, somewhat self-conscious smile. "Your mistress seems quite desperate," he said kindly.

"Yes, sir," she said, swallowing. The ticking of the long-case clock in a corner seemed to mock her, accusing her with every beat, *Li-ar, li-ar, li-ar!*

Lord Burke tapped his pen on the top of his desk once, twice, three times, and glanced at the letter again. He reached into a desk drawer for a sheet of stationery, twisted the lid from a jar of ink. After he had blotted his pen and scribbled several lines, he raised his head again.

"Please give this reply to Mrs. Hammond," he said, folding the paper and stuffing it into an envelope. As he held it out to her, Rachel rose to her feet and took it.

"Thank you, sir," she managed.

Already opening up a leather-bound account book, he nodded. "Will you need someone to take you home?"

"Mrs. Hammond hired a cab for me," Rachel said.

"Very considerate."

~

Rachel had no sooner stepped into the parlor when Mrs. Hammond and Mr. Moore rose from the sofa. "Did he answer?" Mrs. Hammond asked.

Rachel pulled the envelope from her apron pocket and crossed the room. Mrs. Hammond snatched it from her, broke the seal.

*"Dear Mrs. Hammond,"* she read aloud.

*"Please accept my condolences on your husband's tragic passing. Your inquiry regarding worthy charities is most welcome, as so many of our city are in dire need. As soon as possible I shall ask my solicitor, Mr. George Cromer, to call upon you with information concerning the organizations which I sponsor.*

*"Regretfully, I must decline your kind invitation for tea, for I do not make calls. However, I commend you on your generosity, especially during a most trying time.*

*"With warm regards,*
*Adam Burke"*

Crumpling the paper into a ball, Mrs. Hammond said, *"Now* what are we supposed to do?"

Mr. Moore took the letter from her and straightened it out again. He asked Rachel, "Were you allowed to see him?"

"Yes, sir—in the kitchen. Then he invited me to his study and wrote his reply."

"And he did not suggest inviting Mrs. Hammond to visit?"

"He had cut his hand," Rachel offered, hoping that would suffice to end their questions. "With a letter opener. It was bleeding."

"Oh dear." Mrs. Hammond looked worried. "While opening *my* letter? Perhaps that prejudiced him against—"

"No, missus. Before that."

"Think hard, Rachel," Mr. Moore ordered, a little frown tugging at his thin lips. "Did he say *anything* to you concerning the letter's contents?"

Rachel searched her memory for something, anything,

which would satisfy him. "He said that my mistress seems quite desperate . . . and that it was considerate of you to hire a cab for me."

"Well, that's *something.*" Mrs. Hammond turned to Mr. Moore. "What should we do next? Should I call on him without an invitation?"

"No, not yet." He returned to the sofa and sank back into the cushions. "We can't afford to waste time, but we mustn't spoil everything by becoming *too* hasty. We'll just have to make alternate plans."

Mrs. Hammond looked up at Rachel. "Go cook supper."

~

Grateful to be away from the two, Rachel fetched an onion from the larder. As she arranged slices over the fish in the baking dish, she realized she had neglected to mention Lord Burke's scarred face. The thought brought inexplicable relief to her guilty conscience . . . as if by not mentioning his appearance, she was allowing the man a small measure of protection. By the time the flounder was in the oven, she had figured out why. If Mrs. Hammond learned of the scars, she would assume—perhaps accurately—that Lord Burke was desperate for a beautiful woman's company. And Rachel knew how bold her mistress could be.

She wondered about the scars. His face had not repulsed her, though it was unsettling at first glance. Perhaps it was his kind demeanor which had softened the effect of the deformity. Scars and all, Lord Burke's face was far more pleasant to look upon than Mrs. Hammond's or Mr. Moore's. While they both had handsome features, the effects were diminished by the predatory look about the eyes.

~

"The way I see it, we have two options," Gerald was saying, a hand caressing the back of Corrine's neck. "One, we can wait for this Mr. Cromer to call, and you can turn the charm on him."

"But we're not interested in the solicitor. . . ."

"Indeed, but surely he would inform his client how beautiful and charming this wealthy widow is. Men mention such things to each other. Then afterwards you'll send Lord Burke another letter—along with a bottle of good wine—expressing your thanks and asking him for tea."

"But he'll only turn it down again. He said he doesn't make calls."

"True. But a man of his title and wealth has surely been tutored in the social graces. Simple manners would *compel* him to return the invitation."

Corrine considered this, nodded. "I suppose we've no other choice."

"But then . . ." Gerald pursed his lips thoughtfully. "How do we know *when* Mr. Cromer will call? Lord Burke may not consider the matter urgent, particularly since your letter declares you have to wait for the estate to be sold before you can make any donations."

"It was *your* idea to include that."

"I know—and it served its purpose. I just don't like waiting when money is involved."

*You mean when gambling debts are involved,* Corrine thought. It was hard to keep her temper in check whenever he brought up the subject of their desperate financial straits. *We've earned thousands of pounds, but it disappears as quickly as it comes!*

Yet she forced herself to hold her tongue, fearing a repeat of yesterday's episode. She watched him, absorbed in thought with pale eyes half closed. Why was she so dependent upon him? While he was handsome, in a callous sort of way, men much more handsome had expressed interest in her.

Perhaps it was because he did not fawn and stutter in her company, as did most men. He would leave her in a heartbeat if she pushed too far, and it intrigued her that someone would have that sort of power over her.

"Our only other option," Gerald began after a while, "is to send another letter saying you would rather receive the information from him personally."

Corrine frowned. "Wouldn't he think that odd?"

"Oh, I'm quite sure he would, at first." Moving his hand from the back of her neck he said, "But what if you wrote that you appreciate his efforts and mean no offense—but that you don't trust solicitors?"

The tempo of his words quickened. "You'll confide that your father's trusted attorney embezzled money from his holdings for years, so that when he died, your mother was left virtually penniless."

She gave him a bitter smile. "That latter part is true, actually. My father did leave my mother virtually penniless. But then, that was how he lived his whole life."

Gerald touched the tip of her nose, said gently, "My poor dear Corrine . . . the little ragged girl."

"Our patches even had patches."

"Well, you'll never have to live like that again. And I promise, one day we'll be able to buy you all the fine things you deserve."

36

When he spoke to her so lovingly, Corrine could forgive all his vices. "You can be terribly sweet, you know?"

"Sh-h-h!" He sent a feigned worried glance about the room. "Mustn't ruin my reputation as a rake."

That made her laugh. "You're a rake, I'll grant you."

~

With great relief Rachel closed the door to her garret room after cleaning the kitchen. Mr. Moore's knowing little glances as she served supper—always when Mrs. Hammond's attention was occupied in another direction—had unnerved her to the point where she had dropped the butter dish onto the carpet.

She struck a match to light the lamp upon her bedside night table, recalling how Mrs. Hammond had snapped at her for her clumsiness without even considering the reason. *Why can't she see what's going on right in front of her?*

But then, Rachel wondered, could it be possible that she *did* see and chose to pretend it was not happening? If Mrs. Hammond were to confront Mr. Moore over his covert flirtations, that would undoubtedly bring on a scene, and their scenes could get brutal. Once, Mr. Moore had even blackened Mrs. Hammond's eye!

And that would explain why Mrs. Hammond lost her temper more and more lately with *her*. If only she could assure her mistress that his attention was unsolicited, even repulsive!

Rachel allowed herself a dry smile. *And she would thank me for the information, and Mr. Moore would apologize, and everything would be lovely afterwards.*

And pigs would fly! *Oh Father, please help me escape this madhouse!*

Her nerves felt as taut as harp strings, and she knew she

would not sleep if she could not relax. Moving to the chest of drawers near her washstand, Rachel picked up the round wooden cheese box from the top. Inside her sketches rested with an oblong tin pencil-box. She had no desk, so she sat on her cot with a pillow propped against the wall. The box lid on her lap made an adequate surface. She smoothed the piece of brown paper which had been wrapped about Mrs. Hammond's peppermints.

Closing her eyes, Rachel tried to picture Lord Burke's face. It was too bad that she could not afford watercolors or oils nor the lessons which would be necessary to learn to use them. Much better to capture the expression in his eyes with colored paints. A kindly expression . . . and lonely, she realized.

Pencil portraits upon scraps of paper. Still, that was better than nothing. She didn't know what she would do if she couldn't come up here and sketch.

Tentatively, Rachel began sketching Adam Burke's brow with short, feathery strokes. Using a piece of cotton for shading, she added a shadow to the right side of his face, the dark patch over his eye. She wondered if Lord Burke ever wished he could erase his scars, just as she could on paper if she desired.

*But of course he does,* she said to herself. Why else would he be so reclusive? People could be cruel. Who would want to submit himself to stares and whispers? Hence, the loneliness in his face. *You poor sad man.*

The bells of Saint John's were tolling midnight as she put the finishing touches on the sketch. Rachel held the paper closer to the lamp. The resemblance was remarkable, scars and all. There were times, rare ones, when the work of her hands filled her with a wonderful sense of awe.

Weary to the bone, she placed Lord Burke's portrait atop the others in the box. He seemed to stare back at her with thoughtful expression. "Be careful, sir," she whispered.

# 4

A light misting rain fell Friday morning. Still, a graying man with lanky build was on his knees thinning a patch of marigolds in Lord Burke's garden. He nodded up at Rachel, and as if reading the question in her mind, explained, "The rain softens the ground, makes it easier."

She smiled, nodded back, and went on to knock at the kitchen door.

"Why, good morning, Miss Jones," Mrs. Taylor said, opening the door a bit wider.

"Good morning, Mrs. Taylor," Rachel said, dipping into her apron pocket for the envelope. "Pardon me for disturbing you again, but I've another message."

The cook took it from her hand and leaned her head to the side. "Now, are you quite *sure* you want this delivered?"

Rachel's cheeks caught flame. "Yes, please."

"I can't give it to Lord Burke right away," Mrs. Taylor said, not unkindly. "He's having a meeting with his minister."

"He attends church?" The words slipped out before Rachel could realize how thoughtless they sounded. Quickly she explained. "Forgive me. I just assumed he never went anywhere."

"You assumed right," the cook said with an understanding

smile. "See now, miss, I've better things to do than stand chatting in doorways. Why don't you come in and have a cuppa? Lucy will be glad to see you."

~

"You see, Lord Burke hasn't set foot inside a church since he moved into this house," Mrs. Taylor explained as she poured steaming tea into three Blue Willow china cups. "Having those scars . . . well, he doesn't like it when people stare."

"How did he get them?" Rachel asked.

"He was injured in Sevastopol, during the war. And so we have chapel here, every Sunday, in the drawing room."

Rachel understood. The services at Saint Luke's had been held in the foundling home's dining hall. A church could be anywhere people gathered to worship, Reverend Stockbridge had said.

"Do the servants attend?" she asked.

"We do," Mrs. Taylor replied. We've a tidy little congregation. And with Lord Burke and the good Reverend Morgan and his family, we add up to more than the 'two or three' the Good Book mentions."

Rachel nodded. She would have liked to have lingered in this kitchen, soaking up the hospitality. And she *had* been instructed to wait for a reply if possible. But delivering the letter was bad enough. She could not bear the thought of having to lie to Lord Burke a second time.

She was just opening her mouth to thank them for the tea when Lucy asked, "Where do you go to church, Rachel?"

"I haven't in a long time," Rachel admitted.

The girl's eyes grew large. "Why not?"

"Lucy . . ." her mother cut in. "It isn't polite to ask."

"I don't mind." Rachel smiled across the table at the girl. "I work Sundays."

Mrs. Taylor clucked her tongue sympathetically. "Well, if you're ever caught up and missus will give you a little time off, you could think about joining us here. Lord Burke is a lamb. He wouldn't mind."

Lucy's face lit up. "That would be so nice! And you could have lunch with us afterwards."

The very thought of such kindness moved Rachel to the point of blinking away tears. "Thank you for asking," she replied, pushing her chair out from the table and standing. "But I'm never caught up."

She bade them farewell, and was out the door and on the way to the hansom, no longer caring that Mrs. Hammond and Mr. Moore would be furious that she had not waited for a reply.

~

"Checkmate," Robert Morgan said, snatching the king from the black square.

Thirty-year-old Adam Burke blew out his cheeks. The *Jaques* boxwood-and-ebony set had belonged to his late father. He had beaten Robert with this very set more times than he could count during the years they shared a staircase at King's College in Cambridge. But Robert's wife of six years, Penelope, had learned the game before she even went to school.

"I think it's cheating, taking lessons from your wife," Adam said as they replaced the chess pieces for another day. "You ought to be thinking up your own strategies."

Robert's thick fingers handed over Adam's king. "Naturally,

you wouldn't allow Penelope to teach you if she were *your* wife."

"Well, that would be different," Adam said, continuing the playful argument they had had several times in the past. "It's expected for a layman to take advantage of a situation, but a minister should be above all that."

"Expected to take advantage of a situation, Adam? I never figured you for an opportunist."

"Only when it comes to chess."

"Yes, but once you start rationalizing in one area, it seeps into others, and then there go your morals out the window."

Adam shook his head, grinned. "I have *you,* my preacher friend, to made sure my morals remain seep-proof."

"That reminds me; Bishop Harrison called me in for another talk yesterday."

"And . . .?"

"The same subject. He isn't quite sure that it's proper for us to be holding services here when it's only your pride keeping you from St. Andrew's."

"Only my pride?" Adam studied his friend thoughtfully. "And what did you say to him?"

Robert leaned forward, his stocky body rigid in the wooden chair. "Are you sure you want to know?"

"Quite sure."

He sighed. "I asked if he thought it was wrong for our ministers to visit the prisons. After all, John Wesley himself preached at Newgate many times."

"Why did you ask that?"

"Think about it."

Adam blinked. "Are you saying I'm a prisoner?"

"Aren't you?"

"Certainly not," he replied tersely. *"They* can't leave. I stay home of my own volition."

Robert shook his head slowly. "I don't think you can leave either."

~

When Adam didn't reply, Robert looked at him with eyes full of compassion. They had become fast friends almost twelve years ago at Cambridge. After graduation, however, they had gone their separate ways—Adam to the British army, and Robert to the ministry.

Seven years ago, he had received with great joy the news that his friend was moving to London. He remembered the shock, however, when he called on him for the first time. The Crimean War had left its mark on Adam's face and, much worse, had scarred his heart.

"I'm sorry if I hurt you," Robert said softly, rising from his chair. He walked over to where his friend was seated and laid a hand on his shoulder for just a second. "I'll show myself out."

"See you Sunday?" Adam mumbled, still looking straight ahead.

"But of course."

"Robert?"

Robert paused in the doorway. "Yes?"

"Pray for me."

"I always do, my friend."

~

Adam listened to Robert's footfalls fade away against the marble floor in the corridor, then got up and crossed the room to a small mahogany secretary against the wall. From the bottom drawer he brought out a black velvet pouch trimmed with gold. He returned to his chair and untied the cords. Reaching inside, he brought out a tintype of a young woman in a small silver frame.

As he had done so many times in the past, he automatically covered the right side of his face with his hand. The young woman's eyes were focused at something just a shade to the left. She was exceedingly beautiful, with delicate features, laughing eyes, and flaxen hair.

He sniffed and was immediately disgusted with himself for the tears. Still he drank in the image of the face he had once loved until he could stand it no longer. Resting his head against the back of the chair, he closed his eyes. His imagination took over, dredging up memories that were at the same time sweet and bitter.

"Kathleen . . ." The name escaped his lips as a groan. *Why did you break your promise?*

She was distressed to the point of weeping when his artillery regiment received orders in the fall of 1854 to transport to Crimea and reinforce the troops already there. *But she was proud of me, too,* he thought. He had been able to see that through her tears.

Though he had not been a vain man even then, he was glad that Kathleen enjoyed being seen with him. Clad in the uniform of his regiment—dark breeches and a pale blue tunic faced with yellow and heavily braided in silver—he often escorted her down the cobbled lanes of Gloucester, enjoying the pressure of her white-gloved hand resting in the crook of his arm.

After he received his orders, there was no time to plan the

elaborate wedding of which she had dreamed. She had tear-
fully promised him that she would never love another man
and would marry him when he returned.

Thirteen months later he was lying on a pallet on the dirt
floor of a field-hospital tent, his face ravaged by exploding
shrapnel during the siege of Sevastopol. Fortunately, he had
thrown his left arm over his eyes just as the Russian shell hit
the ground in front of him, saving his eyesight while doing
only minimal damage to the arm sheathed in the sleeve of his
winter greatcoat.

Kathleen had received word of his injuries—and to Adam's
great joy, she did not act repulsed when he finally came home.
Even as they walked through town in the light of day, she
took his arm as in old times. After a short while, though, he
began to sense a coldness in her feelings toward him. Whenever he brought up the subject of wedding plans, she would
answer evasively, citing some delay such as the seamstress who
was to construct her gown becoming ill. The smile upon her
lips did not mask the overwhelming resignation he sometimes
caught in her eyes.

*It's just your imagination,* he had reminded himself frequently.
After all, he had worried for weeks about her reaction to his
disfigurement. More than once, back in the hospital tent, he
had awakened in the middle of the night drenched in sweat
and heart racing from a nightmare in which Kathleen recoiled
in horror at the sight of him. He was just being too sensitive,
looking for monsters which weren't there.

Then, five weeks after his return, Adam found out by accident that his instincts were correct. He had ridden horseback
over to her family's country manor house and found his

younger brother Edward's favorite roan gelding tethered to the carriage rail out front.

Recent occurrences began assaulting his mind, such as the day before when Kathleen had accidentally addressed him as "Edward" over tea in her mother's garden. She had become flustered, and he teased her about becoming forgetful.

With the clarity of hindsight, Adam realized Edward had seemed uncomfortable in his presence since his return, never quite looking directly into his eyes. He had attributed his brother's actions to his facial injuries and figured that Edward would grow used to his appearance in time. Then they would again enjoy the camaraderie they had shared as children.

But with all the pieces falling into place, he wasn't so sure anymore. With a heavy heart he had slowly dismounted and tethered his horse. Anger began to quicken his steps, and by the time he reached the door and brushed past the startled housekeeper, his blood was pulsing in his temples.

He stopped just outside the closed library door, suddenly feeling foolish. Surely there was a logical explanation. After all, Kathleen and Edward both loved him. Just as he was about to knock on the door and confess his folly, their muffled voices reached his ears.

Despising himself for stooping so low as to eavesdrop, Adam had put his left ear against the door. Kathleen was weeping, he realized. He could hear the voice of his brother, comforting her.

"I don't have Adam's fortune, but we could live quite comfortably for the rest of our lives with my grandfather's legacy. And with your dowry . . ."

"There would be no dowry, can't you see?"

"But I can't imagine your father's cutting you off. You're his only child. He wants you to be happy."

She gave a desperate bark of a laugh. "Even so, how can I turn my back on Adam now . . . the way he is?"

"That's not your fault." Edward's voice was gently reasoning. "Don't you think it kills me, the thought of hurting him? But he's a grown man . . . old enough to know these things happen."

"But what of everybody else? Everyone tells me what a 'good soul' I am, being so loyal . . . when I know, deep down, they're glad it's me that's stuck with him and not them."

"Adam's wealth still makes him attractive to women. I know at least a dozen who would jump at the chance to marry him." Exasperation crept into his brother's voice. "Anyway, who's more important—me or your father and your silly friends? I can't believe you're even still considering this marriage!"

Kathleen and Edward. The only woman he had ever loved. And his brother! Why hadn't he seen it earlier? When he had first stepped off the train at Gloucester Station and into their arms, why wasn't he aware that he had just become an intruder into their lives?

It took every ounce of willpower Adam possessed not to throw open the door. As it was, he scarcely remembered the five-mile ride back home. When he got there he wandered from room to room, ignoring the uneasy quietness of the servants, and searching—for what, he did not know.

He wished then that he had not surrendered his commission in the army. He belonged among men who were accustomed to looking at wounds and were, for the most part, unencumbered with such deceitful emotions as pity.

Burke Park, the Jacobean mansion and three thousand acres on the River Severn, was legally his since the deaths of both his parents almost seven years before. His older sister, Audrey, had married and moved away when he was just a child, and he had no obligation to support anyone in the family. He could have turned Edward out and allowed him to find out for himself just how long the funds from Grandfather's legacy would support Kathleen's expensive tastes. *Just part of the afternoon,* he consoled himself by toying with the idea. When his brother returned, Adam refused to see him and instructed the servants that he would not see Kathleen either if she came to call.

Mercy and reason won out. It only took a week for Adam to realize that this was no kind of life, and that bitterness would scar his insides as devastatingly as the shrapnel had scarred his face. He decided to leave, and arranged with a solicitor for the servants to be kept on—except for Mr. Taylor and his family, who agreed to go with him. As for Edward, he could even remain with an adequate allowance each month.

Adequate but not extravagant. Enough to run the estate. Adam would not punish his brother, but neither would he finance the kind of life Kathleen was expecting. She was unashamedly pampered by her parents and used to the finer things of life. *Her dowry will be considerable,* he had told himself bitterly. *She can provide the silk gowns and trips to Paris!*

The next consideration had been where to go. At first it seemed that the best way to remain anonymous would be to move somewhere even deeper into the countryside. Perhaps he would buy a crumbling medieval castle somewhere, moat and all, on the top of a cliff. Then it dawned upon him that, while he intensely wanted to get away from people's covert glances and sometimes even bold stares, he did not want to live in perpetual isolation.

That was when he decided upon London. In such a busy, bustling city, neighbors would be more apt to mind their own business. He would have access to his newspapers and journals, and he could even take his one-horse runabout out for rides at night if he wished. And his friend Robert Morgan lived there.

Still, it was several weeks before he could make himself send word to Robert of his new residence. His friend had a natural empathy for people, and Adam did not want his pity. His fears were put to rest upon their reunion, for the minister had simply enveloped him in a bear hug and exclaimed, "I never thought I'd see the day when *I'd* be more handsome than Adam Burke!"

Robert was just the tonic he needed. And his old friend's patient but persistent reasoning over the next couple of years brought him to the saving knowledge of Jesus Christ. But Adam balked adamantly at attending any sort of public worship gathering. The very thought of imposing his disfigurement upon others, even fellow believers, made his blood go cold. He could just picture mothers whispering to their children to stop staring and well-intentioned men pretending not to notice his scars when shaking his hand. Worst of all would be the looks of sympathy sent in his direction—sympathy shaded with just a subtle amount of relief that it was he and not the onlooker who bore the ugly scars.

After weeks of trying to get Adam to change his mind, Robert came up with the idea of having worship services right here at the house. The servants would be the only other members of the congregation besides his wife, Penelope, and later, his daughter, Margaret. He could come to Adam's every

Sunday after he had preached at St. Andrew's, his own tiny church on King Henry's Road.

"This is just temporary," Robert had warned. "Sooner or later, you're going to have to get used to having folks look at you. If they have pity in their eyes, so be it!"

The "temporary" arrangement had lasted four years now. So far Adam had been successful in getting Robert to continue. What he would do if Robert made good on his threat to stop conducting the private services, he did not know. One day, perhaps, he would have to stop living like a hermit, but he was determined to put that day off for as long as possible.

In the meantime and after much prayer, Adam had forgiven his brother and Kathleen. After all, they were married now, with two children. But he could not quite yet bring himself to discard her portrait.

~

"What do you mean, he didn't send a reply?" Mrs. Hammond said when Rachel walked into the parlor empty-handed. "Did you not ask if you could wait for one?"

Rachel met her mistress's glare with as blank a face as possible and replied, evasively, "He was meeting with his minister."

"His minister?" Mr. Moore folded the *London Times* and dropped it to the carpet beside his chair. "But I was informed he doesn't go anywhere, not even to church . . . even though he supports Methodist charities here in town."

"That's *good* news, then." Mrs. Hammond settled into the sofa cushions. "If he doesn't answer my letter with an invitation to call, then I'll just arrange to make his acquaintance at church. After all, how many Methodist chapels can there be in north London?"

Mr. Moore turned his attention back to Rachel. "Did you happen to hear the name of this minister's church?"

"No, sir, I didn't," she replied truthfully, for it was not likely that the little worship meetings at Lord Burke's house had a name. The thought of Mrs. Hammond engaging in a wild-goose chase, visiting chapel after chapel, gave her such satisfaction that she had to struggle to keep the knowledge from her expression.

As it was, Mr. Moore must have noticed something, for his icy blue eyes were studying her. A smile thinned his lips. "Come, sit here with us."

Crossing the room with feet that had suddenly turned to lead, Rachel chose a wing-back chair as far away from her employers as possible.

"Over here."

When Rachel had perched uneasily on the edge of the ottoman near his chair, he spoke again, his voice still gentle. "Why do I have the feeling that you're hiding something from us, our dear Rachel?"

Much to her chagrin, she realized that her hands were beginning to tremble. She clutched them together in her lap and hoped he had not noticed. "I've said nothing but the truth, sir."

"Then why am I having some doubts?" The tone of his voice became quietly menacing. "You wouldn't lie to your benefactors, would you?"

*You're not my benefactors!* her mind screamed, though she managed to keep her face expressionless. *You only took me from the orphanage so you wouldn't have to pay somebody decent wages to do your dirty work!*

"Rachel?"

"I wouldn't lie to you, sir."

Mr. Moore drummed long, slender fingers on his crossed knee, clearly enjoying himself. "I wonder," he began, his eyes sparkling, "if you ever had a strap put to you in that children's home?"

Indignation burning in her chest, Rachel shot to her feet. "You will *never* strap me!"

A stunned expression crossed his face. "My word . . . our girl has a temper!"

"Why don't you leave her alone, Gerald?" Mrs. Hammond, who had been quietly sitting there for the past few minutes, finally spoke up. She yawned. "This conversation is starting to bore me."

"What?" He turned incredulous eyes to her. "She's obviously holding something back from us, and you—"

"No, she's not." Flashing Rachel a look of scorn, Mrs. Hammond said, "She's too dim-witted to plot against us . . . and I'm starving. Let her go fix lunch."

Moments later, Rachel's hands were still shaking as she chopped parsnips over the pot of mutton stew upon the stove. But her soul blazed with a new intensity, brought on by the victory she had won over Mr. Moore and Mrs. Hammond in the parlor. The fact that it had been a small victory at best could not put a damper on her spirits.

She had not told them everything!

# 5

Mrs. Hammond was waiting in the kitchen when Rachel returned with her basket the following morning. "What took you so long?" she demanded.

"I didn't think I was taking a long time," Rachel replied softly, but firmly. The older she grew, the more suspicious her employers became. What did they expect her to do—sprint all the way to market and back?

"This was just delivered." Mrs. Hammond held up a piece of paper. "Gerald hasn't seen it yet, but when he wakes, he'll be furious!"

Setting her basket on the table, Rachel opened the letter that was thrust upon her.

> *Dear Mrs. Hammond,*
>
> *I am distressed to read of your past troubles with your father's solicitor. While I can assure you with all candor that Mr. Cromer is a decent, honest man, I can certainly understand your reluctance.*
>
> *Enclosed is a list of the charities I have been privileged to sponsor. Most are maintained by Methodists; however, there is also a Catholic-run soup kitchen which strives to meet the vast*

*number of the unemployed Irish. If you desire to visit any of these worthy establishments, please send word and I shall write the proprietors to contact you.*

*If I may be of further service to you, please do not hesitate to send word.*

*Sincerely,*
*Adam Burke*

*P.S. My cook has invited your maid, Miss Jones, to our Sunday services here in my home. Please inform her that she is most welcome. We meet at eleven and share the noon meal afterward.*

~

Corrine watched the girl read, and when she looked up from the page, snatched the letter from her. "I'm going upstairs to give Gerald this. You lied to us after all."

*"Please* don't," Rachel begged, putting a hand upon her sleeve. "You didn't ask about the meetings at his house."

"You *knew* we would want to have that information." Shaking Rachel's hand away, Corrine was about to wheel around and head for the stairs when she remembered Gerald's threat to use a strap on the girl. She paused—not so much from compassion, but because of the disturbing realization that he would get a sick enjoyment from inflicting such a punishment.

"I don't know what I'm going to do about this," she said, lowering her voice but still glaring at the stricken face in front of her. "He needs to know about that invitation."

Frantically Rachel suggested, "You could just show Mr. Moore the list of charities Mr. Burke sent *with* the letter."

"But he'll know that a man like Adam Burke wouldn't send a list without some sort of note. And he *has* to know about the Sunday meetings so he can help me figure out a way to get invited. It appears that that's the only way I'm going to be able to meet this man."

"What if you—"

"Hush!" Corrine rubbed her temple, tried to think. "Perhaps there's a solution to both problems. Go change into your good clothes. And quietly!"

As Rachel's soft footfalls faded upon the steps, Corrine went to the writing table in the parlor. Gerald would sleep at least another two hours, perhaps three. She would compose another letter, thanking Lord Burke for the list of charities and for inviting her maid to Sunday worship.

She wrote the letter, adding,

> *I long to find a place to worship as well, Lord Burke. Might I impose upon your generosity by accompanying Rachel this Sunday?*

A bold move, but as he did not take hints very well, she had no other choice.

"What about Mr. Moore?" Rachel asked warily when Corrine handed her the envelope.

"I'll say you and I were invited to Mr. Burke's meetings when you delivered my letter thanking him for his list."

"Oh, thank you!" Rachel cried, and threw her arms around Corrine. Then, as if realizing what she had done, took a step backward. "I'm sorry, missus."

Corrine frowned. "Are you trying to wake Gerald? Just make sure you get back here with an invitation for *both* of us."

When Rachel was gone and there were still no signs of life upstairs, Corrine went down into the kitchen. She helped herself to a chocolate biscuit from the crock, and then another. The look of gratitude on Rachel's face came back to her.

Strange. For those few seconds, Corrine had felt something that was completely new to her. She couldn't identify it, but it was an unsettling feeling. And not entirely unpleasant.

~

Sunday morning Rachel woke even earlier than usual, for she had to lay fires, cook and serve breakfast, clean up the kitchen, and then help Mrs. Hammond with her gown and hair. By the time she was able to hurry upstairs and dress, Mrs. Hammond—already in a dark mood from having to wake so early—was downstairs fuming over the possibility of being late.

The fleeting bond she had felt with her mistress just a few days earlier had vanished with a fury, for Mrs. Hammond was more demanding and insulting than ever. Rachel couldn't imagine what she had done to deserve such scorn. Was it because she had caused her to keep a secret from Mr. Moore? Or because she, a servant, had dared to touch her?

After hanging her work dress in her wardrobe, Rachel slipped the yellow-sprigged muslin over her head. The joy of having a new dress was tainted with the knowledge that it was just more ammunition for the pursuit of Mr. Burke. "It wouldn't be proper to send her to church, or whatever it is, dressed in a maid's uniform," Mr. Moore had said to Mrs. Hammond over dinner two days ago. "And we can't have her showing up dressed like a beggar woman. The man obviously has a soft spot for servants. He might get the idea that you mistreat her."

Rachel fumbled with the tiny horn buttons behind her back. It seemed to take forever, but she had no intention of asking for Mrs. Hammond's help, not with Mr. Moore hovering about. When she finally finished, she coiled her long hair into a chignon at the nape of her neck and fastened it with a comb. She grabbed her drawstring bag from the foot of her bed and left the room.

Mr. Moore stood at the second-floor landing, looking up at her. "It's time to leave," he announced, giving her an appraising stare with eyes that were still puffy from hours spent the previous night in a smoke-filled gin house. "Why did you put up your hair?"

His presence was unsettling. Had he intended to climb the stairs? She resolved to keep her door locked *any* time she was in her room.

"Rachel. Your hair?"

"You didn't tell me not to fasten it up," she said with as much defiance as she dared. *Besides, Mrs. Hammond's the bait,* she added to herself.

He seemed about to say something, then glanced at the stairs below him and sighed. "You best be on your way."

"Yes." She waited until he turned to leave, determined that he wouldn't be behind her on the staircase. It was bad enough she had to face his lecherous scrutiny every day—she didn't want the feel of his eyes moving down her back.

~

*What in the world possessed me to invite guests?* Adam upbraided himself as he held his left cheek taut for the razor. In the hands of Hershall, his valet, the sharp instrument glided skillfully over the soapy lather covering half of his face.

It wasn't so bad that the young maid who had delivered those letters from her mistress was coming—after all, she had already seen his face. But manners had forced him to invite this Mrs. Hammond, too. He could kick himself now for allowing Bernice to bring about this change in his comfortable, safe routine.

Though he resented this turn of events, he had to remind himself that this was not the fault of the two women, who were probably on the way to his home at that very moment. How could he fault anyone for wanting to worship?

He sighed as Hershall wiped the traces of soap from his face with a warm towel. He was a gentleman, and he would do everything in his power to make his guests feel welcome. But deep down, he would be praying that by next week they would find a church of their own.

~

"We really should have a coach and driver," Mrs. Hammond fussed as she and Rachel stood on Lord Burke's porch. She looked exquisite in an azure-and-gold-striped gown, her glossy dark hair cascading in ringlets from behind a matching silk bonnet. Around her neck hung a costly strand of pearls—a gift from a prior suitor. "If Gerald wouldn't go through money as if it were water, I wouldn't have to travel around in rented carriages with only a maid to accompany me."

Rachel kept her expression stoic. She had been looked down upon for so many years that she sometimes wondered if there would come a day when she would actually *believe* herself worthy only of contempt. She had seen such unfortunates, even some who were younger than she, whose expressions showed a resigned acceptance of being beaten down by life.

People grateful for any crumb of kindness, even when it came from an abusive hand. She straightened her shoulders. *Father, please let me die before I ever become that hopeless!*

She was wondering if she had rapped loudly enough on the brass knocker when the door swung open. A middle-aged woman with striking amber-colored eyes welcomed them into the entrance hall and took their wraps.

"Will you come this way, if you please?"

The drawing room, to the left of a long central corridor, was some twenty-five feet square and elegantly furnished. Above the rich cherrywood wainscot, the walls were painted pale sage green with a handsome white cornice. A tiered chandelier of delicate brass hung from a carved ceiling medallion. Three rows of shield-back chairs were arranged upon a Brussels rug.

"Please have a seat," the servant said. "Will you have some tea?"

"No, thank you," Mrs. Hammond replied for both of them.

"Good morning, Mrs. Hammond, Miss Jones."

Rachel turned toward the doorway. Clad in a black frock coat and silk cravat, Lord Burke appeared a little unsettled at the sight of Mrs. Hammond. Not that that was anything unusual, for she had that effect upon men.

"Welcome to my home," he said, entering the room.

"Good morning, Lord Burke." Mrs. Hammond smiled and held out a gloved hand. "You seemed surprised. You *were* expecting me, weren't you?"

She did not seem taken aback at his disfigurement, but then, she was expert at appearing any way she wished to appear.

"Indeed, Mrs. Hammond," he replied, bowing slightly over

her hand. "I just didn't expect such a beautiful woman to be gracing my home."

To Rachel's surprise, he was able to take his eyes off Mrs. Hammond and address her. "Bernice and Lucy will be in shortly, Miss Jones," he said with a crooked smile. "They'll be glad to see you. Would you ladies care to have a seat?"

Without having to even think about it, Rachel knew that Mrs. Hammond would want her as far away from herself and Lord Burke as possible. She walked over to the back row and took a chair. Mrs. Hammond, of course, moved to the middle of the front row, where she could be the center of attention. Lord Burke chose the chair to her right, and Rachel wondered if it was so that Mrs. Hammond would not have to look at his scars.

"I'm so grateful to you for extending this invitation to me as well," she could hear Mrs. Hammond say softly to Adam, her eyes fixed unwaveringly on his face. "And may I say that I admire your concern for your servants' spiritual well-being?"

Stifling a sigh, Rachel found herself wishing Lucy and Bernice were here. Mrs. Hammond's worries over being late had been for naught, for even the minister had not yet arrived.

"They're more than just servants," Lord Burke was saying as Rachel tried unsuccessfully to drown out their conversation with her thoughts. "They're my brothers and sisters in Christ as well. I can't imagine not including them during worship services."

"What a refreshing way to look at it," Mrs. Hammond said. "I believe you'll find Reverend Morgan a true expositor of the Word."

"How good it is to hear that, Lord Burke." She was practically gushing now. "Such an answer to prayer!"

"Where did you attend church in Nottinghamshire?" he asked.

Mrs. Hammond hesitated for an appropriate second or two before replying. "I'm afraid to confess I allowed grief and bitterness to cause me to become a virtual recluse after my husband's death. But when my maid came home with the news of your small gathering, I realized how much I had been longing to worship again."

From the back row, Rachel felt a little sick to her stomach. And the way Mrs. Hammond was gazing at him—as if he were the most handsome man on earth! Her mistress would show her true feelings once she got home to Mr. Moore. Many times in the past she had heard them laughing at Mrs. Hammond's description of Squire Nowells' portliness or some other man's bowed legs or bad teeth.

What was worse by far was the way Lord Burke was looking back, his head tilted slightly towards her, as if he couldn't get enough of her words. Rachel was so absorbed in watching that she was a little startled when Lucy and her mother came in. The girl looked freshly scrubbed and pretty in a pink silk dress, her red hair falling into sausagelike curls at the sides of her face. Mrs. Taylor wore a gown of eggplant-colored calico and a narrow-brimmed straw hat, and leaned to whisper, "Good morning, Miss Jones!"

"Good morning, Miss Jones," Lucy echoed.

"Good morning!" Rachel whispered back. "And do please call me Rachel."

"Only if you'll call me Bernice," the cook said.

"I was praying you wouldn't change your mind," Lucy said.

Bernice smiled and added, good-naturedly, "After all, you got a history of doing such."

Rachel smiled back. Not since the orphanage had she experienced the lightheartedness that comes from enjoying a private joke with friends, and she found it much to her liking.

Other servants began to filter into the room. Two middle-aged women she supposed to be housemaids took seats in front of them on the second row. They turned and smiled at Rachel as Lucy introduced them.

"Glad to have you with us," said parlormaid Marie, the woman with the striking eyes who had answered the door earlier. The other woman, Dora, was thinner, but with the same amber eyes.

"Parlormaids," Lucy whispered. "And they're sisters as well." The two were joined shortly by an older woman with sharp features who nonetheless gave Rachel a shy smile before seating herself.

"Irene," Lucy informed Rachel. "She's chambermaid. I'll introduce you later . . . she's a bit bashful."

Rachel wondered what they must think of Mrs. Hammond, who was still regaling Lord Burke with her melodious voice. *She must have practiced all morning,* she thought. Usually her mistress used a more sultry tone with her victims, but she'd obviously figured that Lord Burke would require special treatment.

The man Rachel had seen in the garden on her first visit walked through the doorway, dressed in black frock coat and trousers. Standing, he was huge, with weathered face, steel grey hair, and thick mustache. He made a beeline toward Bernice and settled into the chair beside her.

"Papa's the gardener," Lucy whispered. "He thinks mum hung the moon, even though they've been married eighteen years."

Rachel leaned forward just a bit so she could watch the couple from the corner of her eye. The man had Bernice's hand clasped in his great paw. She had not even thought to wonder if the cook had a husband. Growing up in the orphanage and then living with Mr. Moore and Mrs. Hammond had given her very limited exposure to *real* families. She didn't know whom she envied more—Bernice, for her loving husband, or Lucy, for having a mother and father.

The sound of knocking drifted faintly from the front of the house. "That would be Reverend Morgan," Lucy said. Conversations faded to an expectant hush. Minutes later a manservant ushered in a stocky man, apparently younger than his lack of hair suggested; a young woman with blond hair caught into a topknot except for the sausage curls falling before her ears; and a curly-haired girl of about three.

"Good morning to you all," boomed the minister as he led his wife and child to chairs in the front row. "I hope we haven't kept you waiting too long."

"Worth the wait, sir!" Bernice's husband said.

"Papa always says that," Lucy whispered to Rachel.

Lord Burke introduced Mrs. Hammond to Mr. and Mrs. Morgan. The little girl turned to stare over the back of her chair at those seated behind her. When her dark eyes latched upon Jack Taylor, she broke into an appreciative grin.

*Why, she's got dimples,* Rachel thought, smiling. She hoped the child would look her direction, too, but just then her mother turned her around to face the front.

Reverend Morgan noticed Rachel, however, as he came to stand in front of the group. He gave her a quick smile, then asked that everyone rise for prayer and hymns.

"Dear heavenly Father," he began, "we thank thee for

allowing us to worship together, and we humbly ask thy pardon for our sins. Give us the desire to do thy will in every task that we undertake, and an appreciation of the blessings thou hast bestowed upon us. In Jesus' name, amen."

When all heads were raised again, Irene, the housemaid with the sharp features, slipped out of her chair and walked over to a mahogany piano in the corner of the room. Mr. Morgan nodded, and she began to play, her features softening with every note.

"Come, thou fount of every blessing, tune my heart to sing thy grace. . . ."

Rachel remembered the hymn from her orphanage years. It felt good to blend her voice in worship with others after so long. She could not help but wonder how Mrs. Hammond was managing. After all, she *had* written to Lord Burke how much she missed attending church. Leaning slightly to the right so she could see past the housemaid in front of her, Rachel noticed that her mistress held her head bowed slightly, as if still praying. Of course! She would probably explain, if asked, that she was so caught up with emotion that she had to thank God again for allowing her to be here.

It would most likely work, too, for Lord Burke glanced over at her occasionally as he sang. She had witnessed that same look on too many other men's faces: that mixture of concern and admiration. She breathed a quiet sigh and wondered, *Are all men blind?*

# 6

The theme of the sermon was discernment, the Scripture reading from the forty-sixth chapter of Psalms: "Be still and know that I am God."

"Most Christians assume that prayer is the process of sending up requests—for health, guidance, prosperity, forgiveness of sins, and the like," Reverend Morgan began, in a voice filled with authority and yet gentleness.

"Some even go further and add thanks for the blessings and even trials God has sent their way. These are all good and worthy things, but listen to the tragedy of it. Our Creator Father welcomes us into the throne room for fellowship, and all we can do is chatter, say our amens, and leave! How sad! How impolite!"

Rachel realized her lips were parted and closed them. Having had very little opportunity to glean spiritual insight from others since leaving the orphanage, she basically was on her own when interpreting the Scriptures. Hearing these thoughts was like lapping cool water after a long thirst. She forgot to look at Mrs. Hammond and Lord Burke and kept her attention focused upon the pastor, loathe to miss even a word.

Reverend Morgan smiled directly at her, as if reading her thoughts, and his voice gentled even more.

"Yes, God speaks to us through the holy Scriptures, but he longs to speak to our hearts if we'll but listen. From listening comes wisdom, discernment. Discernment to see situations, not just on the outside as most men and women do, but with heavenly insight he has given us during our times together."

He smiled again. "If you'll forgive my flippancy, precious ones . . . how can we top a deal like that?"

And then he bowed his head and closed his eyes, as did the rest of the tiny congregation. Rachel lowered her head as well. For years she had prayed for a way to escape Mrs. Hammond and Mr. Moore. But had she ever really listened, in case God was sending an answer?

*Forgive me, Father,* she prayed. *Speak to me please. I'll listen.*

For a little while no one made a sound, not even the child on the front row. At length a quiet amen came from the minister, and people began to raise their heads.

Lord Burke stood, clasped the minister's hand, and turned to smile at the small congregation. "Shall we move to the dining room?"

Rachel knew they had been invited to lunch, but it seemed so unnatural for servants and their employers to be dining together. Why, in six years she had never shared a meal with Mrs. Hammond and Mr. Moore. As she followed Lucy and her parents into the hall, she touched Bernice on the shoulder. "May I help you in the kitchen?"

"No thank you, child." The cook smiled. "We lay it out ahead of time."

"Lord Burke doesn't want us to have a lot of work on Sundays," Lucy explained. "It's just cold meats, cheese, fruit, and the like."

"By the way, may I introduce my husband?" said Bernice,

nodding towards the man beside her. "Jack, this is Rachel Jones."

"I'm pleased to meet you," Rachel said, wondering if she was supposed to offer to shake hands. She had read in *Servant's Magazine*—a halfpenny a copy, and published by the Committee of the London Female Mission to provide guidance to women in domestic service—that the woman was supposed to offer her hand first. But he was so much older than she that it seemed he should be the person to make the first move.

He solved her dilemma by scooping up her hand into his huge rough one. "Jack Taylor here, missy."

"I'm pleased to meet you, Mr. Taylor."

"Jack, if you please," he said, resting an arm on Lucy's shoulder. "Now let's go have some of that lunch my two lovely ladies have prepared."

A spacious dining room lay across the hall from the parlor. The walls were cream colored, with one end dominated by a black marble fireplace with large open grate. Silver, crystal, and jasperware gleamed from a long sideboard against the north wall.

Reverend Morgan, Lord Burke, and his valet—a short man named Hershall—were standing behind their chairs at an oval dining table when Rachel walked into the room with the Taylors. The other women were already seated. Corrine sat three chairs down from Lord Burke . . . and did not appear happy about it. What must have been even more disconcerting to her mistress was the fact that sisters Marie and Dora sat between them. Irene, the older maid who had played the piano, was on her other side.

Reverend Morgan pulled out a chair for Rachel beside his

little girl. Lord Burke held the next chair for Lucy, and Jack Taylor seated his wife before taking his seat.

Once everyone was at the table, Lord Burke said grace. Lucy's description had not given justice to the meal, for there were dishes of cold mutton, peeled prawns with horseradish, pickled beetroot, bread and cheese, dried figs, and rhubarb pudding. Conversation flowed freely, and Rachel imagined that this must be the same kind of comfortable intimacy that large families shared.

The minister's little girl, whom Rachel had overheard addressed as Margaret, was a delight. A copper pot had been placed upside down in her chair, and in her pink calico dress, she sat perched upon it like a queen. Her mother, on the other side, had served the child's plate with small portions of food. But Margaret was more impressed with the figs upon Rachel's plate and asked for one.

"Margaret . . . ," her mother scolded. "That's not polite. You don't even like them."

"I like, Mummy," the girl said.

"It's all right, Mrs. Morgan," Rachel said. "May I?"

"If you don't mind."

"Not at all." With her knife Rachel cut away the bit of hard fruit leading to the stem. When she set it upon the girl's plate, Margaret scooped it into her mouth. She chewed with bemused expression, swallowed, and then pointed to Rachel's plate.

"More?"

"I'll serve you your own this time," Mrs. Morgan said, but winked at Rachel as her husband passed her the dish. "And what do you say to Miss Jones?"

"Thank you?"

"You're welcome," Rachel answered, warmed by the

family-like atmosphere. "And might I say that you have lovely manners for one so young."

"Aside from begging for food at the table," said Reverend Morgan. "Have you any brothers or sisters, Miss Jones?"

"No, sir."

"I'm surprised. You seem to have a way with children."

"At the orphanage . . . ," Rachel began and immediately wished she hadn't. She had to complete her sentence, however, because every ear seemed turned her way. "The older children helped out with the younger ones." She could just imagine Mrs. Hammond's irritation, and willed someone to say something, anything, which would divert the attention away from herself.

Instead, Mrs. Morgan looked at her with sympathetic interest. "An orphanage? Here in London?"

"It was outside Canterbury."

"How old were you when you lost your parents?"

"I believe I was two," Rachel replied quietly. "A cholera epidemic, I was told."

"Do you remember them at all?"

This question came from Lord Burke, and Rachel did not even need to look at Mrs. Hammond to know the cobalt blue eyes would be sending her signals to cease prattling on about herself. But what did she expect her to do? Not answer at all?

"No, sir," she replied. And because she had to go home with Mrs. Hammond later, she thought of a way to make amends. "Mrs. Hammond here generously provided employment for me when I was thirteen."

Mrs. Hammond jumped in quickly. "It was really quite impulsive of me," she confessed, her lips curved slightly in a self-effacing smile. "My husband and I were visiting friends in the area, and we had no need for another servant. But when I visited the charity home and saw that Rachel was about to be set out on her own, my heart went out to her."

She sent Rachel a manufactured look of warmth. "Isn't it wonderful how, when you set out to do a good deed, it turns into a blessing for yourself? When I decided to leave Nottinghamshire after my husband died, I knew I could not manage without my Rachel—she's been a hard worker and cheerful companion. In fact, sometimes I feel that she's more like a sister than my maid."

At the far end of the table, Jack Taylor was wiping his eyes with his napkin. "That's right good to hear, ma'am. Ain't it somethin' how the good Lord works things out that way!"

Even though he was just a servant, Mrs. Hammond smiled at him. "Frankly, it never ceases to amaze me."

From beside her, Irene looked at Mrs. Hammond as if she were an angel from heaven. "I wish somebody like you would have hired me when I was a young one," she said with a quiet voice. "Not everybody's as good to their servants as you or Lord Burke here."

"I'm so sorry." Mrs. Hammond sighed, reached over to pat the woman's bony hand with her small white one. "Unfortunately, some members of the upper class need lessons on treating others decently."

Lord Burke leaned forward. "What were you doing at the orphanage, Mrs. Hammond?"

"Why, charity work, Lord Burke," she replied. "I believe I mentioned in our correspondence how much I relish being involved with helping those less fortunate."

There were nods of approval from half the people at the table, and the other half looked appreciative . . . except for

Bernice. Rachel noticed with surprise that the cook's face wore an appraising expression as she listened to Mrs. Hammond's words.

"You know," began Lord Burke, "that might be the answer to your dilemma."

Mrs. Hammond lifted her eyebrows. "I beg your pardon?"

"I sponsor an orphanage on Wellington Road, to the west of Regent's Park. Someone with your compassion for children could do some great things there."

"You flatter me," she murmured, lowering her eyes. With another sigh, she raised them again. "Unfortunately, my financial situation is static until my estate is sold."

Lord Burke's good eyebrow lowered as if he were in deep thought. "Your letter . . . ," he finally said. "You don't mind if I mention your letter, do you?"

"Of course not." Except for little Margaret, the other guests and servants had ceased chewing to listen.

"You wrote that time was weighing heavily on your hands." His lips quirked into a lopsided smile. "You could do some good with the children at the orphanage. It would cost you nothing but time."

"With the children?" A hand automatically went up to the pearls about Mrs. Hammond's neck, and Rachel could detect a slight tremor at the corner of her mouth. "You mean . . . visit them?"

"Oh, more than just visits," said Adam, still smiling. "Think about how much good you could do by mothering the little ones a bit. I know for a fact that the nurses haven't the time to sit and rock the infants or to hold the others in their arms."

He looked at the minister's wife. "You still go, don't you, Mrs. Morgan?"

"Yes, and what an excellent idea," Mrs. Morgan said to Mrs. Hammond. "Think of all the children who go to bed every night without a mother's touch. I'm only able to visit the orphanage once a week, what with tending Margaret and my mother, but it warms my heart to add some love to those little lives."

"Now there's a heartwarming thought, Mrs. Hammond." At the far end of the table, Bernice had finally decided to speak. "And you certainly have the experience."

"Experience?" The corners of Mrs. Hammond's mouth were curved upwards, but her eyes were anything but smiling as she turned her face toward the cook. "But I have no children, dear."

"Yes, ma'am," said Bernice, smiling back benignly. "But you mentioned that you met Rachel when you was doing some charity work at an orphanage . . . didn't you?"

"Oh, that!" Mrs. Hammond waved a hand and gave a little laugh. "How silly of me. I had it in mind that Lord Burke was speaking of babies, when my experience has been exclusively with older children."

"There are all ages at St. John's," said Mrs. Morgan, wiping her daughter's mouth with her napkin. "Would you care to accompany me this Tuesday?"

"This Tuesday? I believe I have—"

"Or we can go another day if you prefer."

Mrs. Hammond's shoulders sagged a bit, but she lifted her chin and said, "Tuesday's fine."

~

Rachel sat as still as possible in the hired coach, lest Mrs. Hammond take notice of her and decide to vent the wrath that was surely building up in her mind. At present the woman clenched her crocheted reticule in her lap and wore a definite frown. That made things even more ominous, for Mrs. Hammond was too wrinkle conscious to allow herself to frown for very long.

Unfortunately, a vegetable cart on High Street had overturned just moments before, forcing the coach to a dead stop. Drivers of omnibuses, landaus, coaches, and drays yelled curses at the hapless merchant, who, with the aid of a few sympathetic passersby, was trying to right his cart and retrieve at least a portion of his wares. It was as if Mrs. Hammond's final nerve had snapped, for she turned venomous eyes upon Rachel.

"You weren't going to mention what a freak of nature Lord Burke is, were you?"

"He's not a freak of nature," Rachel argued quietly. "He was injured in the war."

"Were you hoping I would appear shocked and ruin everything?"

That had entered Rachel's mind, but she did not dare confess it. Evasively she replied, "You never asked me about his looks."

"But you knew that information would be important. And I suppose you're just gloating inside over the mess you've gotten me into!"

"Me?" Rachel gaped at her. "How did I—"

"You just *had* to tell that charming little story about my taking you out of the orphanage, didn't you!"

A dull ache started pounding Rachel's left temple. "I assumed you would want me to say it."

Mrs. Hammond's small nostrils flared. "But I certainly did

not want to get trapped into visiting such a dreadful place. You knew all along that would happen, didn't you?"

"How could I know that would happen?" For years Rachel had borne the blame for everything that went wrong in Mrs. Hammond's life. Now she set her jaw and forced herself to stare back. "Why would I even *wish* to do that?" she asked in an even tone, hoping to appeal to any sense of reason that her mistress might possess.

"So that you can stay home with Gerald while I traipse over to the slums with the minister's moonfaced wife!" Mrs. Hammond folded her arms beneath her lavish bosom. "You've wanted to get me out of your way for months now, and don't think I don't know it."

"Stay home with Mr. Moore!" Rachel could hardly force the loathsome words past her lips. "That's not true!"

"I've seen the way he's been looking at you!"

Rachel shivered, said in a bleak voice, "I can't help that."

"Oh, can't you? And what kind of looks are you giving him when my back is turned?"

"Giving him?" A cold nausea gripped the pit of Rachel's stomach at the very notion. "I . . . I'm not!"

Mrs. Hammond was eyeing her sharply and seemed to take her reaction as proof that her accusations were true. "Well, from now on, you're not to be alone in the house with him. And that means you'll accompany us to that orphanage."

"Yes, missus." Relief made Rachel go limp against the back of the seat.

"And don't let me catch you making those doe eyes at Mr. Moore again, or so help me, I'll kick you out with no refer-ences!"

~

Hours after his guests left, Adam Burke was reading in his library when Bernice appeared in the doorway. "Sir? May I have a word with you?"

"Come in, Bernice," he said, lifting his feet from the ottoman and preparing to rise.

"Oh, don't go getting uncomfortable for me," she scolded lightly. "Next thing, you'll be bowing like I'm the queen of England."

He smiled and propped his feet back upon the ottoman. "Queen Bernice. I like the sound of that. Will you have a seat, Your Royal Highness?"

She nodded and eased into the chair across from him.

"Are you in pain, Bernice?" Adam asked before she could speak.

She waved away his concern. "Bit of rheumatism, sir."

"Are you taking anything for it?"

"It ain't so bad that I have to do that. But I didn't come to talk about *me,* sir . . . if you please?"

"Very well," said Adam, closing his copy of Ruskin's *The Stones of Venice.* "What's on your mind?"

The woman hesitated as if searching for the right words. "When I came to work for your family, I was but fifteen. You were but five years old. Do you remember those days?"

"Of course. You were the . . ."

"Scullery maid," she finished for him. "But I was determined not to spend the rest of my life scrubbing pots and pans, so I watched Mrs. Dorsey every chance I got. And I asked questions. When she got too old to cook and went back to live with her family, I was given a chance at her job."

"I remember slipping into the kitchen to beg sweets off you," Adam said, smiling. "You never lectured me over spoiling my appetite."

"Well, I should have been sacked for that!" Bernice said, but smiling. "Mrs. Dorsey was just worried I'd spoil you children."

"I don't think you spoiled me . . . do you?"

"Heavens, no! You turned out to be the best of the bunch." Her ruddy face flushed deeper. "I'm sorry, sir."

Adam knew why she was so embarrassed. His parents' disillusionment with marriage and each other had caused them to seek fulfillment in other areas—such as running the estate and restoring old maps for his father, gardening and needlework and paying calls on friends for his mother. Obviously neither had considered child rearing a project worthy of investing time, not when a nursemaid could be procured for lower wages than a good parlormaid. Such parental neglect had cast a pall over every aspect of his young life. Older sister Audrey had married in haste, and then years later the rift had happened with his brother, Edward, over Kathleen.

"Please don't apologize," he said. "There aren't any skeletons in my family closet that you've not met. Now, what is on your mind?"

"May I speak freely?"

"But of course."

Bernice shifted in her chair. "It's that fancy woman."

Lifting his one good eyebrow, Adam asked, "Do you refer to Mrs. Hammond?"

"Yes . . . her."

Adam leaned his head back against his hands and grinned.

"And what of her? Are you about to suggest I invite her for
.tea?"

"Now, don't be making sport of me, sir. You know I
wouldn't be in here if I didn't care what happens to you."

"Of course you wouldn't." Adam moved his feet from the
ottoman again and sat up straight. "Forgive me, Bernice."

She waved a hand. "It's all right. But I've got to warn you
about her."

*So I was right,* Adam mused. Over lunch he had sensed a
coldness emanating from Bernice toward the woman. "You
weren't impressed with her, were you?"

Bernice's lips tightened for a second before answering. "I try
not to judge folks, Mr. Adam. Most people have *some* good in
them."

Adam smiled again. "You've always looked for the best in
people."

She looked down at her roughened hands. "Oh, well, I do
try. But this Mrs. Hammond . . ."

"Yes?" Adam said as she hesitated.

"I don't see any good in her at all. And I think she's after
your money."

"My *money?*" Bernice looked so worried that Adam
couldn't resist another tease. Putting a hand to his chest, he
said, "You mean she's not chasing me for my looks?"

"Lord Burke!" The cook pulled herself out of her chair.
"I can see you're not interested in hearing what—"

He was on his feet in an instant, hurrying over to put a
hand upon her shoulder. "I'm sorry again, Bernice. Here you
are, trying to help me, and all I can do is make jests."

"Well, certain things don't need to be laughed at."

"You're right again. Now, please sit down."

79

She complied but fixed him with a wary expression. "Are you ready to listen?" When he nodded, she continued. "I overheard her speaking with you before the meeting. The things she says just don't ring true."

"You mean about longing to worship again and the like?"

"That's just what I mean—and that bit at the table about visiting orphans!" Bernice snorted. "You can tell she hasn't a charitable thought in her head. Why, it's plain to see even her maid is afraid of her."

"Miss Jones, you mean."

"Yes. The first time that girl came over here with one of Mrs. Hammond's messages, she looked like a frightened rabbit. Then she went and changed her mind and almost snatched the letter back from Lucy. Would have happened, too, if you hadn't walked in the kitchen."

Adam nodded. "Come to think of it, I remember she looked a little worried. Why is that, do you think?"

"I think the girl knows what her missus is up to, and feels badly about it. You probably aren't the first rich man this Mrs. Hammond's tried to get her claws into."

"That's a good possibility."

Bernice looked up. "You mean . . ."

"It only took a little while to figure it out." Adam gave her a knowing wink. "Five to ten minutes, and I knew all about her."

"But how? Even my Jack thinks she's a saint from heaven."

"I questioned her motives right away when she started flirting with me. I'm not exactly the kind of man that women throw themselves at."

"M'lord, I wish you wouldn't say that," Bernice implored with expression pained. "There's someone out there for you."

He shrugged. "Perhaps. But getting back to Mrs. Hammond, I noticed myself what you said about her words not ringing true."

"Are you disappointed?" Her tone was sympathetic. "After all, she's still a beautiful woman."

Adam shook his head. "I didn't find her beautiful."

"You didn't?"

"Well, perhaps at first. But not after I discovered the greed in her eyes."

"And all that talk about getting her to visit the foundling home?" The cook grinned. "You were just pullin' her along?"

He smiled back at her. "I was. But come to think of it, it might do her some good, don't you think?"

Bernice looked doubtful. "If she doesn't end up poisoning the poor little orphans."

"Do you think I should tell her not to come to the meetings again?"

She thought that over and shook her head. "Perhaps they'll be good for her. We know God can change even the most rotten heart. Just look at my Jack. When he first came to work for your family, I thought he was the worst rakeshame I ever saw."

"He's a good, decent man now."

"And the girl . . . Rachel," she continued. "If you take back Mrs. Hammond's invitation, she seems the type that would keep the girl away from here, just for spite. I have a feeling that Lucy and me are the only friends she's got."

"Then it's decided," Adam said. "We'll continue the invitation indefinitely."

Bernice nodded. "And I'll pray for that woman's soul!"

# 7

At nine o'clock on the morning of the twenty-first of April, Rachel answered Penelope Morgan's knock. "Good morning, Mrs. Morgan," Rachel said, holding open the door. As was standard procedure, she had already transferred Mr. Moore's hats and cloak from the hall tree to upstairs. "You didn't bring your little girl."

The minister's wife, dressed in a simply cut but attractive gown of fawn-colored poplin with narrow yellow stripes, stepped into the hall. "My husband helps our housekeeper look after Margaret and my mother on Tuesday mornings. My mother lives with us—she's an invalid."

"I'm sorry."

"Thank you." Mrs. Morgan smiled. "But Mother wouldn't want you to feel sorry for her. And she rather likes having Robert to herself. He reads to her, or at least attempts to, with Margaret tugging at his sleeve."

"I can't imagine such a sweet girl causing much trouble."

"Very kind of you to say, Miss Jones. We rather dote upon her, if that's not obvious."

Rachel led the woman into the parlor and offered her a place on the sofa. "Mrs. Hammond asked if you would mind

83

waiting." She knew that her mistress, still upstairs fussing with her hair, would be in no hurry to come down.

*"Just offer her tea and keep her entertained until I get ready,"* she had instructed. *"I don't want to spend a minute more than necessary at that dreadful place!"*

"That color you're wearing really shows off your eyes," Mrs. Morgan remarked after declining Rachel's offer of refreshments. "Is that a new dress?"

"Yes, ma'am." Rachel absently brushed the folds of Nile green broadcloth gathered at her waist, and the starched new apron—more stage props for the drama that she and Mrs. Hammond were acting out. Still, when she considered the alternative of staying under the same roof with Mr. Moore—at present asleep upstairs—she did not mind so much playing the part of pampered servant today. She had avoided him as much as possible since Sunday and had taken to locking her room door even on the rare occasions she went up there in the daytime.

She was disappointed that Margaret had not come, for in her apron pocket was a sketch of the little girl. She had portrayed the tot seated on a cooking pot in a chair, smiling as she held a fig in her fingers.

Her hand inside her pocket, she touched the linen paper she had trimmed from an envelope Mrs. Hammond had thrown away. *You could give it to her mother now,* she thought. She would miss out on seeing the little girl's face as she recognized herself, but seeing Mrs. Morgan's reaction would be almost as gratifying.

*That is, if she likes it,* she thought. Virtually hiding her talent under a bushel as she did, she was still quite shy over bringing it out into the open.

The minister's wife was beginning to look a little anxious, occasionally glancing at the doorway. She smiled, though. "Won't you sit, too?"

"Oh—yes." Rachel sat in the nearest chair and folded her hands in her lap, wondering what she could possibly talk about that would interest someone as near perfect as a minister's wife must be. They had nothing in common. After all, Rachel had been such a belligerent child—from necessity, for the meek children in the orphanage were tormented incessantly by the others. The meekness came later, when Mrs. Hammond and Mr. Moore cowed her into submission.

And still, she rebelled inwardly. Had Mrs. Morgan, kind and gentle, ever despised anyone the way she hated Mr. Moore? The very idea seemed absurd. What would the good lady think if she knew the servant sitting before her often entertained thoughts of her employer choking to death from a poisonous batch of tea?

"Did you enjoy the service Sunday?" Mrs. Morgan asked at length, while Rachel was still drawing up the courage to present the portrait.

"Oh, yes," Rachel replied. Aside from the tongue-lashing in the carriage on the way home, it had been one of the most splendid days of her life. "Last night when I prayed . . . I listened for a long time."

"Indeed? My husband will be pleased to hear it. And did God speak to you?"

"I'm not sure," she confessed. There had been no decisive message. And yet still, a sweet presence had lingered even after she slipped under the covers.

Even though she had not added the latter part, Mrs. Morgan

said, "Sometimes the message is just that he's there. It's quite a comfort, when we feel like the loneliest person alive."

Rachel leaned her head, studied the woman's serene expression. "But you're not alone. You have your family."

Sadness washed over Mrs. Morgan's round face. "Anyone who lives long enough will eventually find herself shut up in a low place where no human comfort can touch. For me, those times came after each of four stillborn babies."

Tears stung Rachel's eyes and blurred the woman's image briefly. "I'm so sorry."

Mrs. Morgan gave her a stricken look. "Oh dear . . . I don't know what made me say that, Miss Jones. I shouldn't have burdened you."

"No, really. You've not burdened me," Rachel assured her, dabbing the corners of her eyes with her gloved fingertips. Actually, her feelings were mixed: profound sadness for the kind woman and her husband, and gratitude that someone of Mrs. Morgan's caliber would consider her worthy of a confidence. With that came a wave of guilt that she would even think of herself in the face of such loss.

"I'm glad you were able to have Margaret," Rachel said at length.

"Margaret." The name was a verbal caress from Mrs. Morgan's lips. "Robert put her into my arms five weeks after the last stillbirth. I resented him, even resented the baby for not being the little one I had carried for seven months. He agreed to take her back to the foundling home . . ."

Rachel's breath caught in her throat. "The foundling home . . ."

Mrs. Morgan smiled. "I've since come to realize that God often places treasures in places we don't think to look. Robert simply asked me to hold the little bundle for an hour, just to make certain of my feelings."

"You decided to keep her," Rachel breathed, though of course that was obvious.

"And it took less than an hour. We plan to adopt more children one day, after Mother . . . well, when we're more able to give them more time."

*Why couldn't I have been adopted by someone like you?* passed through Rachel's mind.

"But I've gone on about ourselves enough," the minister's wife said, settling back against the cushions. "Tell me more about yourself, Miss Jones."

"About myself?"

"Yes. What do you do in your spare time—do you enjoy needlepoint?"

Rachel shook her head. "Some of the girls took to it in the orphanage, but I confess I never had the patience for it. I'm fond of reading, whenever I can get a book. And I like to sketch."

"You do? Well, what do you sketch?"

"People." She took a deep breath, rose from the chair, and brought the paper out of her pocket. Handing it over to Mrs. Morgan, she said, "I drew this last night."

"Why, this is very good!" Mrs. Morgan put a hand up to her cheek. "Look how you've even shown her dimples!"

"I may have made the arms a mite too short."

"No, it's perfect."

"Would you care to have it?"

"Would I care to—why, I'd *love* to have it!" The woman looked up at her. "My dear, I think it's perfect, and I have a little silver frame that's just begging for this. But I insist on paying you."

"Oh, no. It's a gift."

"Are you sure? Because it's obvious you worked hard on it."

"I'm sure." Rachel smiled at her. Even if she were inclined to accept payment, money would be a pale comparison to the praise being heaped upon her.

"Well, I thank you! I can't wait to show Robert . . . and I'd love to see some of your other sketches."

"You would?" Rachel's spirits crashed almost as soon as they had lifted. Margaret's portrait was on about the nicest cut of paper she had ever used. She couldn't show a fine lady such Mrs. Morgan a cheese box full of scraps and bits. She was just going to have to buy a sketchbook.

She had been saving for a new pair of shoes to replace the leather work slippers that were wearing out. The pair of laced boots she was wearing now had been bought as part of her fancy maid's uniform and were to be used only when Mrs. Hammond wished to impress someone. There always seemed to be something she needed, and she had considered drawing paper a luxury. But some good vellum paper would be so nice. Maybe the shoes could wait a bit longer.

"They're not very fancy," she finally said, in answer to Mrs. Morgan's request.

Mrs. Morgan waved aside her worry. "Oh, but that doesn't matter. Quality is much more important than 'fancy,' don't you think?"

Rachel's heartbeat quickened. Besides Mr. Solomon, no one had ever expressed an interest in seeing her sketches. But the pleasure on Mrs. Morgan's face over the portrait of her daughter gave Rachel new courage. "They're upstairs. But I can fetch them quickly, if you don't mind. . . ."

"I'm sure they'll be worth the wait," Mrs. Morgan assured her.

Two minutes later, Rachel was back with her cheese box. She placed it on the sofa beside the minister's wife and took a seat on the other side. Only after she opened the box did she remember Lord Burke's portrait at the top of the stack. Cheeks burning, she reached for some papers at the bottom and piled them on top of the others. "This was a boy who cleaned our chimney once. . . ."

She had almost said, *in Treybrook,* but then remembered that Mrs. Hammond claimed to be from Nottinghamshire. She hoped Lord Burke's portrait would stay hidden. She wasn't quite certain why the thought of having it discovered was so unsettling. Was it because Mrs. Morgan might assume she had some romantic interest in the man? Or was it because she didn't want *him* to find out from her and assume the same thing?

"These are simply incredible!" Mrs. Morgan was saying, taking out several of the papers and spreading them in her lap. "What talent you have, Miss Jones."

"Thank you," Rachel told her, pleased in spite of her uncomfortable predicament. While Mrs. Morgan studied the sketches in her lap, Rachel caught sight of Lord Burke's face, half hidden by other papers. Pretending to sort through the sketches, she deftly withdrew it and slid it between the box and cushions. She was just breathing easier when the rustling of skirts and crinoline sounded in the corridor. Mrs. Hammond breezed through the doorway in an apricot-colored silk, a smile pasted upon her face.

"My dear Mrs. Morgan."

The minister's wife looked up from the sketches with apparent reluctance. "Good morning, Mrs. Hammond."

Mrs. Hammond approached her visitor, preceded by an invisible cloud of *Vivre le Jour*. "Do forgive my detaining you," she breathed, bending to kiss Mrs. Morgan's cheek. Without batting an eye she added, "I feel so foolish! The hem of the gown I started out with got caught on one of my dressing table latches and ripped, so I had to change into another one. I'm almost feeble without Rachel to help me dress."

"You should have called for her," Mrs. Morgan said. "In fact, we both could have helped."

"Oh, heaven forbid! I couldn't have you left down here all by yourself—and I don't ask my guests to do servants' work. I hope you haven't been too bored."

Mrs. Morgan lifted the sketch of Margaret from the arm of the sofa. "Quite the contrary. See what Miss Jones drew of my daughter?"

"My word . . . ," Mrs. Hammond said, giving Rachel a surprised look.

"You mean, you weren't aware of her talent?" Mrs. Morgan turned to Rachel. "I wish I had more time to look at these, but we're expected at the orphanage. May I see them again sometime soon?"

"Yes, thank you," Rachel answered, returning her smile and hoping she had not angered Mrs. Hammond by bringing out the box of sketches. *After all, she did order me to entertain her. If only Mrs. Hammond weren't so touchy about anyone getting attention besides herself!*

"Well then, we should be going," said the minister's wife,

gently replacing the sketches in the box and gathering her reticule from the arm of the sofa before standing.

"Do you mind if Rachel comes along?" Mrs. Hammond
asked. "It would be such an enriching experience for her."

Mrs. Morgan cast a doubtful glance at Mrs. Hammond's
wide crinoline skirt, but said, "But of course. We'll just have
to squeeze together a bit in the coach."

As the two women started for the door, Rachel slipped the
portrait of Lord Burke beneath the stack in the box and
replaced the lid. Not having time to return them to her room,
she was about to carry the box into the seldom-used dining
room when Mrs. Hammond turned to her and ordered, "Just
save that for later."

"If you please, it'll only take me—"

"We mustn't keep the children waiting any longer," Mrs.
Hammond interrupted. But pleasantly, for Mrs. Morgan's sake.

~

The brick, three-story St. John's Orphan Asylum sat across
Wellington Road from Lord's Cricket Ground, where children of a more privileged class frequently gathered to play.
Mrs. Hammond, Penelope Morgan, and Rachel were ushered
through the entrance door by a pewter-haired man who
walked with the aid of a cane—Mr. Garland, administrator of
the home. "Mrs. Morgan," he said, beaming as he took her
hand, "I was beginning to worry that you weren't going to be
able to come today."

Mrs. Morgan leaned forward to plant a kiss upon his spotted
cheek. "Well, we're here now. And we'll just stay a little
longer to make up for the time."

Rachel noticed the crestfallen look which swept across Mrs.

91

Hammond's face. Nonetheless, her mistress recovered with typical speed and held out a gloved hand while Penelope introduced her to Mr. Garland.

"I'm pleased to make your acquaintance," she said sweetly. Rachel could read her mind. Any acquaintance of Lord Burke could possibly become an ally.

Servants were almost never included in the civilities that members of the middle and upper classes practiced with each other, so Rachel was surprised when Mrs. Morgan gave her name to Mr. Garland as well. *Servant's Magazine* or no, she extended her hand to the man, who warmly took it in his own.

"There is a nursery for the tiniest infants on this floor, as well as the kitchen and serving hall," Mrs. Morgan said after Mr. Garland took his leave. She began leading them toward a wide staircase. "An office and washing-up room. Upstairs are two classrooms and beds for the rest of the children."

A bittersweet déjà vu struck Rachel as she took in their surroundings. The building itself was old—it had once housed a textile factory—but appeared clean and well maintained. "Do they stay inside all the time?" she asked on the staircase. She hoped not, because her fondest memory of the orphanage in Kingston was of the huge yard shaded with oak trees which were perfect for climbing.

"Goodness, no. With Regent's Park so near, the children are brought out in groups to play. Those who are old enough."

"What are we expected to do here?" Mrs. Hammond asked with a stiff smile.

Mrs. Morgan reached the landing and stepped aside. "The school-aged children are at lessons."

Cocking her head, Rachel detected the familiar sound of trebled voices reciting something in unison . . . the continents?

"We'll be with the younger ones," the minister's wife said.

~

"Babies?" Corrine cleared her throat. *Not babies. Please, no. . . .*

Mrs. Morgan smiled. "Not the very youngest—they're downstairs." She started walking again, leading them down a long, paneled hallway. Corrine could hear muted sounds of recitation behind wooden doors.

The minister's wife paused in front of the last door on their left, turned to her and Rachel. "Mr. Garland believes that children not only need their physical needs looked after, but their spiritual needs as well. But how can you teach them about *God's* love if they haven't experienced the most basic human love, that of a mother to her child? The nurses here have all they can do just keeping them clean and fed. The children are desperate for love and affection."

Corrine faltered, shook her head. "I . . . I'm sorry. But I don't think I can do this. As I said before, I only have experience with older children."

"Well, let's see," said Mrs. Morgan, pressing a finger against her chin thoughtfully. "Perhaps you could help the oldest ones study Scripture or arithmetic drills. Most likely the teachers could use another hand."

Corrine glanced back over her shoulder at one of the classroom doors from which was coming a muffled recitation: "By faith Abraham, when he was called to go . . ."

"On the other hand, the young ones probably need us the most," she declared quickly.

The door opened into an enormous room lightened by six

windows on the opposite wall. Indentations in the planked floor indicated where giant looms had once sat, and against two walls were rows of little iron cots. The third wall was taken up with a dozen metal cribs, lined front to back like cars on a train. Some twenty or so chattering little ones from the ages of one to three years played in the middle of the floor, tended by two tired-looking women. Several tots had looked up when Mrs. Morgan opened the door and were now watching the callers with a mixture of expectancy and curiosity. The two nurses raised hopeful eyebrows at Corrine and Rachel, then glanced at each other. One, a tall, dark-haired woman, set down the infant whose nappy she had just changed and, walked over to them.

"Always a sight for sore eyes, ye are, Mrs. Morgan!" she said in a thick Irish brogue.

The woman still held the wet nappy bunched up in her left hand as she offered her right one to Mrs. Morgan. The minister's wife shook the hand that was offered without hesitation. Cringing inwardly, Corrine put both gloved hands behind her back and pretended to stare at the windows against the far wall.

"Good day, Mrs. O'Reilly. May I introduce Mrs. Hammond and Miss Jones?" Mrs. Morgan said while patting the tops of little heads which had begun to cluster around her. "They've kindly offered to accompany me every week."

Corrine's heart jumped in her chest. *Every week!* She had to say something, make some excuse—and quickly—before she found herself stuck here every Tuesday for the rest of her life. "Not *every* week, I'm afraid," she corrected. "I mean, we'll *try,* but sometimes I have other appointments."

"Well, we're grateful for any time ye can spare," Mrs. O'Reilly said. She pointed to the barely visible form of a tot of about two lying under one of the cribs. "The little mite just arrived yesterday, and she's a pitiful thing. Maybe one of ye could sit and just hold her for a bit."

"Mrs. Hammond—would you care to?" Mrs. Morgan asked. "There's a rocking chair over there in the corner."

Corrine was about to reply that she did not wish to wrinkle her dress, but the minister's wife was already leading Rachel to a group of older tots. With stifled sigh, she gathered her skirts and walked over to the crib. She bent at the waist to try to get a look at the child, who had crept farther back out of her reach.

"Come out, please," she said in as soothing a voice as she could manage under the circumstances, while drumming fingertips against the metal railing of the crib.

When no movement came from underneath, Corrine said, "It certainly can't be healthy under there. If you wish me to sit and hold you, you'll have to come out."

Mrs. O'Reilly appeared at her side. "You'll have to coax her a bit, dearie," she whispered. "Her mum left her out on our doorstep yesterday, and the baby's grievin' for her. Perhaps if ye let her see you holding out your arms?"

"Well, I certainly can't crawl down there and get her with this dress on, can I?" Corrine snapped. Turning back to the crib, she tried to soften her voice this time when she called to the child, but to no avail. Finally she straightened and blew out her cheeks. "Isn't there something else I can do around here?"

"I tell ye what," said the Irish woman. "Why don't ye go sit down, and I'll bring her over?"

Corrine clenched her teeth and nodded, then moved with resignation to the rocking chair in a corner. With her crinoline billowing about her, she could only perch on the edge with her reticule behind her. Seconds later Mrs. O'Reilly followed with the crying and struggling little girl. "Here ye go, ma'am," she said, lowering her into Corrine's arms.

"Do ask her to stop crying," Corrine said over the wails. Any hopes she had of keeping her dress unspotted were crushed by the sight of the child's wet eyes and nose.

"Perhaps a lullaby would do it," coaxed Mrs. O'Reilly before walking away. "I've got to finish changin' nappies now—yer doin' fine."

Wrinkling her nose in disgust, Corrine reached back into her reticule for a handkerchief. "There, there now," she said stiffly as she wiped the little face. The child only cried louder, taking in deep, shuddering breaths between sobs.

"Oh, why don't you just shut up!" Corrine hissed through her teeth, then immediately glanced up. Relieved that no one had seemed to have noticed, she softened her voice. "We mustn't cry now, child," she cooed, wondering how so much noise could come from any body so tiny.

The weeping continued. Surely someone else could deal with this brat! She tried to catch Rachel's eye, but the maid was seated on the floor with her back to her. Two or three children were piled in her lap and others on the floor at her side as she told a story. Mrs. Morgan was in a chair across the room, rocking a baby. Mrs. O'Reilly and the other nurse bustled about, too busy to look over at her. The only thing that kept Corrine from setting the little girl on the floor and leaving was that word would get back to Lord Burke.

"Very well now," she soothed awkwardly, drawing the child closer. The child stopped struggling but held her little body stiff as she continued to cry.

Then Corrine remembered Mrs. O'Reilly's advice about the lullaby. She began humming a tune while gingerly rocking the chair—and sure enough, after a while the child relaxed against her, staring up at her face with half-closed eyes. Encouraged by the change, Corrine wiped the little nose again and started singing in a low voice bits and snatches of a song she had learned sometime in childhood.

> "... and so he asked the mighty ship at sea,
> 'Were you once a little boat like me?' ..."

When the child's eyelashes finally touched her pale cheeks, Corrine supposed she was asleep. Just then the child opened her eyes for an instant, raised her arm, and touched Corrine's chin with her little hand. A faint sigh escaped her lips, and she closed her eyes, her arm falling back to her side.

A hollow feeling rose up in Corrine's chest, the feeling that often came in the stillness of night before the brandy she took to soothe her nerves could put her to sleep. *My little girl was only a little older than this when I—*

She shook her head abruptly, trying to push the thought aside. But a picture of Jenny kept coming to her mind. So small and delicate the child had been, with huge gray eyes that regarded her mother with a mixture of fear and longing. She would be ten years old now. Did Jenny remember her at all? Or had she, over time, come to think that her aunt Mary was her mother?

*No!* Corrine's teeth clenched so hard her jaw began to ache. *I won't think of such things!*

But she could not force her eyes away from the child who lay sleeping in her arms.

# 8

In the kitchen, Gerald Moore made a pot of tea and finished the bread and marmalade and ham Rachel had left out for him. Corrine had not known what time they would return, but he assumed that he still had a couple of hours alone.

He was on his way into the parlor to read *The Times* when he spotted the round wooden box. He dropped his newspaper into his chair and moved over to the sofa. Setting the lid aside, he picked through scraps of paper and studied the faces.

*Rachel,* he thought with wonder, for they were certainly not his nor Corrine's. *And she even seems to capture their personalities!*

A great emptiness gnawed in his chest. Here was someone, a servant, who used the talent she had been given—by whom, he wasn't sure. The fact that she had not the proper equipment or lessons did not hinder her from trying to perfect her craft.

He had talent, too . . . once. A star student at Oxford's Exeter College, his idols were Thomas DeQuincey and Sir Edward Bulwer-Lytton. Prose flowed effortlessly from his pen like wine from a cask, and he imagined that one day every library in Great Britain would contain his novels.

Then trouble had come during summer holiday at his

family's estate in Lancaster. Just as he had been ready to start his third year at University, the girl from the village, the wheelwright's daughter, had come to him with the dreadful news that she was carrying his child. Gerald's father had grudgingly offered money to appease the girl's family. But the simpleminded soul, who had taken his declarations of undying love to heart, was insisting upon marriage.

The thought of becoming chained throughout life to such a creature haunted Gerald's dreams. He woke up one morning with the idea that he would go mad if the problem were not resolved. Pretending to have renewed affection for the silly lass, he had asked her to meet him at a certain spot in Bowland Forest where their earlier assignations had taken place. He had only wanted to reason with her without her father and brothers about. But she had made him angry with her babbling on about how happy they would be as a family . . . so angry that he lost all sense of reason and pushed her down a ravine.

Naturally he hurried down to help her, full of apologies. The sight of her, lying stiffly, eyes wide and mouth open, gasping for air, filled him with such panic that he ran through the forest for home. He was able to slip into the house with no one spotting him. His father was long-time friends with the high sheriff of Lancaster, and her death was declared an accident—a terrible, unforeseen accident. With no one to place Gerald even near the scene of the crime, no one could hold him accountable.

He had been bluffing two weeks ago when he warned Rachel that his father would come through in a pinch. A great deal of money from his father's hand had pacified the girl's father somewhat, but the bitter result of Gerald's rage was expulsion from Oxford and estrangement from his own family—his father handed him a cheque for a thousand pounds and made it clear that was all he could expect from him henceforth.

Over the years Gerald found replacements for writing. While decks of cards and bottles of gin did not give him the same satisfaction as penning a flowery description of a sunset, they demanded nothing from his soul. Yet he wondered, in his low hours, how different his life might have been. *If only* . . .

He frowned, despising himself for wallowing in self-pity. Sentiment was for fools, and he was no one's fool. Turning his eyes back to Rachel's sketches, he thought what a shame it was that he could not profit from her talent. He had seen artists, with their pencils and sketch pads at Hyde Park, doing hurried portraits for sixpence or even less. But that wasn't the kind of money he was interested in; and he certainly didn't want her discovering that she could earn a living another way.

A piece of paper caught his eye. He reached for it and brought it close. *Lord Burke,* he guessed. Corrine had described him as hardly looking human, but Rachel's rendering of the man showed handsome dark eyes and a studied intelligence.

*Why did she draw him?* And come to think of it, Rachel had seemed more reluctant than ever to play her part this time. Was it because she had some feelings for the man?

He studied the sketch. Impossible. Most of these sketches were of freaks and beggars . . . this was just another one of the freaks.

But if Rachel *did* have some feelings for the man, wouldn't that double their chance of success? The fact that she was just a servant was hardly a hindrance. Though marriages between the classes seldom occurred and were frowned upon, many a squire's son—himself included—had learned to find his way up the servants' staircase in the dark. She was growing more beautiful every day. What man could resist having *two* lovely women from which to choose?

Gerald smiled. He liked those odds—and he didn't mind sharing, not where money was concerned. He tossed the scrap of paper back in the box and began to close the lid when a sudden thought erased the smile from his face. If this Mr. Burke took an interest in Rachel, what would prevent him from luring her away from them? She was nineteen years old now and not so easy to control as she once was. It would be useless to forbid her to leave if she had somewhere else to go.

*And then what?* Gerald had always taken for granted that Rachel's forced involvement in all of their schemes would guarantee her silence. Often he reminded her that if he and Corrine were ever arrested, they would make certain the authorities knew about her as well. It was a bluff, of course—the last thing they would need was another wit-ness—but an effective one, aided by the tremendous load of guilt Rachel obviously felt.

Still, she was no longer the naive little girl they had taken from the orphanage. What if one day she realized that, as a young servant obeying orders, she would most likely not be held liable for anything they did?

*We can't risk that,* he thought. *She has to stay dependent on us.* As hopeful as he had just been about using Rachel to gain access to Lord Burke's money, he just couldn't do it. He would have to tell Corrine to make certain *she* was the one who got Burke's attention. Even if that meant leaving Rachel at home.

Which wasn't such a bad deal, come to think of it.

~

"Is your mistress all right?" Mrs. Morgan whispered in Rachel's ear. They shared one seat so that Mrs. Hammond could have the one facing them. Ever since the coachman had assisted her inside, Mrs. Hammond had sat staring through the window, seemingly at nothing in particular. "Do you think that the child's situation made her sad?"

Rachel glanced at her mistress. *More likely she had a fight with Mr. Moore last night.* She was aware that Mrs. Hammond had left her husband and baby several years ago, but Rachel had never seen her express any regret for having done so. Why would she feel any more for a child who was a stranger to her?

"I'm not sure," she whispered back. Still, she thought she had seen Mrs. Hammond's eyes glistening when Mrs. O'Reilly finally took the sleeping baby from her arms.

~

"My dear Miss Jones!" Mr. Solomon's face was wreathed in smiles Thursday morning as he made his way to the front of the shop. "I had so hoped you would come today!"

Rachel shifted her heavy market basket over to her left arm. "You had?"

"I want to show you something," he said with a wink. Taking the basket, he led her to his worktable at the back corner. "It was brought in yesterday to be cleaned and reframed."

On the table lay a canvas portrait of a middle-aged man clad in the type of hunting coat worn in the late eighteenth century. Browns, grays, and flesh tones were the primary colors, with a splash of deep scarlet for the jacket.

"Have you any idea who painted this?" he asked.

Rachel drew closer to study the signature scrawled in the left corner. "Reynolds?" Impressed, she looked up at Mr. Solomon. "Sir Joshua Reynolds . . . I've heard of him but I've never seen any of his work."

"You still haff not, my dear—not in this place, at least. Although I did manage to acquire and sell one of his paintings just last February."

"Then who is it?"

"His younger sister, Frances. She never achieved the fame that her titled brother did, but she was quite good for an amateur artist."

"A woman?" Rachel shook her head incredulously.

Mr. Solomon smiled again. "And surely you haff heard of Rosa Bonheur of France?" When Rachel nodded, he said, "So you see, it is possible to be a woman *and* a great artist."

"Yes, it is," she murmured. "But how did she do it?"

"Talent first, of course," said the man. "But talent alone will seldom suffice. Mademoiselle Bonheur was trained by her father, and I assume Miss Reynolds's brother was generous with practical advice."

Rachel leaned over the portrait again and studied the texture of the paint on the canvas. "He almost looks as if he could speak to us, doesn't he?"

"And what would he say?" Mr. Solomon chuckled. "'Please help me . . . I haff been trapped in this portrait for eighty years?'"

Smiling, Rachel retrieved her basket from him. "I have to go home now," she said. "Thank you for showing this to me."

"Of course." He walked with her toward the front. At the door, he said quietly, "You know, I would still like to see some of your sketches."

"But why?" She shook her head. "They aren't anything you could sell."

"Let us just say I am curious. You haff an eye for quality work. Usually God awards such a love for beauty with the talent to create more beauty."

"And what will you say if you don't like my work?"

The old man gave her a beatific smile. "I will advise you to draw for your own enjoyment and not to waste your time trying to sell it."

Rachel wasn't taken aback by his answer. Somehow, the fact that he would be honest and not try to spare her feelings made it easier to consider asking his opinion. But still, what would it change? She couldn't afford the lessons necessary to advance her skills, not to mention paints and canvases.

"One day," she promised. "By the way, may I buy a sketchbook?"

~

"You can't be serious." Corrine sat at her dressing table, blending French rouge into her fair cheekbones with her fingertips. She had to be careful not to overdo it, for women who wore makeup were considered immoral. "Why would a man like Lord Burke even look Rachel's way?"

"I'm not saying that he would," Gerald said. "It's just a possibility that we need to look out for now that she's more . . . mature."

"But she's just a maid. She scrubs *floors* for a living."

"And that's why I'm not overly concerned." He rose from the chair, picked up a hairbrush, and began pulling it through her dark hair. "But we still don't know a whole lot about this Burke's character. Even though he's a praying saint, some men are attracted to lower-class women. Didn't you say he was chummy with his own maids?"

Corrine leaned her head back and closed her eyes, enjoying the feel of the brush. "But not in that sort of way. Besides, he could hardly keep his eyes off *me* last Sunday."

"And who can blame him?" Gerald said. "I'm sure you're right. It's just that when I found the man's portrait, I started wondering if there was something we needed to watch out for."

"If Rachel drew his picture, it's because she apparently draws everyone she sees."

"I didn't see one of me . . . or you."

"Well, his scars must have interested her. But she knows better than to get infatuated with someone with whom I'm involved." Opening her eyes again, she studied his reflection. "By the way, what were you doing in her room?"

The brush ceased moving. "I wasn't in her room, if you must know. She left her sketches in the parlor yesterday. By the way, I believe this house is leased under my name. Is it not?"

"Well, yes, but I just don't want . . ."

"The girl needs to be watched so we'll know she's not plotting anything against us. I can't help it if you're uncomfortable with that."

Corrine sighed, studying in her reflection the fine lines around her eyes that seemed to have appeared overnight. "You just . . . seem to be taking a great deal of interest in her lately."

Smiling, Gerald resumed brushing her hair. "If that's all you're worried about, you needn't. I'm only interested in one woman, and she's right here with me."

She closed her eyes again, trying to convince herself that she had only imagined the coldness coming from him lately. Then she remembered the way he had been looking at Rachel. She wasn't making it up.

"So, are you still going to take her with you when you drop in on Lord Burke?" Gerald asked after a while in a casual voice.

Turning to take the brush from his hand, Corrine nodded. "I think that's best." *For more reasons than one,* she thought.

~

Two hours later, Dora was showing Rachel and Mrs. Hammond through Lord Burke's front door. She led them to chairs in the parlor, then told them she would see if Lord Burke would be able to receive guests.

Presently he stepped into the room, wearing a black waistcoat over a white shirt and gray worsted trousers, and said cordially, "Good afternoon, Mrs. Hammond, Miss Jones."

Holding out her hand, Mrs. Hammond said, "I beg you'll forgive my impulsiveness—popping over unannounced like this."

Lord Burke approached to take her extended hand, then nodded at Rachel before taking a seat in a chair. "There is nothing to forgive. It's not every day that I get a visit from two lovely women."

"You flatter me, Lord Burke," Mrs. Hammond said, then corrected quickly. "*Us*, rather."

He smiled. "What is it I may do for you?"

"You see, we were just out shopping, and we came across a lovely apron." Mrs. Hammond's gloved hand motioned toward the parcel in Rachel's lap. "Gingham and Irish lace. Well, Rachel said right away, 'That would look so lovely on Lord Burke's cook!' Bernice is her name, correct?"

"Bernice. And so you bought it," observed Adam, folding arms across his chest.

"Didn't I mention before how impulsive I am?" she said. She brushed the wrinkles from her maroon sateen skirt. "Anyway, we were about to start for home when Rachel said, 'I don't think I can wait until Sunday to see Bernice's face when we give this to her!'"

Taking a moment to send an affectionate look in Rachel's direction, she continued, "As we haven't anything else pressing, we chatted it over and decided to drop in. Are you sure you're not terribly angry?"

*Chatted it over?* Rachel thought bitterly. *When did we do that?* Aware that Lord Burke was looking her way, she made sure her expression was sufficiently bland to please Mrs. Hammond.

"Of course I'm not angry," Lord Burke was saying. "And it was so kind of you to think of Bernice. I'll send for her right away."

"Oh, don't do that," said Mrs. Hammond. "I'm sure she's busy. Besides, since it was Rachel's idea, I thought it would be nice if she took it to her."

Lord Burke shrugged. "Certainly, if that's what she would like to do." To Rachel he asked, "Can you find your way to the kitchen?"

"I can find it, sir." With the parcel in her arms she got to her feet, relieved to be leaving the room.

~

Lord Burke turned again to Corrine. "How was your visit to the children's home?"

"Oh, wonderful!" she exclaimed. "It was such a joy to bring

some happiness to those little lives. I can't thank you enough for suggesting it."

"Well, it was good of you to go. Mr. Garland has convinced a few other women to give the children some time, but Mrs. Morgan is the most faithful. I admire her for that."

"And so do I," Corrine agreed. "There just aren't enough faithful people in the world today, and they stand out like jewels when you find them."

"Does that mean you'll consider accompanying her every week?"

Covering her discomfort with a smile, Corrine replied, "I insist upon it, actually. Those children need us. And I must confess I was charmed by them—they're so beautiful."

"Yes, I imagine they are."

"You mean you've never seen the children you're helping support?"

"No, I haven't," he answered just a bit tersely.

"Oh dear, have I offended you?" Corrine mentally kicked herself for speaking without thinking. She rushed to explain. "I only meant . . ."

"No offense taken, Mrs. Hammond." He smiled a little, as if to put her at ease. "I believe I mentioned in one of my letters that I seldom make calls."

"Yes, you did, come to think of it." Corrine realized then that her faux pas could turn into a golden opportunity. Softening her voice, she said, "Lord Burke . . . would you mind terribly if I asked a personal question?"

"Of course not."

She shifted in her chair and fixed her gray eyes upon his face. "Your scars . . . is it true that they're the result of being wounded in battle?"

"They are," he replied, but did not elaborate. But at least he did not appear to be offended.

"And are they the reason you don't make calls?"

"I just don't care for attracting stares." His voice softened. "And I wouldn't want to frighten the children."

Careful to put as much warmth as possible in her tone, Corrine said, "You fought for England, Lord Burke. Those scars are medals of honor. And you're still an attractive man. Has no one ever said that to you?"

~

Stunned by his uninvited guest's blatant flattery, Adam could only look away. Her words, however insincere, caused a longing to grip his heart. *Why can't it be true?* he wondered darkly. *There's more to me than just my face. Isn't there a woman somewhere who would be willing to look beyond it and see that I still have some worth?*

Here seated opposite him was such a woman, one who professed a willingness to ignore his disfigurement—but the only worth she cared about was in pounds sterling.

Mrs. Hammond obviously mistook his silence for embarrassment, for she began speaking again. "Forgive my boldness, but if there's one thing I've learned in life, it's to speak the truth when it needs to be pointed out. When I met you this past Sunday, the first thing that came to my attention was how nice your eyes are. Kind eyes, filled with character."

"Well, thank you," he said. Suddenly tired, he wished this woman's maid would come back so she'd leave.

"I've something to confess, Lord Burke," she went on softly. She lowered her eyes. "Lord Burke. I'm not being quite honest with you."

110

Adam raised his good eyebrow. Was she about to turn around and admit that the words she'd just spoken had been pure flattery? Did she have a conscience after all? If she did, it certainly worked fast! "Indeed?"

"No," she murmured, looking deeply ashamed. At length she said, "You see, Rachel and I *could* have waited until Sunday to bring the apron by."

*So this confession's to be as phony as her compliments,* he thought, waiting for her to continue.

"We've just been so lonely ever since we moved to London," she was saying. "And you and your servants are the only people we know . . . besides the Morgans now, of course."

Even though he felt she was lying again, he could not allow himself to be anything but a gentleman. "Are there not women's societies you could join?"

Mrs. Hammond sighed deeply. "Please don't think me a snob, but I find most women . . . well, shallow. All they care about are fashions and gossip."

Adam struggled to keep from smiling. "Do they?"

"You have *no* idea."

"And what made you so different?"

"I take that as a compliment," she said with a little smile. "You see, I grew up an only child, and my father treated me as his equal." She was looking over Adam's shoulder now, with a dreamy cast to her face. "At the dinner table, when the ladies would retire to the drawing room so that the men could light cigars and speak of hunting and Irish home rule and window taxes and India and such, I was allowed to stay. I grew up appreciating the way men look at the world."

"And so you prefer the company of men."

Mrs. Hammond stared directly into his eyes, gave him a self-effacing little smile. "That sounds so . . . so wanton, doesn't it? But actually, I do. So when Rachel and I couldn't bear the loneliness this morning, I immediately thought of you. I did so enjoy your company Sunday."

~

"I should leave now," Rachel said to Bernice and Lucy at the kitchen table, over the rattle of cups and saucers.

"Oh, must you?" Lucy said. "Why, you haven't even finished your tea."

Rachel had to laugh. "That's because you poured another cup before I finished the first one."

"We would enjoy having you stay longer," Bernice told her, her ruddy face marked with concern, "and I do so appreciate the pretty apron. But we wouldn't want you getting into any trouble with your missus now."

Nodding, Rachel thought about Mrs. Hammond's earlier instructions to take as long as possible in the kitchen. *She'd prefer you stay in here all day,* she said to herself. And she would actually rather prefer that herself. *But you've done enough damage to Lord Burke today.*

"Just five more minutes," she said, prompting Lucy to clap her hands. She covered her cup with her hand. "But no more tea!"

~

Gerald was waiting for Corrine's report at home. "And how was your visit?"

Corrine opened her arms. "A kiss first."

He embraced her and pressed his lips to hers. As they

walked into the parlor he said, "I do hope that wasn't your *first* of the afternoon."

"Don't be so impatient—he's not as forward as most men. Besides, that was my first time alone with him."

"And I have the subtle feeling the idea doesn't appeal to you, does it?"

"Kissing him?" Corrine shuddered, and said in a dead voice, "Why should it be any different? I loathed kissing Squire Nowells and Sir Michael. But I always manage to do my part, don't I?"

Putting his arm around her waist, Gerald led her over to the sofa and took a place next to her. "You do, indeed. By the way, where is Rachel?"

"I sent her down to cook supper."

"How did she behave around Lord Burke?"

Corrine shrugged. "The same way she behaves most of the time. Like a deaf-mute."

"Good," he said. "And you said she left the two of you alone."

"Just as we planned. It was a stroke of genius, suggesting I get that apron for the cook."

Gerald kissed her again. "I have my moments."

# *9*

I don't believe anyone can prepare poached turbot like Bernice can," Robert Morgan said as helped himself to seconds. He and Penelope were in Adam Burke's dining room for their customary Friday evening meal with their friend. Across from each other, they sat adjacent to Adam at the end of the table.

Adam nodded agreement. "She says her secret is lemon juice, grated nutmeg, and fresh basil."

"Well, so much for your ability to keep *secrets,*" Penelope said. "I'll definitely try that."

Adam winced. "Just don't tell Bernice, and I won't be murdered in my sleep."

Robert let out a laugh. "As if you would! That woman coddles you to death—I'll wager she would roast a donkey for you if she thought you had a craving for it."

"And when did the good reverend start gambling?" Adam asked.

"All right, I know when to hold my tongue. Just wanted to let you know, if you ever decide you've had enough of the good life and want to let her go, we'll treat her with the respect she deserves."

"I'll bear that in mind. Now will you pass that platter, or do you intend to have the rest for yourself?"

~

After supper the three went to the library, where Adam and Penelope settled into leather chairs while Robert browsed through the shelves. "For a man who never goes anywhere, your collection of books grows every week," the minister said, thumbing through a volume of *The Mill on the Floss* by George Eliot.

"Borrow it if you like," said Adam. "I have an arrangement with Lackington's in Finsbury Square. They send me a crate of the latest books to inspect every fortnight or so. I just send back what I'm not interested in purchasing."

Penelope brought out her reticule. "Oh, Adam, I have something to show you." She reached over to hand him a linen handkerchief wrapped around something hard and flat.

Leaning forward to take the object in his hand, Adam opened the handkerchief and brought out the silver frame. He smiled. "Why, it's Margaret! When did you have this done?"

Penelope smiled. "We didn't *have* it done—someone sketched it from memory. Would you care to guess who?"

He studied the portrait again, looked up at her. "You'll have to enlighten me."

Exchanging smiles with her husband, who had now taken the chair on her other side, she said, "Rachel."

"Rachel. Rachel who?"

"Mrs. Hammond's Rachel. Miss Jones. She gave this to me before we left for St. John's. Were you aware that she's an artist?"

"No, I wasn't." He brought the portrait closer. "She's quite good, isn't she?"

"Quite good, indeed," Penelope agreed. "I must admit I was surprised."

"Did she show you anything else?"

"She has a whole box of sketches. Regrettably, we had to leave before I was able to see many, but the ones I did see were excellent."

"Ah, the lovely Mrs. Hammond," Robert said. He winked at Adam. "I believe she's set her cap for you, my friend."

Adam took one last look at the portrait, then handed it back to Penelope. "I believe you're right."

Robert looked surprised. "Well, it's good to hear you acknowledge that. There was a time when you thought no woman would even want to look at you again."

"That was before I realized how attractive money can be."

"What do you mean?" Penelope asked. "She seemed genuine to me . . . if a bit theatrical."

"Everyone seems genuine to you," Adam said, giving her an affectionate smile. "Why else would you have married old Robert here?"

Robert snorted at that remark. "Why do you think she's after your money?"

"Let's just say I have a strong hunch. Bernice has as well, and I'd consider her the most astute judge of character I know. Mrs. Hammond paid us a call yesterday, you know."

"Did she?" Penelope said.

"Yes, with Miss Jones. Only she sent the girl to the kitchen as soon as propriety would allow—a gift for Bernice was the reason. Then when we were alone, she . . . well, flirted with

me. It was obvious she didn't mean a word of it. She may be
theatrical, as you say, but she's not *that* good an actress."

He added in a wry tone, "I take that back. She'd make a
perfect Lady Macbeth."

"Perhaps you should suggest it," Robert jested, then
sobered up at the sharp look from his wife. "And then, perhaps not."

Penelope shook her head. "I'm surprised, Adam . . . and
disappointed. You certainly deserve better."

"What will you do about her?" asked Robert.

"Nothing."

"Nothing?" Glancing again at her husband, Penelope said,
"But if she's after your money . . ."

"Unless she comes here with a mask and a pistol, my
money's perfectly safe," Adam told her. "And unless she makes
a habit of popping in to see me too often, I'll allow the situation to stay as is. You don't object to allowing her to accompany you to St. John's, do you?"

"Not at all. She actually was a great help last time."
Penelope made a face. "Even if it was only to get your attention."

"So she's still welcome to our Sunday meetings then?"
Robert asked.

Adam gave his friend a nod. "Would you have it any other
way?"

"No, I wouldn't. I can't see turning anybody away from
hearing the gospel, even if she's come for the wrong reasons."

"You're such a good man," Penelope said, smiling at her
husband. She turned to Adam. "And you."

Robert reached for his wife's hand and returned her smile.

"And not to mention Miss Jones," he said softly. "She's not likely to be allowed to come if her mistress is turned away."

"Bernice mentioned that, too," Adam said. "Speaking of Miss Jones, may I see that portrait again?"

~

Groaning, Corrine turned over in bed to lie on her stomach and press her forehead against the pillow, trying to ease the pain gripping the top of her head. The throbbing was so intense that she had left the table before finishing her supper.

She wished Gerald had come upstairs with her. While he had made sympathetic little noises as she pushed her plate away and told him she was hurting, he simply ordered Rachel to help her up to her room and fetch her a pot of strong tea. *He didn't miss a bite,* she thought reproachfully.

She had waved away the tea when the girl returned, opting instead for a glass of brandy. Rachel had to steady the glass in her shaking hands and hold it up to her mouth.

The brandy wasn't helping, even though she had gulped it down a good twenty minutes ago. *Maybe I should have another glass.* Yet she was hurting too badly to raise her head, even more so to reach for the decanter on the bedside table.

*It's your own fault,* she chided herself. *You've got to stop thinking about that child!* She wished now, more than ever, that she had never agreed to visit that dreadful orphanage.

~

"Thank you, sir." Downstairs in the kitchen, Rachel reached for the tray of plates and silverware Gerald carried in. "But I really can clear the table myself."

"And have you climbing up and down those stairs with

your arms full? I just wish I could help you more often, but . . ." His jerk of the head insinuated that Mrs. Hammond was the reason. Something inside warned Rachel not to turn her back on him. She waited until he had left the kitchen before turning to put the plates in the sink. After she washed them and set them in the rack to dry with the glasses, she dunked the copper roast-beef pan down in the water and began to scrub it, keeping her ears alert to any sounds on the stairs. They were stone and easy to slip up or down without making noise, so she turned every few seconds to check the doorway with her eyes as well.

She had just became absorbed in scouring the crust from the pan with a cloth when she felt a presence close behind her.

"You know, your hair is like spun gold," came an oily whisper in her ear. A hand touched her shoulder.

Rachel froze.

Gerald stepped closer and ran his hand down her backbone. "I wonder if you realize how beautiful you are."

With nausea gripping her, Rachel felt in the dishwater for the carving knife. She took hold of the handle and wheeled around, sloshing water on both of them. "Don't ever do that again!" she cried as she held the knife pointed at the middle of his linen shirt.

He eased a few steps backward, held up his palms in a pacifying manner. "You're overreacting, Rachel. I only meant to pay you a compliment."

Obviously, he was struggling not to smile, and it infuriated her even more.

"I know what you meant!" she said as she took a step toward him.

He took another backward step, bumped into the worktable, and began edging sideways. "Oh, come on. Can't you take a compliment?"

"Not from the likes of you, I can't! And if you want to send me to the workhouse, go ahead. One rat to watch out for is the same as another!"

Gerald glanced at the doorway, put a finger to his lips. "Not so loud . . ."

"Leave this kitchen if you want me to be quiet!" Her teeth had begun to chatter and her hand trembled, but she managed to keep a firm grip on the knife.

It was not firm enough. In an instant he lunged. With one arm he pinned her arms to the side, and with his other he pried open her fingers so that the knife clattered to the stone floor.

"Don't you dare hold a knife to me again," he snarled. His breath reeked of gin. "Or they'll be fishing your body out of the Thames the next day."

She could not answer, but stood trembling in his grasp.

His arms tightened around her. "Do you understand me, Rachel?"

"Y-yes."

"Good." He let go of her and stepped back. "Not a word of this to Mrs. Hammond, or you'll live to regret it." At the door he sent her a smile over his shoulder and said, "She wouldn't believe you anyway."

Rachel propped herself against the edge of the table, her knees weak. *I'd be ashamed to tell a soul!*

~

Hours later, Rachel rose from her cot and went over to the dormer window. The night was cloudless, with stars crusting the sky like sprinkled sugar. Beneath them were the dark silhouettes of houses. Not even one window was lit.

*Everyone in London is asleep but me,* she thought, feeling lonelier than ever. She closed her eyes and pressed her forehead against the glass. *Please help me, God,* she prayed silently. *Surely there's somewhere safe I can go.*

For a long time she waited for an answer. She was comforted when a sense of his presence filled the small room. But not when what seemed to be the answer found its way to her heart.

*Wait . . .*

"Wait for what, Father?" she whispered, throat tight. "For them to kill me? Or ruin someone else?"

When the same answer came, she went to bed and wept, from weariness and loneliness, and the realization that her faith was weak indeed.

~

"I'm sorry, but the position has been taken," said the housekeeper at the sixth back door Rachel knocked upon on Saturday morning.

"Already?" Rachel's shoulders fell. "But I just bought this newspaper two hours ago."

The woman sighed and looked past her to another young woman coming up the path. "And you're the sixth person who's applied," she said kindly. "Number seven's coming up behind you."

"Isn't there some work I can do?" she pressed. "I don't need a big salary."

"I'm truly sorry."

"Yes, missus. Thank you for your time."

"Take a little advice, dear," said the housekeeper with a sad smile. "You're a pretty one and polite, too; but you won't get a position without a letter of reference. Why don't you ask your former employers to write one for you?"

"Yes, I'll have to do that," said Rachel, backing up the steps. Thanking the woman again, she turned and nodded at number seven as she passed. The other applicant was young, too, and wore an anxious expression . . . the same look Rachel knew had been on her own face all morning.

When she returned home, Mrs. Hammond was waiting at the kitchen worktable.

"Where have you been?" she demanded. "I had to make my own hot chocolate, and there aren't any pastries left."

The anxiety which been a part of her life for over six years seized Rachel, but she fought against it. "I'm sorry about the chocolate. There were ginger biscuits in the jar last night."

"Well, I get hungry when my head aches. Where were you?"

*Don't back down!* Rachel thought. "I had some errands." She squared her shoulders and met the gaze without flinching. "Now, would you like me to go to the bakery?"

"First I want to know where you've been." Mrs. Hammond motioned to the newspaper tucked under Rachel's arm. "You've been looking for another job, haven't you?"

"I had some errands," Rachel repeated softly. Turning from the angry woman, she reached up for her market basket. "What kind of pastries would you like?"

~

Corrine studied the girl's back. It was obvious that Rachel no longer believed her threat to tell any new employers that she was a thief, else why would she be looking for another position?

*You ought to sack her right now,* she told herself. But then what? What if she decided to go to the police? Or what if she actually did find another position?

Then she would have the problem of explaining to Lord Burke why Rachel was no longer with her at the Sunday meetings. She could always make up some reason, but what if Rachel kept up her friendship with that cook and her daughter and told them the truth? In fact, what would keep the girl from telling them *everything?*

Lord Burke was far too softhearted. He would believe his servants. Then she would have no chance at all with him.

There wasn't time to find another prey. Their money situation was only two or three months away from desperate—that is, if Gerald had only moderate losses at the card tables. She couldn't understand why he failed to see that he was throwing their money away with his gambling. For every quid he pocketed, he lost five the following night.

And he was behaving oddly. Just Sunday past, as she dressed to go to Lord Burke's, she had noticed Gerald staring a little too intently at her strand of pearls. When she returned, she hid them in the toe of a seldom-worn pair of slippers in the far recesses of her wardrobe. The pearls were the prettiest thing she had ever owned and her most valuable possession. She was determined they wouldn't be used for gambling debts . . . or any other of Gerald's debts, for that matter.

There was another reason she wanted to hang on to the pearls, one she did not like to think about. If Gerald ever left her, he would probably take every penny they owned. She had to have some assurance of an income, at least for a while, and selling the pearls would give her that.

Corrine focused her attention upon Rachel again. *She's changing,* she thought. *And she'll leave if we don't treat her differently.* Part of her would welcome such an occurrence. Rachel had grown into a beautiful young woman, and Gerald had obviously noticed. But until they moved on to another town, they couldn't risk her turning on them.

"I'd like some pastries," she finally said. "But I can wait if you're too tired."

Rachel blinked at her. "I beg your pardon?"

"You look tired. Why don't you sit and rest for a while first?"

"I'm . . . I'm not tired," the girl said. "And I can get some eggs while I'm out."

"That would be nice." Corrine started for the stairs, then turned back to face her. "And, Rachel . . ."

"Yes, missus?"

"Why don't you throw that newspaper into the dustbin?"

~

Corrine poured Gerald a cup of tea at the table in the parlor an hour later. Still in his dressing gown, he opened his *London Times*. "Where did Rachel disappear to?"

"Market," Corrine answered, waiting until his attention was focused on the newspaper so that she could add a second spoonful of sugar to her own cup of tea.

"Didn't she go yesterday?"

"She forgot the eggs."

Gerald shrugged. He looked up again, however, when Corrine pulled out the chair across from him.

"I won twelve pounds last night," he announced.

"Really? How much did you lose the night before?"

His expression darkened. "That doesn't matter. I'm on a winning streak now."

She ignored this rationalization. She had heard it all before. "I want to talk with you about something."

"Yes?"

"It's Rachel. Have you noticed anything different about her?"

"Different? How so?"

"She went looking for another position this morning."

"Another position!" he snorted. "I don't even have to ask if she found one."

"She didn't, but—"

"And she won't," Gerald interrupted. "Not if *I* have anything to do with it."

Corrine was tempted to ask why he felt so strongly about keeping Rachel. She was pretty certain that his reasons were not the same as hers. But she was in no mood for an argument, so she took a sip of her tea and said, "We can't expect to keep her forever. One day she'll find another place, with or without references."

Gerald closed the newspaper and turned it over to the back page. He scanned the fine print for a few seconds, then passed it across to her. "So many unemployed servants looking for jobs these days. How many 'situations' advertisements would you estimate are on that page? A hundred?"

"There's something different about her," Corrine persisted. "It's almost as if she's grown up overnight. I'm telling you, she's not as frightened of us as she used to be."

"Pray tell me," Gerald said with exaggerated softness, as if he were speaking to an idiot, "how will her newfound courage change the domestic employment situation in London?"

Corrine shook her head. "I don't know. She seems determined enough to find a way."

~

Gerald thought back to their confrontation in the kitchen and the expression on Rachel's face when she held the knife at him. She would have used it on him if he had not backed off. Perhaps Corrine was right. "What do you suggest?" he asked.

"I think we should start treating her better. That includes a bigger salary."

"But we can't afford—"

"Her salary's a pittance. We spend more on lamp oil than we do on her. What we can't afford is to lose her right now."

He didn't have to be convinced of that. "Then we'll just have to do it."

"Also, we need to let her know right away that we've had a change of heart about the way we've treated her."

Gerald smiled. "Do you mean something like . . . a *religious* conversion, my dear?"

"No." Corrine shook her head. "She would never believe that. Not without your giving up the cards and gin—and letting Lord Burke off the hook. Not to mention . . ."

"I see your point." Linking hands behind his neck, he leaned back in his chair and weighed their options.

"We could just come out and admit that this job-hunting incident made us realize how much we don't want to lose her."

"Good idea." Gerald nodded slowly. "But I believe *I* should be the one to speak with her."

"Alone?" Corrine's eyes filled with suspicion. "Why?"

"I know what you're thinking." He sat up again, reached across the table to take her hand. "And you're wrong. I just feel that I'm the one who's treated her the worst, so the apology should come from me."

"But why not both—"

"Because we don't want to make too much of this. If Rachel thinks we've become desperate to keep her, then she'll start demanding more than we're prepared to give her. I won't have a tyrant for a servant."

Corrine frowned. "I just can't see her behaving that way."

Gerald couldn't see it either, but he didn't want Corrine around when he apologized to the girl. The incident in the kitchen last night was minor in his own mind, but he was sure it was the reason she went out job hunting this morning. And he didn't want her blurting out anything that Corrine shouldn't hear.

"I grew up in a household with servants," he reminded her. "Trust me, you don't ever want them to feel they're not expendable."

"If you insist," Corrine said.

Gerald watched her refill the teacups. *She thinks I don't know she's slipping more sugar into hers,* he thought. She was becoming so predictable. For all her beauty and refined ways, Corrine Hammond was still just a country bumpkin.

# 10

Rachel was cleaning up after Saturday's supper when Mr. Moore stepped into the kitchen.

"Now, don't start getting edgy," he said as she stood poised to sprint. "I'm going out in a few minutes, but I wanted to have a word with you."

She glanced at the carving knife she had kept next to the sink all day, and watched in silence as he pulled out a chair at the worktable. He was dressed in a dark broadcloth frock coat with a diamond stickpin in his silk cravat, his usual attire when frequenting the gaming rooms.

"Will you have a seat?" he asked, motioning to the chair across the table from him. When she didn't move, he said, "I promise to be a gentleman."

Wiping her hands upon her apron, Rachel glanced at the knife again, then walked over to pull out the chair.

"Do you know why I'm here?" he asked when she was seated.

She shook her head.

"I came to apologize for last night. I don't know if you realized it, but I had tossed back quite a bit of gin during the evening, and I wasn't myself. Still, there's no excuse for what I did."

Rachel couldn't believe what she was hearing. *First Mrs. Hammond, and now him!* When she had recovered from the shock, she steeled herself and said quietly, "It wasn't just last night."

Mr. Moore's eyebrows lifted. "Excuse me?"

"You've been . . . making me uncomfortable for a while," she said.

He opened his mouth as if to protest, closed it, and said at length, "Yes, you're right." He lifted his hands helplessly. "I've nothing to say in my own defense either. You've turned into such a beauty that I forgot my manners."

Rachel frowned at him. "You're doing it again."

Appearing to be genuinely surprised, he put a hand up to his chest. "Am I? You mean the compliment?"

"I don't like your saying things like that."

"Then I'll quit." Mr. Moore put a finger up to his lips. "Never again, and that's a promise."

He had certainly never apologized before, for anything. This was because she went looking for another job, Rachel was certain. Whatever his reasons, she realized she might never have another opportunity to speak her mind. She sat up straight. He was going to hear all of it, even if she ended up sleeping at the workhouse!

"It's not just the things you say," she went on. "I don't like you . . . looking at me the way you do."

He grimaced. "I've really been a cad, haven't I?"

"Yes, sir." Her voice was a whisper now, but she still forced herself to meet his pale eyes.

"Then I must make amends. If I promise to leave you alone, will you stop all that non— I mean, will you stop looking for another job?"

Suddenly it dawned upon her that this whole change in attitude was not only to keep her from finding another position. He was afraid she would tell Mrs. Hammond!

"By the way," Mr. Moore continued as if reading her mind, "I confessed everything to Corrine this morning while you were out getting eggs."

Wary of anything he would have to say, Rachel said, "You did?"

"I did." He shrugged. "Go ahead and ask her if you don't believe me."

"What did she—"

"What did she say? After she shouted at me—which she had every right to do—we both realized that we've been treating you rather badly. Me, especially. That's when we decided to raise your salary. Double it, actually."

His thin lips stretched into a magnanimous smile as if he had just bestowed a great favor upon her. "Well, don't you have anything to say?"

"Say?"

"I should think you would be happy. Perhaps even a thank-you would be in order."

She took in a deep breath. "I can never be happy here."

"Why?"

"Because of what you do—you and the missus."

His expression hardened for a fraction of a second; then he leaned forward and gave a labored sigh. "You mean how we make money."

"You extort it."

"Not so," he insisted, shaking his head. "If people want to give Corrine money, then she's not foolish enough to turn it down."

"But she pretends to care for them."

"And you think she's the only woman who's ever chased a wealthy man? My dear child, women do that all the time."

She still couldn't believe he was allowing her to speak frankly. Years of self-loathing over her part in their deeds brought a bitter taste to her mouth. "Most of the men who gave her money were married. And look at Squire Nowells."

"That was unfortunate," Mr. Moore replied, shaking his head. "But Corrine didn't hold a gun to his head. And if a man is unfaithful to his wife, I think he deserves to lose a little money. They've been rich enough to absorb any loss of the funds they've given—I repeat, *given*—to Corrine."

"What of Lord Burke?" asked Rachel.

Mr. Moore sighed. "What of him?"

"He's not being unfaithful to anybody."

"I wouldn't worry about the good and kind Lord Burke. The man obviously gets happiness from sharing his money, and Corrine is just going to make him a little happier."

"By deceiving him."

"By being *kind* to him," Mr. Moore insisted. "You're too young to understand such things, Rachel, but men enjoy having a beautiful woman pay attention to them. Lord Burke probably can't believe his luck right now."

"But she'll leave him one day . . . after she gets his money."

He held up a hand. "After he *gives* her *some* of his money."

"And how will that make him feel?" Rachel persisted. "He'll know he was being used."

"Not at all. Corrine will simply tell him that her husband was found alive, rescued from some remote island, and that she has to return to him." He smiled. "And Lord Burke will be left with the realization that he's not unattractive to women. That should be worth a little expense along the way."

He took the watch from the fob pocket upon his waistcoat and clicked it open. "I'm late for an appointment," he said, picking up his silk hat from the table. He pushed out his chair and stood. "By the way, I forgot to mention that you're to get Sunday afternoons off, too, starting tomorrow. Corrine would still like you to go to those church meetings at Lord Burke's, however. We assume you won't mind that."

He was expecting her to thank him, Rachel realized, but she could not bring herself to say the words.

"Well," he said, perching hat upon head. "Good evening."

She sat there for a little while when he was gone, wondering at the conversation which had just taken place. Did the men Mrs. Hammond pretended to love really deserve what happened to them? Even if they did, did that make what she was doing right? Mr. Moore had made her deceptions sound almost noble.

But it wasn't right. And it wasn't right for her to be a part of it.

~

Gerald turned at the sound of footsteps in the hall. "What is it, Rachel?"

"I would like to know why you won't give me a letter of character," she said.

Gerald replaced his umbrella in the brass stand and studied the face of the girl before him. *I could get lost in those green eyes,* he thought. Deep set and innocent, they almost looked out of place over lips that were full and sensuous. He thought of a line from Byron: *She walks in beauty, like the night.* While he was drawn like a magnet to her innocence, the desire to take it away from her dominated his thoughts more and more lately. *Let you go? Never!*

"You're still wanting to leave us, Rachel? After I gave you my word we would treat you better?"

Rachel nodded. "You can hire somebody else. You said yourself that there are plenty of servants looking for jobs."

*Stall her,* he thought. If he could get her to stay with them a bit longer, he could always think up some way to talk her out of leaving. "How about this?" he finally said. "If you'll forget about looking for another position until we get ready to leave London, I'll have Corrine write you up a glowing letter of character."

He started turning for the door, then had a second thought. "In fact," he added, "how about when we leave here we give you enough money to rent a room somewhere while you look for employment—say for two months?" Gerald stretched his lips into a smile. "It's the least we can do, after all the years of service you've given us."

~

*Perhaps he's right,* Rachel rationalized. *Perhaps Lord Burke does enjoy the attention Corrine is giving him.* She had never thought about it, but it was possible that men needed to feel handsome, just as women wanted to be told they were beautiful. And if the man had enough money to be giving some away, he could probably well afford to pay for Corrine's bolsters to his ego.

"Have we an agreement?" Mr. Moore asked.

Hesitating, she said, "Do you give your word about the letter of character?"

Mr. Moore picked up his umbrella and tipped the brim of his hat with its ivory handle. "You have my word, Rachel."

~

The biblical story of Daniel in the lions' den was the foundation for Reverend Morgan's sermon on Sunday, the twenty-sixth of April.

"Do you think Daniel had absolutely no fear?" the minister asked. "I have to believe that he did fear them. We are created to fear danger—it is one of the gifts God equips us with to keep us alive."

He looked over at his daughter and smiled. "Margaret does not fear second-story windows. She would climb into them if we allowed it. Fearlessness and courage are not always the same. Indeed, believing as I do that Daniel feared the lions makes me admire him even more so. Perhaps one of the things he prayed for in his upper room—thus breaking King Darius's law—was the courage to go through the ordeal, no matter what God would decide the outcome to be."

Again, the words were as water to Rachel's spiritual thirst. It was as if the sermon had been written for her. For she realized it was fear of what would happen to her which led her to give even second thought to Mr. Moore's assurance that Mrs. Hammond's attentions to Lord Burke were somehow paying him a kindly service.

"I thank God that in England, at least, we're not put into situations where we are martyred for our faith," the minister went on. "But, precious ones . . . *to whom much is given, much is required.* And I believe that our freedom compels us even more to stand up for holiness and goodness in the face of those who would have us do otherwise. Let us pray for courage, brothers and sisters!"

*Yes, please, Father,* Rachel prayed silently. *Please give me the courage to do what's right.*

~

"You'll never catch me in one of them underground carriages," Jack Taylor said a half hour later as he slathered mayonnaise on bread for a roast beef sandwich. "It ain't natural, for sure."

At the head of the table, Lord Burke pointed his fork in the gardener's direction. "Did I not hear you say the same thing about trains when we were preparing to move to London?"

"He did," Bernice confirmed. With a sidelong grin at her husband, she related how he had said it wasn't "natural" to be traveling across the country at thirty miles an hour.

The huge man actually blushed. "But that were different. And I'm man enough to admit I was wrong."

Penelope Morgan nodded. "Well, I'm with you, Mr. Taylor. I would be afraid the ground would cave in." She glanced down at the little girl seated on a copper pot in the chair beside her, happily munching on a pickled carrot. "And I absolutely forbade Robert to take Margaret with him."

Stunning in a rose-colored silk gown trimmed with ecru cotton lace, Mrs. Hammond looked at the minister with affected awe. "You actually went down into that tunnel?"

"It's not like a rabbit hole, Mrs. Hammond," Reverend Morgan said. "You should go and see for yourself sometime—the air's just a bit heavy with sulfur, but not unbearably so. And it's lit up quite nicely."

"According to the *Times,* more routes are being planned as we speak," Lord Burke said. "They say that there will come the time when people will be able to go from one end of the city to the other in a matter of minutes."

Rachel noticed the glow in Lord Burke's eyes as he spoke of this latest marvel, the London Underground. *He looks as if he's dying to see it for himself. . . . Doesn't he go anywhere at all?*

He turned his face in her direction and caught her staring. Quickly she dropped her gaze to the sandwich upon her plate.

To her further mortification, he said, "By the way, Miss Jones . . . Mrs. Morgan showed me the portrait you drew of Margaret. You have an incredible talent."

"Thank you, sir," Rachel murmured, still watching her plate and hoping the pleasure on her face wasn't obvious. *An incredible talent,* he said!

"We were wondering if you would mind bringing some of your other sketches next week?" asked Reverend Morgan.

The satisfaction from having had Mrs. Morgan praise Margaret's portrait had left Rachel with a craving for more. She wanted the whole world to look at her sketches and confirm that she had talent, a gift, that brought a spark of light into the drudgery that was her life.

Still, she shook her head. If only she had had time to work in her sketchbook. "Just bits and pieces," she said to the minister. "Nothing good enough to show everybody."

"She's just being modest," Mrs. Hammond said warmly. "She's very talented."

Rachel gave her a grateful look, and Mrs. Hammond smiled back. But her praise turned out to be an attempt to steer the conversation to herself. "I've always encouraged her to develop that talent. In fact, I've asked her to do my portrait."

Softening her voice, she added, "My late husband often asked me to have one made. He would say, 'Corrine, your

137

face should be immortalized on canvas, so that years from now our great-grandchildren will still be able to enjoy your—your beauty.' I put it off though, never seeming to find the time. Now it's too late."

~

Adam watched Mrs. Hammond dab at her eyes with her napkin and thought of a line from one of Sir Francis Bacon's essays. *It is the wisdom of crocodiles that shed tears when they would devour.*

At length the woman lowered the napkin and put on a brave little smile. "Now, would you just look at what I've done—spoiled a lovely gathering with my melancholy memories."

"Not at all, missus," said Marie. "That was touching."

After another few seconds Bernice cleared her throat. "You know, I'd like to have a portrait made of Lucy."

"That's a grand idea," Jack said, while Lucy, seated between her father and mother, put a hand up to her pinking cheeks. He asked Miss Jones, "How much would you charge to draw her picture?"

"Why, nothing," Miss Jones replied. "I haven't colors, though. Does that matter?"

The cook reached over to squeeze her hand. "I saw little Margaret's portrait. Anything you draw will be beautiful. And we'll talk more later about paying you."

"Try if you will, Bernice," Penelope leaned forward and advised. "But she wouldn't take a penny from me."

"I don't charge my friends," Miss Jones said, giving the minister's wife a quick smile.

Silently watching the interchange before him, Adam was

both touched and amused by the girl's reaction to being the focus of everyone's attention. She was positively glowing. *Yet she looks like she'd like to crawl under the table any minute.*

Back when he was a brash, young officer out to conquer the world for England's sake, that sort of modesty would have annoyed him. While he had never been one to lord his position and wealth over people of lower social stations, he often mistook their meekness for signs of weak character.

Now having experienced rejection by those closest to him, he understood the necessity to keep one's feelings sheltered against any possible hurt. *And she's been hurt sometime in her life . . . perhaps back in the orphanage. Or perhaps Bernice is right about Corrine Hammond's mistreating the girl.*

"Why don't you come over one day this week and have Lucy sit for you?" he found himself saying. "I must confess, I've never watched an artist at work—I would be interested in seeing how you go about it."

Before Miss Jones could reply, Mrs. Hammond said, "What a wonderful idea, Lord Burke. We'll be here tomorrow afternoon."

"Sorry, missus," Bernice said, "but we do the baking for the week on Mondays. Takes up the whole day."

"And we have our children's home to visit on Tuesday," Penelope said.

If Mrs. Hammond was disappointed at the delay, she covered it well. "Then those days simply won't do, will they? But Wednesday will be just fine."

Bernice glanced at Adam. He nodded back.

"It's very kind of you to spare her, missus," Bernice said to Mrs. Hammond. "And I'll cook and send you something special to make up for her time away. But you don't have to bother with getting out yourself."

"We'll send a coach for her," Adam said. It would be a hired one, for his one-horse runabout and the market wagon were all that were necessary for his reclusive lifestyle.

"Oh, but I *adore* watching Rachel sketch," Mrs. Hammond said. "It will be a fun outing for me, too. That is . . . if you don't mind my coming along."

She was lying—Adam knew it instinctively. She had probably never watched the girl work. She had probably never shown any interest at all in her sketchings. Until now, when doing so would suit her purposes.

"You don't mind, do you?" she repeated, her smile not quite masking the desperation in her eyes.

He almost felt pity for her. Another quotation came to mind, from the poet Matthew Prior, of over a century ago.

*Virtue is its own reward.*

If that were so, then the *lack* of virtue would be its own punishment. He would not wish to be a predator like Mrs. Hammond if it netted him all the money in England. There was a lot to be said for a night's sleep unhampered by a troubled conscience. And a person did have to account to God, sooner or later.

~

Rachel trimmed the crusts from her sandwich and wondered if she had imagined the disappointment which had briefly shadowed Lord Burke's scarred face. Never had she met *any* man immune to Mrs. Hammond's charms. Could he be the exception?

Come to think of it, she had noticed the same fleeting

expression the day they dropped over with the apron. Was it just possible that he could see through her act? Perhaps Lord Burke's appearance wasn't the only thing which set him apart from most other men. Perhaps the discernment Reverend Morgan had preached about last Sunday was part of his life.

She glanced at the people seated around her. In all the places she had traveled with Mrs. Hammond and Mr. Moore, she had never experienced a household where servants were invited to break Sunday bread with their employer.

*He's a decent man.*

A pang of some indefinable longing touched her heart. She sent a covert glance toward the head of the table again, as Lord Burke and Jack were conversing. What would it be like to have someone as decent and kind as him fall in love with her?

Her mind immediately pushed away the thought. She was still just a servant, after all. They might be dining together at the same table, but for all the difference it made, they might as well be on different continents.

# 11

Tuesday morning Corrine thought of pretending
a headache, which would not be far off the mark,
for she and Gerald had argued last night over what
he deemed her lack of progress with Lord Burke.

Remembering how Lord Burke had looked at Rachel
Sunday finally propelled her out of bed. And, she decided on
her way down to the kitchen, Rachel had diverted enough
attention away from her.

"Don't bother dressing up," she said while raiding the
crockery jar for scones in the kitchen. "You've enough to do
around here."

The girl's face went white. "Please don't leave me here. . . ."

She did not say *with Mr. Moore*, but Corrine knew that was
what she meant. Refusal rose immediately to her lips, but the
absolute misery in Rachel's expression made her reconsider.

"Oh, very well," she said, but held out a hand when the girl
seemed on the verge of embracing her.

*You're going soft*, she said to herself.

~

In the nursery, Mrs. O'Reilly greeted her, Mrs. Morgan, and
Rachel with a weary, "You're balms to our souls, you are."

Mrs. Morgan and Rachel were already enveloped from knees to the waist by the hugs of chattering little ones. Corrine stood a bit off to the side and searched the huge room with her eyes.

"Are ye looking for the little girl?" Mrs. O'Reilly asked.

Corrine frowned, reluctant to admit it. The child had come to her thoughts several times during the week, in spite of her efforts to forget about the orphanage. It was bad enough that she had to *come* here every Tuesday—she resented having it pop up in her mind in the meantime. Still, she couldn't help wondering if the little girl would recognize her.

She had left her crinoline at home this time, too.

Mrs. O'Reilly took a step over to her and pointed to a little bundle in the furthermost corner of the room. The child lay on her side with her knees drawn up to her chest, watching the other children with a listless expression. "She's not wantin' to eat."

"Not anything?"

"She'll drink a wee bit of water now and then, but she won't touch her milk or porridge. We've had to force what we could down her, but it ain't enough."

Corrine looked over at the little body again and winced. "Force her?"

The Irish woman shrugged work-rounded shoulders. "Sounds heartless, but she's got to have nourishment."

The child stirred, lifting her head from the wooden floor. She seemed to scan the room for a few seconds, then closed them again and laid her head back down.

"She's still lookin' for her mother," Mrs. O'Reilly explained. "Perhaps ye could sit with her for a while, like ye did the last time."

"Very well." Sweeping around children, Corrine made her way over to the corner. The child lifted her head again and watched with disinterested eyes. Instead of calling to her, Corrine simply bent down and took her up in her arms. She expected a struggle, but the child lay limply in her arms as if resigned to whatever should happen to her.

Alarmed, Corrine held the girl against her shoulder and sought out Mrs. O'Reilly, who was lying a sleeping infant in one of the cribs. "Why won't she cry?"

The woman turned and reached out a finger to touch one of the child's flaxen curls. "I don't know. But I can tell ye they don't last long when they get to this state."

Corrine was horrified. "Do you not care what happens to her?"

Mrs. O'Reilly's sigh seemed to cause the lines in her face to deepen. "I don't want the child to die, Mrs. Hammond. But if she does, by the very next mornin' we'll have another, just as pitiful, to take her place. If we grieved every time something like this happened, we couldn't work here."

"It just sounds so cold."

"Cold? Meanin' no disrespect, I'll tell ye what's cold—it's when folks have to spend twelve hours a day in the mills or factories just to keep a roof over their heads and a bit of food in their families' bellies. Sometimes there's no place for a little one like this to stay if she's got no other family to help care for her. Then the mother and father have to give her up, hopin' their child'll have a better chance here."

Corrine instinctively tightened her arms around the limp form. "I should think she would get hungry enough to want some food after a while."

Mrs. O'Reilly shook her head. "Most times they do, but

sometimes the sadness gets in the way of the appetite. Don't forget—she don't understand that her mother might have left her for her own good. She just wants her back."

Resting chin against the top of the little blonde head, Corrine carried her over to a rocking chair. The rockers squeaked slowly against the wooden floor as she patted the child's back.

*How sad the world can be at times,* she thought.

And not just for little children.

*I can't even remember the last time I was happy.* Gerald's money from his family, and then the money they started making themselves, had insulated her from sorrow for a while. The excitement of high living had given her little time to reflect upon the emptiness of her lifestyle. But then the sleepless nights started, and the thoughts that raced so furiously in her head made her worry for her own sanity.

She thought back to Robert Morgan's sermons. Though she had successfully blocked out the minister's words, one overall feeling had pierced her heart. She was a sinner. She glanced down at the baby in her lap, whose fair head rested against her bosom. *The worst kind. The kind who abandons her own child.*

What was her daughter, Jenny, doing at this very moment? Was she happy? Did she ever wonder about the mother who had abandoned her?

Corrine shook the thought from her head and forced her imagination to carry her elsewhere, to people with whom she had laughed, dresses she had worn. It worked for a little while, but then the self-incriminating thoughts began to creep back in.

She looked down at the girl, whispered, "You're too young to die. Why won't you eat?"

An idea passed through her mind. The next time she caught Mrs. O'Reilly's eyes, she beckoned for her.

"Yes'm?" the Irish woman said, wiping her hands on her apron.

"What is this child's name?" asked Corrine.

"There weren't no note with her or anything, so we've taken to callin' her Anna."

"Anna." Corrine ran her fingers through the girl's silken hair. "I was wondering if you've tried giving her a bottle."

"She's more than old enough to drink from a beaker."

"I have a feeling I could get her to take some milk. Don't you have bottles downstairs for the younger babies?"

"We do."

Corrine gave the woman a smile. "Do you think you could get one for me . . . with some warm milk?"

Mrs. O'Reilly left the room, shaking her head and muttering to herself, but several minutes later she returned. Wordlessly she handed over the bottle and went back to work.

"Now, you're going to drink some of this, Anna . . . for me," Corrine said. Making soothing little sounds, she coaxed the rubber nipple between the girl's teeth.

The child stared up at her with unblinking eyes, mouth gaping. Corrine began to rock the chair gently again and, for the first time in her life, found herself breathing a prayer. *God, please make her drink—I don't want her to die.*

After several minutes Anna seemed to come out of her lethargy long enough to take a tentative pull on the nipple.

Corrine took in a quick breath. "That's a good girl."

The first hesitant drinks turned into thirsty gulps, and she drained the bottle in a matter of minutes. Setting the empty bottle down on the floor beside her, Corrine hugged Anna to herself and marveled at the great warmth which had come over her.

Mrs. Morgan was making her way over, round face incredulous. "She took the bottle?"

"She did." Corrine smiled up at her. "I believe I could get her to eat something else as well."

"I'll go down to the kitchen and ask for something not too taxing upon her stomach. Some cold porridge or the like." The minister's wife smiled at Corrine. "What a blessing you've been to this child. What's her name?"

"Jen——," Corrine started to say, then realized her mistake. She breathed a quiet sigh. "Her name is Anna."

~

"Miss Jones?"

Poised at the garden steps leading down into Lord Burke's kitchen that afternoon, Rachel looked to the right, where Lord Burke stood wearing dark blue trousers and a simple white linen shirt with sleeves rolled to his elbows. His arms were surprisingly bronzed for someone she assumed seldom went out of doors.

"I *thought* I heard someone," he said. "Good afternoon."

"Thank you. And to you."

"Aren't you sketching Lucy tomorrow?"

"Yes, sir. Tomorrow." Rachel dipped her hand into her apron pocket. "I'm here to—"

He held up a hand. "Let me guess. You're here to deliver a message from Mrs. Hammond."

"Yes, sir," she said again, embarrassed at the amusement in his brown eyes. It wasn't her fault that Mrs. Hammond sent her over so often. "Shall I bring it to the kitchen?"

He shook his head. "I'll take it. Unless you'd like visit Bernice and Lucy."

She would have enjoyed that very much, but instead she walked over to him and took out the envelope. "Thank you anyway. I'm sure they're busy, and I should get back."

Adam took the envelope from her and slipped it into the pocket of his trousers. "Have you time to see something?"

"What is it?"

He laid a finger to his smiling lips. Surprised, Rachel followed him past trellised vines and blooming shrubs. He stopped at a young pear tree and turned to her to whisper, "Have you ever seen robin nestlings?"

"Not since I was a girl," she whispered back.

He gently moved aside a cluster of leaves and stood to the side. Rachel stepped closer to the branch. Five tiny, brownish-pink nestlings, beaks wide open, were clustered together as one wriggling mass among bits of blue-green eggshells.

"Where are their parents?" Rachel whispered, resisting the urge to touch the nest.

"I saw the mother fly away just before you arrived, so she should return shortly." He leaned a little closer to the nest and said softly,

> *"Tell me, thou bonny birds,*
> *When shall I marry me?"*

When he paused self-consciously, searching for the rest, Rachel couldn't resist finishing:

> *"When six braw gentlemen*
> *Kirkward shall carry ye."*

Lord Burke looked surprised, then smiled. Easing back the covering branches, he said, "We should move so the mother can feed them."

That was Rachel's cue to leave, of course. She had embarrassed him by filling in the lines instead of giving him more time to recall them. Or, he simply had other things to do.

"I have to leave now anyway," she said, not quite meeting his eyes, hoping the slight warmth of her cheeks would not intensify into a flaming blush. "Thank you for showing me the nest, Lord Burke."

"But wait," he said, falling in beside her. "You're fond of Sir Walter Scott?"

"More so of his novels than his poetry," she admitted.

"Yes? Do please stop a minute, Miss Jones. I'm no good at conversing at a gallop. Which of his books have you read?"

She stopped beside a trellis bearing tiny green muscat grapes. *He's just being polite.* But yet, there seemed to be genuine interest in his brown eyes.

"I've read *Ivanhoe, St. Ronan's Well,* and the Waverley series," she replied. The cottage Gerald had rented in Treybrook, while the owners were touring the Continent, had had a modest library, and Rachel had slipped a succession of books up to her attic bedroom.

"I'm impressed," Lord Burke said. "Which do you prefer? Reading or sketching?"

She had never thought to ask herself that. "Well, both, sir."

It was simply easier, most times, to get her hands upon a pencil than a book besides the penny dreadfuls that Mrs. Hammond allowed her to read whenever she finished one. Still, they were better than no book at all.

"And who is your *favorite* author?"

Rachel knew she should not take up any more of his time. But he was so easy to converse with, and he did not leer at her the way Mr. Moore did. Besides, it would be rude not to answer his question. "I like Charles Dickens very much, sir. But I've only read *A Tale of Two Cities* and *Oliver Twist.* They were in the house we stayed in in Treybrook."

"But that's in Humberside. Isn't Mrs. Hammond's estate in Nottinghamshire?"

"She rented the other one for the summer," she lied, hating herself for doing so. Would the prophet Daniel have even been tempted to lie? She was certain he would not have.

If Lord Burke noticed the discomfort in her expression, he did not show it. "You know, I have several Dickens novels. Would you care to borrow some?"

"Oh, but I couldn't, sir." How could she accept more generosity, knowing she was aiding Mrs. Hammond's deception of him? The courage she had prayed for since Sunday's sermon had failed to visit her yet.

He looked disappointed. "It would please me if you would. I've read them all, and there is nothing sadder than a closed book."

*Oh, there are sadder things,* she thought. But of course, he would be aware of that.

"Perhaps one?" she said, mostly because he was expecting it, even though the thought of having another Dickens novel in her hands was wonderful.

"I'll have one for you tomorrow." He studied her for a second. "Hmm. *David Copperfield* would suit you, I think. Does that sound all right?"

"Yes, sir." She looked down at her hands because the appreciation in his expression was unsettling. She was aware that she did not deserve it. Still, she managed to say, "Thank you, sir. You're too kind."

And thought, *If only you weren't!*

# 12

Corrine was reclining on the sofa, halfway through *A Cousin's Betrayal* when Gerald entered the parlor. "Back so soon?" he said, rubbing his hands down the front of his wrinkled linen shirt.

She closed the book and swung her feet around to the floor. Turning her cheek up to accept his kiss, she tried not to inhale, for his breath was foul. "I've been home for three hours. When did you get home?"

"Oh, sometime this morning," he said, taking a place beside her. "The game went longer than I planned, but don't worry, nobody saw me enter the house."

"You played cards *all night?*"

Gerald yawned, causing Corrine to turn her head briefly. "Where's Rachel?" he said. "I'm dying for some tea."

"She should be back shortly. I sent her to Lord Burke's."

"Indeed? Why?"

"To inform him to expect us at two in the afternoon tomorrow."

"You already settled that Sunday, didn't you?"

"We never discussed an exact time, so I want to be sure he'll be prepared for us. I would hate to get there and find that he's shut up in a room with that minister or taking a nap . . . or whatever it is the man finds to do."

"Clever girl. I believe the fellow is as good as in the net."

"Thank you," Corrine said, as warmed by the compliment as she was repulsed by his breath. She would ask him to go back upstairs and brush his teeth once she made certain his apparent good mood would last a while. He could get so touchy at times.

And it seemed this was to be one of those times, for he glanced at the penny dreadful in her lap. "How can you read such rubbish?"

"Rubbish? This is a good story—I can barely stand to put it down."

Crossing his legs, he settled back against the cushions and gave her a condescending smile. "Let me guess. The heroine is a poor baroness whose fortune was stolen by an evil cousin."

"She's not a baroness," she said defensively, yet she brushed the book from her lap to the space beside herself and the sofa arm. Gerald could be an unbearable snob sometimes, just because he came from wealth and had some education. It rose to her lips to remind him that the author of *A Cousin's Betrayal* had at least gotten *published,* but she thought better of it.

Gerald yawned, covering his mouth with a neatly manicured hand. "How was your mission of mercy today?"

"It was a good visit," Corrine found herself saying. She described how she had managed to coax Anna into taking some milk and even a bit of porridge.

"You can't imagine how . . . useful it made me feel. I believe she would have allowed herself to starve if I hadn't gotten her to drink from the bottle."

"I'm not surprised," Gerald said.

*Then again, he can be terribly sweet.* Corrine smiled at him. "You aren't?"

"You've had *men* eating out of your hand for years now . . . why shouldn't children as well?"

Gerald had looked at her with that knowing expression countless times, but today there was something in those pale eyes which made her feel dirty and cheap. As she did at the children's home, she had to force herself again to put such thoughts out of her mind.

"Why do you do that?" he asked.

"Do what?"

"Jerk your head like that." He frowned. "I've seen you do it several times lately."

Corrine pressed her lips together. How could she explain to someone with seemingly no regrets for anything he ever did the need to quiet the voices in her head? How accusations sometimes seized her mind so violently she had to shake her head in an attempt to get rid of them?

"I didn't realize I was doing it," she offered as feeble explanation.

Gerald took up her hand and put her fingers to his lips. "We'll have to work on that before it becomes a habit. You don't want Lord Burke thinking you have a tic, do you?"

Though embarrassed, she raised her chin and said, "I'll work on that. But don't worry. He probably doesn't look for flaws as diligently as you do."

"Are you saying I'm too critical?"

Carefully, she replied, "Well, you can be."

"Then I apologize, my love," he conceded. "I just want what's best for you."

"I appreciate that. But . . ."

"But what?"

Corrine squeezed the hand that still held hers. "I need your encouragement, Gerald. Now more than ever."

"Why more now?"

Closing her eyes for a second, she admitted, "Because I've been feeling so . . . ugly lately."

He chuckled.

"Why is that so funny?" she asked, irritated.

"Because you know very well that you're beautiful!"

"I'm not referring to my face. I feel ugly *inside* sometimes."

~

Gerald stifled another yawn and began to wonder when Rachel would return. He had had nothing to eat since rising, and while he wasn't terribly hungry, he wished for a cup of tea. Corrine seemed determined to prattle on and on about whatever had brought on her blue mood, and he could not change the subject without hurting her feelings.

*How tedious it must be to be a woman!* To go through life weighing every emotion, every thought . . . what a bore! Men were made of much sterner stuff, which was why he preferred their company.

*Most of the time, at least,* he thought, smiling to himself.

" . . . understand that?" she was saying, looking at him.

He dredged up a comforting smile. Better to allow her to air out whatever was troubling her now. *Then hopefully she'll shut up for a while.*

"I think I understand," he replied, letting go of her hand so that he could put an arm around her shoulders. "Having to become involved with religion at Lord Burke's has affected you. What did that preacher say that's gotten you so melancholy?"

"Nothing, I suppose." Corrine shrugged. "But there are times I can't help but wonder about the people we've . . . hurt. Like Malcolm's widow."

"Mrs. Nowells? She's most likely happy that the old bore's not about anymore, don't you think?"

"Perhaps she loved him."

"And perhaps not. Now, what can we do to get you into better spirits?" He rubbed his chin. "What if I took you to the theatre? Here we are living in London, and we haven't even been yet."

"I don't think so."

"There's no danger of coming across Lord Burke, if that's what you're—"

"I'm not in the mood," Corrine said listlessly.

Exasperated, Gerald fought the urge to leave the room. She would only become sullen and not speak to him afterwards if he did. He sometimes felt trapped. Although he was becoming increasingly bored with Corrine, he knew that keeping her happy allowed him the lifestyle he preferred. The idea of actually *laboring* for his living was much more abhorrent than the problem of boredom. One day he would put away the gin and cards and finish his novel, he promised himself often. He would show his family—the world—of what greatness he was capable.

But until then, he was dependent upon the woman beside him. He tried another tactic to cheer her. "Tell me again about this child you got so attached to."

Her expression took on a happier cast. Seconds later, though, Gerald regretted his choice of subject.

~

"You want to do *what?*"

Under the weight of Gerald's incredulous stare, Corrine lost a little of her nerve. "It would be just until I'm satisfied she's eating regularly."

"But *every* day?"

"Only until she gets stronger. You don't object, do you?"

"I certainly do. I realize you were pressured into going there once a week with that woman—and it's likely working in our favor. And I'm glad you had a good day. But that would be overdoing it, don't you think?"

"I don't see how. You sleep away the most of the day anyway. You would hardly know I'm away."

He moved his arm from her shoulders, turned to her, softened his voice again. "Have you forgotten *why* we came to London, Corrine?"

"Of course I haven't forgotten. But I have enough extra time. How can an hour or so at Saint John's interfere with that?"

"The plan is to get *all* the time you have committed to Lord Burke," he said. "Not to go around wet-nursing a little bas—"

"Gerald!" Anger clouding out caution, Corrine said, "The child would have *starved* if I hadn't gotten her to take the milk. I must say you surprise me . . . begrudging a helpless little orphan. If you would do something good for someone *once* in your life you would understand how I feel."

In the silence which followed, Gerald stared at her, sighed, and shook his head. "It's really quite ironic, don't you think?"

"Ironic?"

"I mean, what would the good people at that orphanage say if they knew?"

"If they knew what?" Corrine asked warily.

"If they knew what kind of mother you really are." He feigned a sympathetic smile. "How you left your own child—*Jenny* was her name, wasn't it?"

Breathing suddenly became labored. "Why are you—"

"I wonder how many times your little daughter cried for you?" he went on, relentless in his cruelty. "Perhaps she refused to eat, just like your new little friend. You don't think she starved to death, do you?"

"Gerald, how could you?" Tears burned Corrine's eyes. "I'm not going to sit here and—"

Quick as breath, Gerald reached out and clasped her chin with his hand. Roughly jerking her face around to just inches from his, he hissed with foul breath, "I just don't want you to forget what kind of person you are. And what your purpose is."

"I haven't forgotten." She attempted to pry his hand from her chin, but he was stronger. With his other hand he grabbed hers and pulled them down to her lap.

"Stop, Gerald!" she cried stiffly, squirming in vain. "Or I'll pack my things and leave. . . ."

He merely held tighter, watching her struggles through half-closed lids. Slowly he moved his thumb around to her bottom lip and pressed it against her teeth. "And go where, pray tell?"

"I don't know. . . ." Every time Corrine tried to pull her hands away, he tightened his thumb against her lip. Her gums were aching. "Just stop hurting me!"

Gerald began bearing down harder with his thumb. "This *hurts,* you say?"

With tears coursing down her cheeks, she attempted a nod but could not even move her head. She knew he could be cruel, even striking her in rage once in a great while, but he had never been physically brutal in such a calculating manner. There was a disturbing satisfaction in his pale eyes.

Though tears blurred her vision, Corrine wondered if she was seeing him clearly for the first time. "Please," she whimpered. *"Please stop."*

~

Rachel stood in the corridor holding the tray. The steam wisping from the spout of the teapot had dwindled down to a ghostly thread. If she didn't serve the tea soon, she would have to go back downstairs and brew another pot.

She hoped that the lowering of the voices in the parlor was a good sign. She had witnessed countless altercations between the two, but never *voluntarily*.

Mr. Moore's voice made her flinch.

"I didn't spend all that time training you to have you turn into Florence Nightingale!"

Rachel breathed a sigh and turned again for the service staircase. How long had they been at it? Usually their fights ran out of steam after a while, as did the teapot. Perhaps they would be finished by the time she had made another pot.

Another sound made her pause. Mrs. Hammond's voice, filled with distress. Did she ask him to stop hurting her?

*None of your business,* Rachel thought, and yet found herself turning again. She moved closer to the closed door, held her breath and listened.

"I'm sick of having to cater to your every whim!" Mr. Moore was shouting. "You were a low-class *nothing* until I taught you how to get what you want!"

The answering sob sent a chill up Rachel's spine. She

remembered the strength in Mr. Moore's hands when he wrestled the knife from her hand in the kitchen.

*You have to do something,* she told herself. Hoping the tea was still warm enough to serve, she edged open the door and walked into the parlor.

"It's about time!" Mr. Moore exclaimed, releasing Mrs. Hammond's hands and getting to his feet.

Rachel dared a glance toward her mistress, quietly weeping with hand up to her mouth. "I'm sorry, sir," she said to Mr. Moore, and she lowered the tray to the table. "I'll just pour—"

"Never mind," he seethed. Ignoring Mrs. Hammond, he stalked to the open doorway and through it, only to reappear a fraction of a second later and point a finger at Mrs. Hammond.

"You *will* concentrate your efforts on Lord Burke! And if you mention leaving me again, I'll fix it so *no* man will ever want to look at you!"

He shot Rachel a thunderous look. "And the same goes for you!"

~

Even the parlor windows rattled when the front door slammed. Mrs. Hammond flinched at the sound, and in spite of herself, Rachel's heart again went out to the woman who had treated her with such indifference and scorn for so many years.

"He's gone, missus," she said gently, kneeling in front of her. "Did he hurt you?"

Eyes red and wet, Mrs. Hammond moved her trembling hand from over her mouth and frowned at it. "My lip's not bleeding, I don't think."

"I'll get some cool water for it so it won't swell." Rachel took off for the kitchen, returning minutes later with a wet dish towel. Seating herself beside Mrs. Hammond, she said, "Here now. Hold this over your mouth for a while."

"It won't swell. He's too smart to do anything to ruin my looks."

Nonetheless, she took the wet cloth. Rachel watched her alternately press the cloth to her lips and wipe her eyes with it.

"Why do you stay with him?" Rachel asked.

Mrs. Hammond shrugged. "I love him."

"But how can you love someone who hurts you?"

"You're too young to understand." She let out a mirthless laugh. "I deserve someone like Gerald—a man who pretends to love me while he sends me to the beds of other men."

Heat rose in Rachel's cheeks.

"I've embarrassed you, haven't I?" Mrs. Hammond said.

Rachel shook her head, but she felt her cheeks burn hotter.

"You see how jaded I've become?" She rubbed her eyes with the cloth and sank back into the cushions. "The things decent people only whisper about have become so commonplace in my life that I mention them without blinking an eyelash."

"What will you do?" Rachel asked.

Her mistress handed the cloth back to her. "Why, have a glass of brandy and go to bed."

"That's all?"

She shrugged again. "What else would you suggest?"

"I would—" Rachel stopped abruptly. She had always thought of Mrs. Hammond as a strong woman. But would a strong woman accept a situation which obviously made her unhappy? After all, she had enough money to go somewhere else, and she didn't have to wait for character references.

"You would leave." Mrs. Hammond gave her a bitter smile. "Is that what you were going to say?"

"Yes, missus. We could pack our things right now."

"We? You mean you would go with me?"

"I wouldn't stay here alone with him."

"And where would we go?"

"Why not the place you came from? I could work . . ."

"Home?" Mrs. Hammond cut in. "My dear, my family would not welcome me. And besides, it's the first place Gerald would look."

"Then just tell him you don't want to be with him anymore."

"Did you not hear what he said before he left?" Mrs. Hammond shuddered visibly. "He wasn't joking."

"You mean he would . . ."

"I don't even want to imagine what he's capable of. Why do you think his family disowned him?"

Rachel knew, or thought she did. She had heard Mrs. Hammond throw that up to him during one of their arguments. "A girl in Lancaster?"

"Gerald didn't want to marry her, nor did he like the notion of a child who looked like him running about for everyone to snicker about. He tried to get the girl to go with one of his servants to see a midwife who could . . . get rid of the inconvenience."

~

Corrine watched the rapid succession of emotions that moved over Rachel's face. The girl couldn't possibly understand. But Corrine did. She herself had been to such a woman three times since she started living with Gerald. Three times she had submitted to that frightful old crone with sour breath and rotting teeth.

Not for the past three years, though. Which meant she could probably no longer conceive. But then, that was good, wasn't it?

Rachel's voice brought her back to the present. "Do you mean he wanted the girl to give the baby away?"

"He didn't want the child *born*," Corrine answered flatly. "But when she refused to go see the woman, he took her off in the woods and . . . she stumbled and broke her neck."

For one second, two, Rachel stared at her. "He *killed* her?"

"He claims it was an accident." Corrine realized she should not be saying any of this, that Rachel had enough damning evidence against them. But the pump had been primed, and it was like taking a tonic, giving air to some of the fury she had stifled for years. "But I don't believe it."

The girl shook her head, did not try to hide her expression of pity mingled with disgust. "And you *love* him?"

Corrine sighed. How could she admit that Gerald's past had made him seem irresistibly dangerous and exciting! Warmth crept through her cheeks. She so seldom blushed. Perhaps she did have some remnant of conscience, after all.

She eyed Rachel with wonder. "You came in here because he was hurting me, didn't you?"

"Yes, missus."

"And yet I've treated you so badly. Why did you do it?"

The girl shrugged. "I couldn't bear hearing you hurt."

"Thank you." Tears stinging her eyes, Corrine reached for her hand. "How I wish I were like you."

"Like me, missus?"

"Like you. Clean. Pure."

At length Rachel said, "I'm not so innocent as you think me. My thoughts are so murderous sometimes that they frighten me."

"Your *thoughts?*" Releasing Rachel's hand, Corrine rubbed her own forehead. "I wish that were my only sin."

"I watched you with that child this morning."

"One act of goodness in my whole life." Corrine gave a dry laugh. "Weighed against more horrible, selfish actions than I can count."

Suddenly she felt drained, crushed by the terrible burden of her own awareness. Unsteadily, she rose. "I'm going to bed."

Rachel got to her feet as well. "Is there anything I can do for you, missus?"

"Can you stop me from dreaming?"

"From dreaming?"

"The thoughts that torment me in the night. Can you make them go away?"

Somberly, the girl shook her head. "No, missus."

"Then there's nothing you can do for me." Halfway across the parlor she paused to say over her shoulder, "On second thought, bring me up some brandy. The decanter in my room is empty."

# *13*

The inside of The Golden Lion was dimly lit and smelled of beer and cigars and gin. A low murmur of voices came from the dozen or so patrons leaning against the bar or seated at tables with cards fanned in their hands. They would become raucous as the night wore on and the pub filled with workers fresh from their shifts at factories. Someone would eventually invite Gerald to join a game starting up at one of the tables, but for the moment his mind was not on gambling. He tossed back a gulp from his third glass of gin and allowed it to burn his throat.

*I'm sick of Corrine and her whining!*

And now she was feeling guilty, of all things! What next? Changing her mind over taking Lord Burke's money?

He frowned, took another drink. What happened to the old days, when Corrine's beauty and total self-absorption fascinated him? Like a sponge she had soaked up his efforts to refine her manners, and set out with a vengeance to snare any unsuspecting prey he pointed out to her.

Now she was no fun—no fun at all!

And Rachel, who bewitched him with her unawareness of her own beauty. He was aware of why she had dashed into the middle of their argument, of course. Some sense of duty toward Corrine, who certainly wouldn't have done the same for her. Rachel was growing less easy to control now, and one day she would succeed in finding another place to go.

He took another gulp of the gin. Corrine would behave now. He had seen the terror on her face when he threatened to ruin her looks. He would do it, too. *Then she would be a perfect match for Lord Burke, wouldn't she? And I could teach Rachel to take her place.*

He just had to make certain Rachel was fully aware of the consequences of leaving him.

And he would, too. He drained his glass and pushed out his chair.

But for now, he would order another drink.

~

*"Can you see them?"*

Adam blinked into the darkness surrounding his four-poster bed, trying to identify the sound which had jarred him from his sleep. When the cobwebs cleared from his thoughts, he realized that *he* was the one who had spoken.

He could not remember ever talking in his sleep before. He could recall his words, but the dream which had prompted them hovered at the edge of his mind, teasing him with bits and pieces of vague scenes. Finally he decided it didn't matter. Turning his pillow, he rolled to his other side and closed his eyes again.

Just as the drowsiness deepened his breathing, a vision from the dream drifted back into his mind. He saw a deliberately chaotic scattering of flowers in all colors and hues. *Mother's garden,* he thought.

*He was walking in the garden, dressed in the scarlet uniform of his regiment, a sword sheathed at his left side, his father's silver medal of valor from the Battle of Navarino on his chest. At his right was a woman in an iridescent gown that was even more brilliant than the flowers. He could not see her face, for a light breeze caused her long golden hair to billow about her cheeks. She allowed him to hold her hand, but he was hurt by her silence as he unsuccessfully tried to make her speak.*

*They approached one of the wrought-iron benches, sheltered by a dogwood tree in full bloom. He helped her to take a seat, then heard a faint rustling overhead. He craned his neck and peered up into the branches of the dogwood. Its blossoms had transformed into hundreds of white butterflies, moving their wings as if keeping time with some melody silent to human ears.*

*Smiling as he stood before her, he reached for the woman's hand again. She would speak to him once she saw the butterflies. But now he could see her face, and he was speechless, stunned into silence by the luminosity of her emerald eyes. She seemed to understand that he was struggling to find his voice, and lifting her other hand to his scarred cheek, she whispered his name so softly that it felt as a caress.*

*His heart pounding within his chest, he pointed up at the branches. "Butterflies . . . ," he managed to say.*

*He watched her take a quick breath and stare upward with an expression filled with awe and delight.*

*"Can you see them?" he asked. But then the woman and the butterflies vanished.*

~

Lying in the stillness of the dark, Adam tried to recall who the woman was. At first he was certain that it was Kathleen because of the golden hair—and because she had visited so many of his dreams over the years. Then he remembered the shining green eyes and the wondrous smile.

*Miss Jones?*

*Why her?* he wondered. Yet he found himself closing his eyes again, trying to recapture that picture in his imagination. Perhaps if he lay still enough, the dream would return.

~

"A Joseph Price to see you, sir."

Two hundred miles north of London in the farming village of Treybrook, Humberside, Squire Malcolm Nowells III wiped his mouth with a napkin and nodded to Ramsey, his butler.

"I'll see him in my study." From the head of the table he sent his wife an apologetic look. "Excuse me, dear—pressing business."

His wife, Louisa Nowells, glanced at his half-finished plate, then at their eleven-year-old son. "But little Malcolm's birthday . . ."

"This shouldn't take long," Malcolm said, already pulling his considerable bulk out of his chair. "How about if I join you for cake in the conservatory in an hour?" He picked up his cane from where it hung on the back of his chair and limped out of the dining room.

He was settled behind his desk in the study when Ramsey opened the door and ushered a gentleman into the room. "Mr. Price," he announced with the same air of formality he used when heralding the presence of all of the Nowellses' guests. His duty performed, he stood aside to wait for any further instructions from his employer.

"That will be all, Ramsey," Malcolm said. He waited until

the butler had closed the door before motioning to a chair. "Please have a seat, Mr. Price."

His visitor was a a tall, muscular man in his early forties, with thick dark hair and neatly trimmed beard. Taking the chair, he said, "I'm accustomed to dealing with Mr. Fawcett. But he sent word this morning that you wished to speak with me directly." Though his clothes were the tweeds of a country dweller, his elocution and manners spoke of an educated background.

Malcolm straightened his game leg and leaned forward, resting his elbows upon the desk. "I have great trust in Fawcett—he was my late father's solicitor."

"Please accept my regrets—"

"Yes, thank you," Malcolm said, waving aside his condolences. "Fawcett informs me you've found something out."

"About Mrs. Hammond, you mean."

"No . . . about how many silk hats Lord Palmerston has in his dressing room!"

Mr. Price smiled benignly. "Yes, that was an obvious question. I do beg pardon. As for Mrs. Hammond, I've got some interesting news."

Malcolm's eyebrows lifted. "Yes?"

"She travels with a man. I've traced them back to Manchester, Shrewsbury, and Rotherham so far. Fortunately, Mrs. Hammond feels secure enough to use the same name. Whether it's her real one, I cannot tell yet."

"Of course she feels secure." Malcolm's frown was bitter. "Her victims aren't able to publicize her notoriety or go to the authorities without calling attention to their own indiscretions. Did any of the other men . . ."

"Take their own lives?" Mr. Price shook his head. "None

in the towns I've mentioned. I don't know about other places yet."

"How did you get this information?"

"Mainly servants, Squire Nowells. Most are eager to supplement their wages . . . and more than willing to talk about their employers."

Giving a snort, Malcolm said, "I imagine some are. I'm certain *my* servants would be more discreet, however."

His visitor smiled again. "Be sure to relay my best wishes to your son on his birthday. And allow me to express my regret at the riding accident nine years ago, which cost you the partial use of your right leg."

"Ramsey!"

"Rest assured, your butler is tight-lipped. He barely spoke to me except to ask for my hat."

"Then who . . . ?"

"It doesn't matter. Nothing of a scandalous nature was offered—not that I would have listened."

"You're rather insufferable." Malcolm leaned over his desk as far as his girth would allow and gave the man a warning look. "You'll learn your place if you wish to stay in my employ."

~

Joseph Price picked up an onyx paperweight from the desk and turned it over in his hands. That was the trouble with gentry, he thought. They were too used to having people bow and scrape in front of them.

"My place is where I choose to be," he replied. "If you no longer require my services, you have but to say the word."

Squire Nowells made some sputtering noises, then sighed

and held up a hand. "I need your services," he said meekly. "But I must say I'm not accustomed to doing business with your type. Do you always insult the people you work for?"

"I wasn't aware that I had insulted you. If you feel that I have, then I apologize. Now, do you want to know about the man with whom Mrs. Hammond travels?"

"You have his name?" asked Malcolm, perking up immediately.

"Found it out four days ago, after several false leads. Your solicitor's instructions were to come with a report when I came across something significant."

Malcolm nodded. "That's extremely significant. Who is this cad?"

"He presented three different identities to the landlords in the three cities I mentioned."

"Then how . . . ?"

"How did I find his name?" Joseph smiled and sat back in the chair. "I reasoned that a scoundrel such as this man would be more than familiar with the gaming and liquor establishments. I found circles of men who had gambled with him. Gin is a sure way to loosen lips. He used the name Gerald Moore in Rotherham and Shrewsbury. In Manchester I traced the same name to a tailor's shop he frequented."

The huge man beamed across the desk at him. "Fawcett was right—you're worth every penny. And do you know where he and the woman are now?"

"I have an idea they headed for London after your father's tragic death."

"How do you deduce that?"

"This Mrs. Hammond is an extraordinarily beautiful woman, I've been informed. That has worked in my favor during this whole investigation, for quite a few train attendants and stationmasters have recalled seeing a woman whose description matches hers."

"London would make sense," Squire Nowells said. "It would be easy to remain anonymous there. Do you think you can find them?"

"I'll find them," Joseph assured him. "But it's not going to be easy. In fact, I should have left for the city as soon as I found out about Mr. Moore. I'm wasting valuable time here."

"I had a reason for requesting that you see me when you came up with something solid." Squire Nowells pursed his lips, hesitated, then lowered his voice. "There is something you and I need to discuss."

Joseph lifted his eyebrows. "Something that Mr. Fawcett couldn't tell me?"

"Fawcett's a good man, as I've said, but his ideas and mine differ on how to . . . handle the situation when you find the woman and her companion."

"Meaning . . ."

"I don't want the authorities involved."

~

Joseph had always striven to live his life with integrity and honor. His career as a detective had, in fact, initially grown out of a strong moral sense and his desire to help others. After six unfulfilled years of lecturing in the mathematics department in King's College, Cambridge, he had traveled about the British Isles, picking up odd jobs when his funds ran low. He had been serving as a gardener on an estate in Stockport when his employer expressed a longing to find his wayward son. Joseph felt sorry for the man and set out to try and reconcile the family.

He discovered that he had a knack for tracking people down. It took him only three months to find the son and another week to convince the prodigal to go home to his family.

The grateful father had numerous contacts among the upper class, and news of Joseph's skill spread. Before long he was never at a loss for clients. He relished the freedom and adventure his occupation afforded, and he considered himself the most fortunate man alive.

Price was not in any sense religious, but he had never done anything that conflicted with his own high standards. He knew what the gleam in Squire Nowells' eyes meant, and he didn't like the idea one bit.

"I'm not an assassin, sir," Joseph declared flatly. "If that's been your purpose all along, then you're to be disappointed."

Malcolm Nowells III drew himself up in his chair. "My father was a decent man who made the mistake of listening to the flattery of a beautiful woman. I will not rest until she and her lover are punished."

"Then you should be contacting Scotland Yard."

"Why? So those two vultures can bring further humiliation to my family with a public trial? Have you any idea how much sensation a case like this would cause in the whole of England?"

"I can understand your desire for revenge, but—"

The man's fist pounded his desk. "Justice!"

"Very well . . . justice. But I've seen the inside of several prisons in my line of work, and they aren't pleasant places to spend the rest of one's life."

A weary sigh escaped Malcolm's lips. "There is another reason I don't want the authorities involved. My mother was devastated when my father killed himself. Not only did she lose a husband of thirty-five years, but she discovered he was being whispered about by her 'friends.' They pretended to believe my story about Father's being depressed for months before he died, but Mother wasn't fooled. Now she doesn't want to leave the house. Just sits in her room all day."

He regarded Joseph with pleading eyes. "Don't you see? Mother couldn't live through the gossip this would stir up again, and I'm not ready to lose another parent."

Joseph was quiet for a long time. He had killed once before, but only in self-defense, when a trio of thieves attacked him on the road to Birmingham. While he took no pleasure in killing one of the men and gravely injuring the others, it had not interfered with his sleep afterwards. Criminals like that would have ended up killing some innocent person one day, if they hadn't already. But to take two lives in cold blood—and one of them a woman?

"I can't do it," he finally said. "As much as I sympathize with your family, I just can't. Perhaps you should pay me what you owe me so far and get someone more . . . experienced to look for them in London."

Mr. Nowells reached into his vest pocket for a key. Wincing at the pain in his knee, he bent down to unlock his bottom desk drawer, then took out a fat envelope and tossed it on his desk towards his visitor. "Two hundred pounds."

"Mr. Fawcett has already given me two payments, so you don't owe me near that amount."

"This is a bonus," said Mr. Nowells. "In addition to what I already owe you. Plus that amount again if you're successful."

The implications dawned upon Joseph. "You mean if I kill these people."

Mr. Nowells stared back for a second, nodded.

Joseph picked up the envelope, counted out ten ten-pound notes and shoved them in his waistcoat pocket. Handing back the rest, he said, "I've worked hard on his case, and there is still more to do. I'll thank you for the bonus. But when I bring them back, you may do with them what you like. No doubt you'll find someone else around here eager to earn that other hundred pounds."

# 14

The silence between Corrine and Rachel became a living thing, a third presence which filled every inch of the space between them. Not until the carriage reached Clifton Hill did Corrine speak, though she could not bring herself to meet Rachel's eyes.

"I suppose you know Gerald came back." With her thumb she traced the patterns of the beads on her reticule.

"I heard him this morning," Rachel replied softly.

"I had no choice. You know that."

"I know."

"Anyway, he promised never to hurt me again," Corrine said, still moving her thumb along the beads. *As long as I do as he says.* She said nothing else until the carriage pulled up in front of Adam Burke's gate, but when the driver came around and held up a hand to help her to the ground, she shook her head.

"I'm not getting out."

Rachel looked up from gathering her sketch pad and pencils. "Missus?"

"I've been worried over Anna all day. What if she won't eat for anyone else?"

"But Mr. Moore . . ."

Corrine stared across at the Lord Burke's house. Surely that Irish woman could coax Anna to take a bottle just as well. *You can't save every orphan in London.*

She had only to recall the feel of the little hand clasping her chin, and the decision was made. "He won't know. I won't be gone long. I'll come back here afterwards, then we'll ride back together."

"How will I explain to Lord Burke?" Rachel asked. "He's expecting you as well."

Uncertainty muddled Corrine's thoughts again, for only a second. She smiled at Rachel and, with a voice filled with irony, answered, "You can say that the kindhearted Mrs. Hammond is visiting orphans. That should impress him."

~

Lucy, looking very grown-up in a honeysuckle pink silk dress, stood where her mother had positioned her in front of the marble fireplace in the drawing room. The girl held a bouquet of daisies from the conservatory, their stems wrapped with long trailing pink ribbons.

Shortly after Rachel had taken a seat in a comfortable wing-back chair, Lord Burke and Bernice asked if she minded their placing chairs on each side. Having never sketched before an audience, she felt nervous at first, but she maintained her composure by concentrating on Lucy and the sketchbook in her lap.

"Those are her eyes, all right . . ." Bernice breathed minutes later when Rachel had penciled in the girl's last eyelash with short, feathery strokes. She put a hand up to her mouth. "Beg pardon, Rachel!"

Rachel smiled at her. "It won't disturb me if you wish to

talk." Now that she had gotten off to a good start, her mind relaxed and allowed her hands to take over.

"I'm curious." Lord Burke leaned closer to watch. "Do all portrait artists begin with the eyes?"

"I'm not sure, sir. It just seems the right place to begin."

He nodded. "That makes sense. After all, they're the most expressive parts of our faces. I would imagine you'd want to get them right before starting anything else."

"I've heard it said that the eyes are the window to the soul," Rachel said quietly, sketching Lucy's right eyebrow.

"And so they are," Lord Burke said.

"It's going to be a beautiful picture, Rachel," Bernice said. "Thank you again for doing this."

"Oh, I should be thanking *you* for the opportunity," Rachel replied. "I've never had a chance to work with a live model."

"But then how—," Lucy began.

"Lucy, don't speak," her mother admonished. "You can't be twisting your face all up." She turned to Rachel again. "How can you draw without a real, live person to look at? Surely you had models in your art classes."

"I usually just draw from the picture in my mind. And I've never even seen another artist work, much less had any lessons."

"So who taught you?" Lord Burke asked.

Lifting the point of her pencil, Rachel shook her head. "I've just always known how. When I lived at the orphanage, I used to take bits of coal and draw on any flat stones I could find."

"Then it was God who taught you," Bernice said with conviction.

"And he's obviously a good teacher," Lord Burke said.

"Thank you," Rachel whispered past a lump in her throat. Their kindness could be overwhelming at times. She would store in her mind the memory of this day, like one of her sketches, to be taken out and savored during the lonely times.

~

Adam watched, fascinated, as Rachel penciled in Lucy's nose and mouth. The girl was talented, there was no doubt.

*And a bit of a mystery,* he thought, for now and again he was given the distinct feeling that she kept much to herself.

"How long have you worked for Mrs. Hammond?" he asked.

"Six years," Rachel replied.

"It was kind of her to go back to see about one of the children." He had been pleasantly surprised and wondered if he had misjudged the woman. Or was this a ploy to make him think more highly of her?

Whatever Mrs. Hammond's motives, he was still glad that Rachel had come alone. There was a sadness behind those lovely green eyes, but also an intelligence that was obvious in spite of her bashfulness.

He studied the confident set of her mouth. A honey-colored lock had worked its way out of the chignon at the nape of her neck, and it bounced slightly every time she looked up at Lucy. *She's a beautiful girl,* he thought. *And I doubt if she even knows it.*

He wondered how old she was. Sitting there with her brow wrinkled in concentration, she didn't seem so young, so incredibly far from his own age.

*What are you thinking!* he chided himself.

For just a moment he had forgotten his situation. If not

a freak of nature, he was a freak of war. He had no right to think that way about any woman. His heart suddenly felt heavy in his chest.

"I've some work to attend," he said, abruptly getting to his feet.

Bernice's round face filled with dismay. "You're leaving?"

"I'm looking forward to seeing the finished project." He noticed that Rachel's pencil had stopped moving. Had he hurt her feelings?

"It's lovely so far," he added kindly. With that, he turned and left the room.

~

"Rachel, must I keep smiling?" Lucy said through stretched lips and closed teeth. "My whole face aches. . . ."

"Oh, Lucy!" Rachel winced and looked up from the sketchbook, where she had just penciled the lace upon on the girl's collar. "I'm finished with your face!"

Bernice chuckled. "Well, you *warned* us you never used a live model before."

Lucy was not amused. "I feel more like a dead one—and I don't think I'll ever be able to smile again. May I take a peek at my picture?"

"When I'm finished with the bodice of your dress," Rachel said.

Fifteen minutes later, she walked over to the fireplace and held the sketchbook for Lucy to see. She was rewarded immediately when the girl's face lit up.

"I look like a princess!"

Rachel couldn't resist teasing. "I thought you couldn't smile anymore."

Lucy grinned in response. As Rachel returned to her chair, Lucy leaned forward and took a quick glance at the grandfather clock in the corner. "It's been over an hour now. When you finish my dress and shoes, may I sit?"

"You've stood for longer than that in the kitchen," Bernice admonished.

"But I was working. It's harder to stand still like this."

Rachel smiled at the girl. "Just a bit longer."

"What about the fireplace? Will you draw that, too?"

"I think it would look nice in the background. But I won't need you to stand in front of it once I get it outlined."

"Then how long will it take after that?"

"Not long at all, I think. Fireplaces are probably easier to draw than people."

"And they don't *complain* nearly as much." Bernice directed a pointed look to her daughter. She then turned to Rachel. "What about you? Surely you're worn out. Why don't you stop for some tea?"

Rachel nodded, feeling the strain of the last hour. "Some tea would be nice, thank you."

"I'll bring it here," said the cook, already on her feet.

She was back fifteen minutes later with a tray. Rachel had put her pencils down on the carpet next to her chair, and Lucy was holding the sketchbook up to admire her portrait.

"Let's sit here at the sofa, like proper ladies," Bernice told them.

Rachel took a place at the opposite end of the sofa from Lucy, allowing Bernice to sit in the middle. "Am I keeping you from your work?" Rachel asked, realizing that the cook probably had not known how long the portrait would take.

"Not at all," Bernice answered. She leaned forward to fill

the three cups at the table in front of her. "The bread was baked Monday, and I started a mutton stew right after lunch. Dora's stirring it every now and again."

"Lord Burke doesn't eat fancy when he has no guests," Lucy said, biting into a chocolate biscuit.

"He likes his meals simple," her mother agreed. She poured a dash of milk into Rachel's cup and handed it over. "By the way, we'll have to show him Lucy's portrait. I know he'd like to see it."

Rachel wasn't so sure about that. "Perhaps you shouldn't disturb him."

~

*Am I imagining the flush to Rachel's cheeks?* Bernice wondered. *Surely she isn't afraid of Lord Burke, of all people!*

Come to think of it, Lord Burke was acting strangely, too—getting up and dashing off like he did, almost like he was nervous. But why would he be nervous?

"Hmm . . . ," she said, doing a little arithmetic in her head.

"What is it, Mother?" Lucy asked.

"Nothing." But she could not help but smile to herself. Lord Burke needed a wife, someone to love, even if he pretended otherwise. Why not Rachel? Even though there was an age gap of about twelve years, Rachel was *certainly* more mature than his former fiancée had been, that shallow-brained Kathleen Hardgrove. But knowing Lord Burke, he would need a little prodding in the right direction.

She drained her tea and set saucer and cup back upon the tray with a *click*. "Lucy, bring the tray to the kitchen when you two are finished. We'll allow Rachel some privacy while she sketches the fireplace."

"I really don't mind the company," Rachel said.

Getting up from the sofa, Bernice shook her head. "We've work to do. You don't need us here in the way."

"But you just said the stew's already in the pot," Lucy protested.

"It needs stirring." Ignoring the ache in her hips from sitting for so long, Bernice leaned to pat Rachel's shoulder. "You're a lovely girl."

Rachel smiled up at her. "Why, thank you, Bernice."

"And I suspect more people know it than just me."

Straightening, she ignored the girl's puzzled look and left the room. She hurried up the corridor and stopped at the door to Lord Burke's study. *You're a sentimental, interfering old biddy,* she said to herself. *You'll only make him angry.*

*At what risk?* She smiled. He could rant and rave, but her position was as safe as a shilling in the Bank of England. She lifted a hand to knock softly.

"Yes?"

Bernice opened the door and stuck her head inside. "Mind if I have a word with you, m'lord?"

"Of course not, Bernice." Lord Burke looked up from his ledger. "Is the portrait finished?"

"Almost."

"Will you have a seat?"

"I've sat long enough," she replied, standing inside the door. "I just wanted to ask you something; then I'll leave you alone."

He set aside his pencil. "Ask away, then."

"Have I been a good servant to you?"

"The best," he said with crooked smile, then leaned his

head. "But . . . you're already aware of that. What is this, Bernice? Are you about to ask for a raise?"

"My salary's more than adequate," she replied. "What I came to ask is a favor."

He folded his hands atop the open ledger. "Very well. What can I do for you?"

"Go watch that girl finish the picture."

"Miss Jones?"

Hands on her generous hips, Bernice nodded. "I believe you hurt her feelings when you walked out a while ago."

Lord Burke's expression filled with concern. "You think so? But I had things to do."

"Things that couldn't wait?" she gently chided.

"Well, probably not, but . . ."

Bernice walked over to the chair facing the desk and lowered herself into it. "May I speak plain with you?"

"When have you ever not?"

She returned his gentle smirk. "I chat with folks like myself every market day—cooks, maids, footmen, the like. Most complain over how their employers treat them. You expect us to get our work done, but you've never looked down on us for being servants. And I thank our Lord for that."

"Well, God created us all in his image, didn't he?"

"He did, indeed. And some he created more lovely than others."

Lord Burke raised his good eyebrow. "Meaning?"

"Miss Jones. Forgive my being so personal, but I noticed how you looked at her in the room there. I've never seen you take notice of a woman like that since—well, sir, since Miss Kathleen."

His stared at her. "I was interested in watching her sketch, Bernice. That's all."

"Would you be telling me the whole truth, sir?"

"Of course. Why would I lie to you?"

"Maybe it's yourself you're lying to, Lord Burke."

~

*Lying to myself?* Adam thought. He knew that women were supposed to be more sentimental than men, but this was just a little silly.

"Bernice, I can't believe what you're implying. She's just a child."

"She's nineteen, Lord Burke—soon to be twenty."

"I'm old enough to be her father!"

Undaunted, the cook sat back in her chair. "And how many twelve-year-old boys do you know with children?"

He shook his head and wondered for the hundredth time why Bernice seemed to feel it necessary to mother him. Her preoccupation with his well-being could be so irritating at times! "There's no sense in even discussing this. I don't know how you claim I was looking at the girl, but you're mistaken. Besides, I hardly know her."

"Then . . . you don't think she's lovely?"

"All right," he sighed with exasperation. "She's lovely."

Bernice grinned triumphantly. "And wasn't that *you* pacing the whole house this morning, waiting for her to show up?"

"I don't know what you mean." Adam picked up his pencil.

"Oh . . . so it was Mrs. Hammond you were hoping to see?"

"I really have a lot of work to do here, Bernice. Is that *all* you wanted?"

"Well then, sir," she huffed, pulling herself out of her chair. "I suppose I'm bein' dismissed."

"I suppose you are," he replied tersely.

He had never spoken to her in such a harsh tone. He watched uneasily as she walked through the doorway into the hall. "Bernice!" he called out just as the door clicked.

He was about to get up, but then the door opened again, and the cook stuck her head inside. Her expression was blank, but he detected a knowing look about her eyes.

"Sir?" she said.

Adam sighed again. "You're right. I was looking forward to seeing her."

She stepped again into the office. "Why were you too proud to admit it?" she asked gently. "Is it because she's a servant?"

The barb hit home. "You know that's not the reason."

Silence hung between them. Bernice finally spoke—as usual, cutting right to the core of the matter. "Rachel is special. Can't you see that?"

Automatically, Adam's hand went to his leathery cheek. "She deserves better."

"Better than you?" Bernice shook her head. "Someone like you is just what she deserves, sir. And I do believe she cares for you."

"Then what she's feeling for me is pity. I'm not going to take advantage of that."

"Won't you at least come out and see her?"

"Send for me when the portrait's finished. I'll come then."

"Very well." Bernice's shoulders sagged with resignation. "I'll send Lucy 'round to fetch you in a bit."

Before she could leave again, Adam said, "Bernice?"

She turned to face him. "Yes, sir?"

"Do you really think she was hurt when I left the room?"

Giving him another sad smile, she answered, "I'd say it was both of you that was hurt."

~

After Bernice left, Adam tried in vain to concentrate on his work. Finally he closed his ledger. It wasn't polite for him to hide in here. The least he could do was to be courteous. With a sigh, he got up from his chair.

On his way to the drawing room, he stopped at a wall mirror in the hall to adjust his tie. When he had first moved into this house, he would not allow Mrs. Fowler to hang any mirrors, save those in servants' private rooms. After he became a Christian, he realized that vanity was a sin not only of the very beautiful but of the not-so-beautiful as well.

Still, he wondered if he would ever become used to the face staring back at him. He touched the network of jagged wounds on the leathery skin. What woman would want to be close to him?

He almost changed his mind and headed back for the study, but then he told himself that he was being ridiculous. The girl didn't care about his appearance one way or the other. After all, she most likely had dozens of suitors. However, she was a guest in his home, paying a favor to one of his servants—and he would show her that he had manners.

He stepped through the open doorway to the drawing room, wondering where everyone had gone. He heard the rustling of paper then and realized that the wing-back chair was still occupied.

"Miss Jones?"

"Oh, Lord Burke," she answered, turning so that he could see her face.

He went over to the chair at her right. "Bernice says you're almost finished."

"I'm working on the fireplace right now."

"May I see it?"

She handed him the sketchbook. "Incredible!" he exclaimed. Lucy's image stood before the half-finished fireplace. He could see the joy in her eyes from wearing a new frock and being center of attention.

"I really believe this is better than the one of little Margaret," he said and hastened to add, "although her portrait was very good."

"Thank you," she said and smiled. "I think this one's better, too."

"And you say this is the first time you've used a model?"

"It was much easier than relying on memory."

"I should imagine." Handing the sketchbook back to her, he said, "Well, I shan't disturb you. I'll just sit here and watch . . . if you don't mind."

~

Rachel wondered if he could hear her heart beating, for it had started pounding in her ears when he sat beside her again. *Concentrate on the fireplace,* she ordered herself as she put her pencil back to shading another silver vein in the marble.

"I asked Jack to pick you some spring onions from his garden."

"That was very kind of you, sir," she said, touched.

"Are you hungry?"

In spite of being flustered, Rachel had to press her lips to suppress a smile. "No, sir. Thank you."

From the corner of her eye she could see Lord Burke's arms fold across his chest.

"What's so amusing?" he asked.

"Nothing, sir."

"No fair, Miss Jones. Let me in on the joke, too."

She could tell by his voice that he was smiling. She raised her pencil, turned to him, and admitted, "You won't even think it's funny. It was just something that struck me in an odd way."

"And . . ."

He was not going to let up until she confessed her foolishness. She stifled a sigh and admitted, "When you asked if I was hungry . . . my immediate thought was that you were offering to bring the onions in here."

After a second or two he said, "Well, you're wrong, Miss Jones."

Heat rose to her face. "You see, I told you . . ."

"You're wrong when you say I won't think it's funny," he said and began to chuckle. Rachel could not help but smile.

At length Lord Burke gave her an appreciative look. "I'll try again. Have you had tea?"

"Thank you, yes," she replied. "Bernice brought us tea and biscuits a little while ago."

"And then they left you here all alone?"

"They had some cooking to finish."

"I see. And is my company disturbing your work?"

"Not at all, Lord Burke," she answered, and found that she

meant it more than she could convey. *Remember your place,* she reminded herself. He was merely being polite to a houseguest who happened to be a servant. That was the sort of man he was.

"Good," Lord Burke said. "I brought *David Copperfield* down from my library. I hope you enjoy it."

"I'm sure I shall," said Rachel. "Thank you very much."

A silence stretched between them for a few seconds, the only sound being the lead of the pencil raking softly against the paper. At length he said, "Did you accompany Mrs. Morgan and Mrs. Hammond to Saint John's again yesterday?"

"Yes, sir. We had a pleasant visit."

"The Morgans join me for dinner every Friday night. I imagine Penelope will have nothing but praise for the help you've given."

"Not just me, sir." She told him how Mrs. Hammond had persuaded the little girl to take some milk and food. "I believe the child would have starved had it not been for her."

"Hmm. May I ask you something, Miss Jones?"

"Yes, sir," she replied, turning her pencil sideways to shade the mantelpiece.

"Mrs. Hammond—how does she treat you?"

The pencil froze in Rachel's hand. "Treat me?"

"Yes. Is she good to you?"

If he had asked her that question just two days ago, how would she have replied? She thought she *might* have responded to the concern in his voice and poured out her heart to him.

But a lot had changed in just two days. Some things were best kept inside, she realized, especially when there was nothing to be gained by telling them. The relief which had washed over Lord Burke's face when he became aware that Mrs.

Hammond had not accompanied her spoke volumes. He did not care for her.

*Mr. Moore will be furious when their plan fails.* He would blame Mrs. Hammond, of course. What would he do to her?

Two days earlier she would not have cared. But a bond had been formed between them—a tenuous one at best, but strong enough to keep Rachel from betraying her mistress. She had no such loyalty for Gerald Moore. What kept her lips closed about him now was the fear of what would happen if Lord Burke decided to inform the police. Mr. Moore was too cunning to be easily caught, and she feared his revenge more than anything in the world.

"Mrs. Hammond treats me well," Rachel finally replied.

"Are you quite sure?"

She looked at him. "Yes."

"That's good to hear." He sounded relieved. "Forgive my prying, but there's . . . there's a sadness about you sometimes. I worried . . . "

*Worried about me?* Her pulse started pounding in her ears again, and she had to erase a stray pencil mark.

Lord Burke leaned closer. "You're almost finished, aren't you?"

"Almost, sir." She could not help but feel some pride as she tilted the portrait for his inspection. "What do you think?"

"What do I think?" His eyes were on her now, and his voice softened. "Beautiful is what I think."

Rachel's heart jumped in her chest. Why was he looking at her like that?

Awkward silence fell over the room. Rachel tried hard to focus on her work, but she was uncomfortably aware of the pair of brown eyes on her as she put the finishing touches on the mantelpiece.

After a while he cleared his throat. "You know, I'd like to have it framed for Bernice and Jack if they'll allow me. Can you recommend anyone?"

Pleased to have a distraction from the perplexing thoughts dancing about in her mind as well as an opportunity to return Mr. Solomon's kindness, she told Adam about the elderly man and his small gallery. "He says that the right frame is almost as important as the painting itself."

"Do you think he would come here and speak with me if I paid for his time? After his shop closes, I mean."

Rachel nodded. "I believe he would, sir. He's a very kind man."

"Then I'll send a message to him first thing tomorrow morning."

She was finished, and she brushed the stray bits of rubber from the paper. "Do you mind if we show Bernice and Lucy?"

He took the sketchbook from her hands and held it out in front of himself to study. After a full minute he smiled, lowering the portrait. "I'll even get Jack. I want to see their faces."

# 15

"Can't you go any faster?" Corrine called out to the driver of the hired chaise.

The man simply pointed to the road ahead and said something she could not understand.

*Blooming cockneys ought to learn English!* Corrine thought. She glanced over her shoulder at the sun, hovering just above the steeple of All Saint's Church two blocks away. *You shouldn't have stayed so long,* she scolded herself. *Now you'll have precious little time with Lord Burke.*

In spite of her anxiety, she smiled. Anna had not wanted her to leave. After she had coaxed her to take some milk—this time from a beaker—and a little bread, the child had leaned her head against Corrine's bosom and put her thin arms up around her neck.

She couldn't just walk away and leave her like that, so she had decided to rock her until she fell asleep. Every time Corrine thought Anna had drifted off and made an attempt to ease her into Mrs. O'Reilly's arms, the child would wake up and cling more tightly.

She finally fell asleep, but Corrine pictured the child waking up in a crib later and looking for her through the iron bars. *I hope she won't cry,* she thought, fearing she probably would. *She won't understand that I can't stay there. All she'll know is that I'm gone, just like her mother.*

Gerald's cruel words about her own daughter echoed in her mind. Corrine tried desperately to rationalize her own pain and guilt. *Mary was more of a mother to her than I was,* she reasoned. *Perhaps Jenny didn't even realize I was gone.* Deep down, Corrine knew it wasn't true. She had seen the pain in little Anna, and she knew she had done the same thing to her own tiny daughter. But her own wounds went too deep; she couldn't bear to allow her thoughts take her in that direction for very long.

*Think about Lord Burke,* she ordered herself. Gerald was right—her attention had not been totally focused on the man. That had to change.

Crimson streaks were the only evidence of the setting sun in the west when, twenty minutes later, the chaise pulled into the carriage drive on Clifton Hill. Perhaps this would work out after all, Corrine thought. Surely Lord Burke would feel compelled to ask her to stay for supper. And since this wasn't Sunday, the servants, including Rachel, would dine in the servants' hall while she would have Adam to herself.

She paid the driver, brushed wrinkles from her mauve silk skirts, and walked up the cobbled footpath to the front door. The maid Irene—or was it Marie?—answered.

"They're expecting you, Mrs. Hammond. Will you follow me?"

Corrine could hear Lord Burke's voice through the open parlor doorway.

"No, I can't say I ever feared monsters as a boy . . . but I lived in mortal terror of chickens."

And then a young female voice. "*Chickens,* m'lord?"

"Well . . . yes, Lucy. They seemed much bigger in those days."

Then came laughter as Corrine walked through the doorway. Rachel, Bernice, and the girl Corrine recognized as her daughter shared the sofa, while Lord Burke and the gardener sat in chairs.

The picture of contentment sent a stab of pain through Corrine's heart. How long had it been since she had enjoyed the company of friends? Had she ever, really? She had gotten just a taste of it yesterday when Mrs. Morgan and Mrs. O'Reilly watched with amazed expressions as Anna drank from the bottle. And last night, letting down her guard long enough to share her feelings with Rachel—that had been nice, in a way, even though Gerald had made her feel so wretched.

"Mrs. Hammond," Lord Burke said, rising. "You're just in time to see the portrait."

Corrine affected what she hoped to be her most feminine smile. "I'm so glad."

Jack the gardener was standing as well, and approached to hand her a sketch pad.

"Why, thank you," Corrine said sweetly, taking the chair Adam had pushed closer to the circle. She looked down at the portrait, and this time her smile took no effort.

"Why, Rachel, this is beautiful!"

"Thank you, missus."

Corrine looked up at Lucy, seated between her mother and father on the sofa. "And what a pretty model she had to work with."

While the girl blushed, Bernice gave Corrine a grudging smile. "Thank you for saying that, Mrs. Hammond."

"How was the child you visited?" Lord Burke asked after

Jack took the sketch pad from her and brought it over to
Bernice.

Corrine's smile faltered for a fraction of a second. "Much
better. But it seems she won't eat for anyone else."

"Then you plan to go there every day?"

She shrugged and met Rachel's eyes. "I suppose I must.
She's such a thin little waif—we can't allow her to starve."

Just days ago Corrine would have gladly used the sympathy
in everyone's faces to make herself look like a heroine. Now,
however, a lump had settled in her chest. She folded her hands
and tried not to think about the fact that Anna was probably
waking up now, weeping for her . . . or about how she would
hide future trips to the orphanage from Gerald.

From the corner of her eye, she noticed that Bernice
seemed to be studying her. Corrine had known instinctively
from that first Sunday dinner that the cook did not like her—
a situation which had not troubled her for even a second.
Now she found herself wondering what the woman was
thinking . . . and wondering why she cared so much.

"That is kind of you," Bernice finally said in a low voice.

Corrine looked over at her, surprised at the surge of gratitude those words caused. "Thank you, Bernice."

~

"Well, if you'll excuse me, I've things to do in the kitchen,"
Bernice said a moment later, getting to her feet. She turned to
look down at Rachel. "I can't tell you how happy you've
made me."

"Won't you let us pay you?" Jack said, rising from his chair.

Rachel smiled at the two and shook her head. "It was my
pleasure."

At her mother's signal, Lucy got up and followed her parents out of the room.

"Will you stay for supper?" Lord Burke asked Mrs. Hammond. "It's not fancy tonight, but Bernice always cooks more than enough."

"How did you know I was famished?" Mrs. Hammond replied, smiling.

Rachel was aware that this was her cue. In fact, she should have left the room with Bernice's family. She rose from the sofa, her heart surprisingly heavy after the lightheartedness of just minutes ago.

"Excuse me," she said, starting for the door. "I'll go help in the—"

"But the invitation is to you as well, Miss Jones," Lord Burke said, getting to his feet.

Rachel did not have to look at Mrs. Hammond to know the message her blue eyes would be sending. "Really, sir, I'm happy to dine with the others."

"Oh, but I insist. Don't we, Mrs. Hammond?"

"Yes, of course we do," Mrs. Hammond replied with a wooden smile.

"Then it's all settled."

The next thing Rachel knew, Lord Burke was offering one elbow to her and the other to Mrs. Hammond, then ushering them down the corridor to the dining room.

Regardless of the closeness Rachel had felt toward Mrs. Hammond yesterday, Rachel knew that she would suffer a tongue-lashing on the way home again. But there was nothing she could do about that now. Lord Burke had her hand to his side, and she had no choice but to walk with him.

~

A three-quarter moon was suspended in a night sky peppered with stars. Silence stretched between Corrine and Rachel in the carriage Lord Burke had insisted on hiring.

*He's smitten with her,* Corrine thought, glancing at the girl's silhouette, illuminated by gaslights. Not that Lord Burke's actions had made it obvious. He had been the perfect host, dividing his attention between both of his guests. But he had not been able to hide the affection in his eyes every time they met Rachel's.

Then to top it off, he had given the girl a novel and . . . onions! He never asked if Corrine might care to borrow a book. Did he assume she was illiterate?

How long had this been going on? She had never noticed the man paying much attention to Rachel before, but perhaps she had been too sure of herself to even consider that he might be interested in someone else over her.

*Especially a servant!*

She turned again to glare at the girl, but found herself strangely touched by the misery evident on her face even in the darkness. Her mind carried her back to yesterday, Rachel hurrying into the room while Gerald was hurting her. It was a risky thing to do; he could easily have turned on her.

It suddenly dawned upon Corrine why Rachel looked so miserable. *She's figured out that Lord Burke doesn't care for me. And she's wondering if I know it!*

Yet, she was certain Rachel had not had enough experience with men to recognize the admiration that had been in Lord Burke's eyes for herself.

*I wonder how she feels about him?*

She straightened in her seat. No matter how Rachel felt, this was a disastrous turn of events. Bitterly she thought, *You shouldn't have used her this time.*

But then, had not Rachel begged not to be involved from the beginning? What could she have done? And as far as Lord Burke's preferring her, what could Rachel have done to prevent it? Knocked out a few of her own teeth?

Corrine sighed, reminded herself, *This isn't her fault.*

But regardless, she could not afford to give up without trying harder. The alternative would be to admit to Gerald she had failed. Just the thought caused a chill to run up her arms.

"Rachel, are you cold?" she asked abruptly.

"No, missus," the girl replied, but the arms she held to her sides belied her words.

"Why didn't you bring your wrap? Well, I suppose you didn't realize we'd be out so late." Corrine slid close to her. "We'll share mine."

~

To Corrine's dismay, Gerald was in the sitting room, not even dressed in evening clothes. She lifted her face to accept the kiss he brushed against her cheek and asked, "Aren't you going out?"

He shook his head. "After our . . . little disagreement yesterday, I realized that I've been neglecting you. I haven't been spending enough time at home."

He was lying, Corrine could tell. How many other times had she been too self-absorbed to realize his flattery was laced with falsehoods? Something must have gone wrong at his gambling place. Had he lost all their money?

She knew better than to ask.

Gerald smiled and poured two glasses of wine. "You've been gone for hours—I take it to be a good sign."

Corrine had years of practice stretching her lips into smiles. She offered one to him now. "Well, Lord Burke insisted I stay for supper."

"Indeed!" Avarice shone from Gerald's pale eyes. "And what did you and the gentleman find to talk about?"

"Why, *me,* of course."

He looked pleased with her answer. "I have a feeling we're about to strike it rich soon, love."

"Well, he seems rather cautious with his money," she countered quickly. She did not want Gerald *too* optimistic—he was pressuring her enough as it was. While she realized it would be impossible to deceive him indefinitely that Lord Burke had romantic feelings for her, she certainly was not going to come out with the truth until it was absolutely necessary. *If only Lord Burke would leave town!* she thought. Then Gerald would have to find someone else to target, and her problem would be over.

At least her most *immediate* problem, she corrected mentally, and sighed. It seemed that life had evolved into a series of problems, and she could see no way out.

~

Downstairs, Rachel set the basket of onions in the coolest spot in the larder and wondered at the way she had caught Lord Burke looking at her at times during supper. Had Mrs. Hammond noticed?

Had she imagined the affection in his dark eyes? Was this his way of discouraging Mrs. Hammond's pursuit of him? Yet he seemed too principled to pretend interest in a woman just to get another to leave him alone. And those eyes had held the same expression when she was alone with him as she finished Lucy's portrait. That couldn't have been for Mrs. Hammond's benefit.

She rinsed soil form her hands at the sink and scolded herself for having such lofty pretensions. After all, Lord Burke was a kind man, and she was still just a servant. He was just being friendly because she drew Lucy's portrait.

Nevertheless, a picture of his warm brown eyes came again and again to her mind. She knew that tonight when her head touched the pillow, she would close her eyes and allow her imagination to carry her back through this special day.

~

"Sorry, mate. Never heard the name before," said the proprietor of The Toad and Fiddle on Tottingham Court Road.

Joseph Price was not surprised. After all, this was the first place he had looked since arriving in London and procuring lodging. "Would you recall seeing a gentleman with light blond features, thin lips, and a mustache? He would have only been a customer for the past six weeks or so."

Again, the man shook his head. "I hope you find the bloke so he can claim his money, but we get chaps from all over here. After a while, the faces look alike."

Joseph left the address of the inn he had checked into this morning and asked that he be contacted if Gerald Moore should come into the establishment. "It's worth a fiver to me," he added.

With eyes heavy he returned to Warwick Inn on Charing Cross Road late that evening. *Your age is catching up with you,* he said to himself after paying the driver of the hansom. *Ten years ago, you would have made do with a nap now and again.*

He would have to settle down one day, he realized. He was in good physical condition for a man of forty-two, but time had a way of slipping up on a person. And as much as he loved his occupation, sometimes in the still hours of the night in yet another strange town, he wondered what his life would have been like if he had chosen a wife and family instead of wanderings. He would die one day, and then what would remain of the life he had lived?

*It's not too late to settle down,* he thought, knowing that it would probably never happen. He was approaching the front door of the inn when a man's voice startled him.

"Mr. Price, may I presume?"

Squinting, Joseph stepped out of the amber glow of the doorpost lamp. The voice probably belonged to one of the pub proprietors whose memory had been jarred by the offer of five quid.

"Yes, who's there?"

As his eye had adjusted to the blackness, he realized that two men were standing there. One, apparently he who had spoken, appeared to be in his mid to late fifties, while the other was much younger, possibly still in his twenties.

"My name is August Berrington," said the older man. He extended his hand. "Inspector Berrington, Scotland Yard."

Joseph shook the man's hand. How had Scotland Yard learned of his presence in London? And more to the point, why had two of its men come to call?

"I must say you have me at a loss, Inspector."

"Then we must explain ourselves." The inspector introduced Mr. Green, the younger man, and asked Joseph if he would mind accompanying them in their carriage to a café on Regent Street which stayed open for most of the night. "We're interested in the questions you've been asking."

The café, located on the ground floor of an inn called The Sycamore House, still had customers from the theatre crowds. The three men took a corner table, ordered ham sandwiches and coffee, and made small talk until the waiter returned with their food. Here in the light, Joseph was able to study the men seated across from him. Inspector Berrington was a stocky, square-shouldered man, his face dominated by a thick gray mustache. Mr. Green, trim and well dressed, wore wire-rimmed eyeglasses. He seemed to be nervously anxious to please his superior.

"We've had men in pubs all over London today," Inspector Berrington said. "And lo and behold, it turns out that some-one else is making inquiries about a person who matches the physical description of the man we're looking for."

"You don't say?" said Joseph, trying to hide his surprise. In all of his searching for Gerald Moore and Corrine Hammond, he had never had a clue that Scotland Yard was on their trail as well. He had taken for granted that, like Squire Nowells, none of the victims or their families had wanted to involve the authorities because of the publicity involved.

"And why are you looking for this person?" He took a swallow of his coffee. "Assuming that we're indeed talking about the same man."

The inspector directed a significant glance at his young assis-tant, then cleared his throat. "You left your name and address all over town, Mr. Price, which is how we found you. Never mind our purposes. I'd be interested in knowing why you're searching for a man named Gerald Moore. That was the name you gave, wasn't it?"

"You didn't answer my question, Inspector Berrington. What leads you to believe we're on the same trail?"

"We have no name for our suspect," the inspector explained while picking onion slices from his sandwich, "but the physical description exactly matches the man you're looking for. Obviously, we're wondering if he's the same person."

"I don't know if I can answer that," Joseph said. "Not without knowing what your suspect has done."

Inspector Berrington nodded at his assistant. "Mr. Green?"

The younger man sat up straight, obviously eager to do his part. "Some patrons of a pub called The Golden Lion came to us this morning. They said they played cards with a gentleman last night who boasted of murdering a pregnant young woman in Lancaster to get out of marrying her. The man didn't offer his name, but had blond hair, blue eyes, and a mustache—the same description of the man you're seeking."

Joseph had to sit silently for a minute and digest this information. *Could Gerald Moore be a murderer, too? Surely a man who would extort money had very little respect for human life. But—murder?*

"Why the secrecy?" he asked at length. "Why don't you simply post his description?"

"We may be forced to do that soon," Green answered. "But according to the men at his table, he was quite drunk. It's quite plausible that he will not remember his confession."

"And it's possible that he made the whole story up," Mr. Berrington cut in. "Either way, for the time being, we'd rather give him the illusion that his story went no further. If he panics and leaves the city, we may never find him."

*That makes sense,* Joseph thought. "So you aren't giving out *why* you're looking for him."

"No, not yet." The inspector studied Joseph's face with weary eyes. "We gave a phony reason . . . just as you did."

"I beg your pardon?"

"We're aware of your reputation, Mr. Price. You've let it be known that this Mr. Moore you're seeking has come into some money. Why would someone hire a detective of your caliber to find an heir when they usually turn up sooner or later?"

Before Joseph could answer, Berrington went on. "Now we have to wonder if you're looking for Moore for the same reason."

Joseph sighed, ran a hand through his dark hair, and admitted, "My reasons for seeking him have nothing to do with yours. And I'm still not convinced we're looking for the same man."

"That's entirely possible," the inspector acknowledged. "But your inquiries have given us a possible name for our suspect when we hadn't one before. You can understand our eagerness to learn everything we can about this Gerald Moore."

Joseph toyed with the handle of his coffee cup and wondered what the ethical response would be. If indeed Moore was out there murdering women, then certainly he needed to be caught. But his orders not to involve the law had to be considered, too. If he shared what little information he had with Scotland Yard, there was a distinct possibility that they would find Moore before he did.

*But how will you feel if it comes to light that he killed that woman?* he asked himself. *And you've not helped?* He thought about his sisters, Carolyn and Frances. What if a killer were loose in Bristol? Would he not want the police to have every clue available to find the culprit before he murdered again?

He sighed again and looked up at Inspector Berrington. "I still doubt that we're looking for the same man, but I'll give you everything I've learned of the personal habits of Gerald Moore."

"That's very—"

Joseph held up a silencing hand. "But as the reason I'm looking for him has nothing to do with the murder, I intend to keep that to myself to protect the privacy of my client. If you find Moore, you won't need my information to determine whether or not he's your killer."

To himself he added, *And if I find him first, I'll whisk him out from under your very noses.*

# *16*

T here's a Mister Solomon to see you, sir," Dora
announced Thursday morning in Adam's parlor.
Adam set his *London Times* on the carpet beside
his chair and got to his feet. "Already?" He had only sent Jack
with the message an hour ago, asking the art dealer to call at
his convenience. "Please show him in. And ask Bernice if
she'll send Lucy's portrait in here."

A genial-looking man with gray hair and spectacles came
through the doorway at the maid's bidding. If Mr. Solomon
was startled at Adam's appearance, he hid it well. He shook
Adam's outstretched hand before easing himself into a chair.

"I wasn't expecting to see you so soon," Adam told his visitor, feeling guilty at asking an elderly man to take a carriage
ride across town. He had not thought to ask Miss Jones how
old Solomon was. "There certainly was no rush."

Mr. Solomon chuckled, his eyes crinkling at the corners
behind his spectacles. "I haff been training my grandson Levi
to take my place. I'm planning ahead to the time when I'm no
longer able to work, you see. When I received your message,
I decided that it was a perfect time to test the boy's mettle."

Adam smiled. "Are you not worried? A boy running a business alone . . ."

The man laughed again. "My wife tells me I must stop referring to Levi as a boy. You see, he is twenty-three—" He paused, his forehead drawn in concentration for a couple of seconds. "Twenty-*four* years old, and with a wife and child already. My! Time slows down for no one, does it not?"

"No, it doesn't," Adam agreed. He could see why Miss Jones spoke so highly of him.

"Tell me, Mr. Burke, how did you come to know of my shop?"

"From Miss Rachel Jones. She was here yesterday and sketched a portrait of my cook's daughter." Irene came back through the door as if on cue, the sketchbook in her hands. As Adam instructed, she handed it to Mr. Solomon and left the room.

"Miss Jones said we should keep the sketch in the book until it's ready to be framed, so the paper won't crease," Adam said. "Perhaps I should order another book for her so that she may continue to sketch."

"Yes, that is a good idea. Mr. Solomon nodded and lifted the pasteboard cover and smiled. "And you say Miss Jones drew this?"

"Yes, sir."

"I haff been asking her to show me some of her work." He looked up at Adam for a second with an expression of pure delight. "I had a *feeling* that the young lady had talent!"

"Do you know her very well?"

The man shook his head, squinting as he studied the portrait. "I know nothing of her personal life, only that she loves art. On market days she comes to my shop—always hurrying, but still taking a little time to chat with an old man."

Adam became even more interested. He leaned forward

intently. "Why do you think she wouldn't show you her work?"

"I don't know." Mr. Solomon gently closed the cover to Rachel's sketchbook. "Perhaps she thinks because they are penciled sketches, they are inferior. I sell mostly paintings, you see."

"Isn't there a market for sketches?"

Mr. Solomon smiled. "My friend, there is a market for everything in London. But most people want oils or water-colors to hang on their walls."

Leaning back in his chair again, Adam crossed his arms and thought. After a long and mostly sleepless night, he had come to the painful conclusion that he was allowing his heart to run away with him as far as the girl was concerned. She probably thought him a fool at supper last night, the way he could not stop himself from watching her.

But what could be wrong with aiding someone blessed with such a talent? He could well afford to do so, and Rachel did not even need to know that he was involved. "Do you think Miss Jones would be interested in oils or watercolors if I bought some? The paints, I mean, and canvases and whatever else she would need."

Pursing his lips, the man gave his host a quizzical look. "If *you* bought them for the young lady?"

"Anonymously, of course." An idea came to Adam. "Perhaps you wouldn't mind allowing her to assume they're gifts from you? I would be in your debt."

"She admires the oils the most every time she comes in my shop—I think she is fascinated by the colors. But paints would not do her any good, my friend. She would not know how to use them."

Adam tapped his forehead lightly. "But of course. She needs lessons for that, doesn't she?"

"Most definitely," replied Mr. Solomon, pushing his spectacles up on the bridge of his nose. "She is good, but one can go only so far with talent alone. She must learn technique."

"Can you recommend a teacher?"

"I most certainly can. He studied in Paris for two years and is now an associate at the Royal Gallery. The young man is a most promising talent."

"Who is he?"

The old man's smile became angelic. "My other grandson, Reuben Solomon. Would you care to meet him?"

Adam laughed. The man was crafty, too! "I'll take your word for that, Mr. Solomon. Would you mind informing Miss Jones for me?"

"But why do you not want her to know the lessons and paints are from you?" Mr. Solomon asked. "Reuben will charge you a reasonable price, as he is still a student . . . but you may still expect to spend a tidy sum. The giver of a gift of such magnitude should be recognized."

"Because I don't wish to burden her . . . to make her feel unduly grateful to me."

For the first time, the man's old eyes seemed to take notice of Adam's scars. Gently, he said, "You don't wish that she should be *burdened* with feelings of gratitude? Perhaps the young lady would *like* to know that the lessons are from you."

Adam shook his head. "I'll pay extra if you'll deliver the news to her and keep my secret. Do you have her address?"

"I'm afraid I haff not."

"It's written down in my study," said Adam, getting to his

feet. "Her employer sends messages to me occasionally. If you'd be so kind as to wait here . . ."

He stopped just short of the door and looked back at Mr. Solomon. "I seem to have forgotten my manners—may I send for some tea?"

The old man waved a hand in the air. "I would enjoy nothing better, my friend, but perhaps some other time. The clouds were becoming dark while I was on my way here. I do not wish to be caught in a storm."

Adam nodded. "I'll hurry, then."

Smiling, Mr. Solomon added, "Even more important than the rain, I must go back and make sure that Levi has not sold my Delacroix for twenty pounds."

~

Corrine was at her dressing table when Gerald walked into the room, clad in a gray morning coat and trousers.

"You're up rather early, aren't you?" she said, studying him in the mirror.

"I don't know." He yawned. "What time is it?"

"Ten o'clock."

He yawned again, walked over, and massaged the back of her neck. "That early? Well, I suppose staying home at night has its merits. Is Rachel making breakfast?"

"Yes."

He picked up Corrine's perfume decanter containing *Vivre le Jour*, lifted the stopper and waved it below his nose. "I've always loved this aroma. Where are you going?"

"Why, to Lord Burke's."

His eyebrows lifted. "Indeed? He invited you?"

"Of course," she replied airily. "Didn't I tell you last night?"

"No, you didn't."

"Are you sure? Oh, well, he did."

Smiling, Gerald set the perfume bottle down. "I'm pleased you're listening to me. You'll thank me, too, when he lends you enough money to pay your debts until your 'estate' is settled. Then we'll go to Paris."

"Paris would be nice," she said. *But I'll never see it,* she thought darkly. For eight years he had promised to take her there, but he always managed to find another sheep to fleece right away. Even now he was probably searching for Lord Burke's successor.

Gerald was studying her face in the glass. "Is something wrong?"

"Wrong?" Corrine winced as she pulled her brush through a tangled curl. "What could be wrong?"

"I don't know. You're not worrying about that orphan, are you?"

"Not at all."

"That's good." He folded his arms and cocked his head. "Are you sure?"

"Absolutely," she assured him. "Like you said, I just allowed that minister to confuse me."

"I'm glad to hear you've come to your senses. Besides, you can still see the child every Tuesday. I never heard of anybody starving to death when there's food about. She doesn't need you." He sent a frown toward the doorway. "Of course, *I* may starve if Rachel doesn't bring up something to eat. What's taking her so long?"

"She had to get dressed, too. We're leaving right after breakfast."

"Why are you taking her with you? The idea is to spend time *alone* with the man."

"You forget what sort of man Lord Burke is. He thinks I'm a good Christian lady—one who wouldn't travel about town unescorted." Turning to give him what she hoped was a reassuring smile, she added, "Besides, Rachel understands she must disappear as soon as possible. She'll visit with the other servants."

~

The driver of the chaise had to raise the bonnet, for fat drops of rain were beginning to splat the cobbled stones. "We're not really going to Lord Burke's?" Rachel asked after hearing Mrs. Hammond give instructions to the driver.

"I'm sorry—I couldn't tell you before. I was afraid something in your face would show."

The chaise started moving. Rachel looked through the side window toward the house. "Mrs. Hammond . . ."

"Yes?"

"Are you quite sure he believed you?"

"Of course. Why wouldn't he?"

Rachel looked again over her shoulder. The house grew smaller with every ring of hooves upon cobblestones. "I don't know, missus. Perhaps I'm making things up in my mind, but the way he looked at you when I served breakfast seemed . . . odd."

Giving a sigh of exasperation, Corrine leaned over the girl to look through her window. She half expected to see Gerald standing in the street watching them.

"He's probably sound asleep at this moment," she said to Rachel, sitting upright again. "You're just more afraid of him since he threatened us. You know he never goes out in the daytime."

Rachel nodded, but she didn't look convinced. When the carriage was nearing High Street, upon which they would normally turn south for Saint John's, Rachel put a hand upon Corrine's arm.

"Missus . . . please tell the driver to turn right."

"Rachel . . . this is silly."

"Please!"

She had never been so insistent before. Corrine wondered, *Is this a ploy to see Lord Burke?*

Perhaps Rachel was just as smitten with him as he obviously was with her. But even if that was so, surely she would not make up all of this just to be able to see him again. She had never been devious.

"You there! Driver!"

Because the rain was coming harder now, Corrine had to call twice before the man slowed the horse and looked over his shoulder. "Turn north up ahead. We want to go to Clifton Hill instead."

With a shrug the man flicked his whip.

"Thank you, missus," Rachel breathed, settling back into the seat.

"I still think this is ridiculous," Corrine grumbled. "What am I supposed to tell Lord Burke—that we just decided to pop in?"

"We did it once be—"

"I know that," Corrine snapped. "But it isn't proper for a lady to make a habit of it. He'll think I'm too forward."

Rachel bit her lip, hesitated. "But what's more important, missus? What Lord Burke thinks, or what Mr. Moore will do if he finds out you went to the orphanage?"

Corrine resigned herself to looking like a fool in front of Lord Burke. Rachel was an artist, after all. Artists were prone to flights of fancy.

A quarter of an hour later the chaise rocked to a halt in Lord Burke's carriage drive. Corrine sighed, "I hope you're happy, Rachel. Now, we shan't stay here long—I'm still determined to see if Anna is all right."

As the driver was opening an umbrella, the sound of hoofbeats against cobblestones came from a near distance and grew louder. That was not unusual anywhere in London, but in spite of herself, Corrine could not help but glance in that direction.

Rachel grabbed her arm at the same time.

"Mrs. Hammond!" she whispered.

Through rain that had thickened into sheets, Corrine could still see the hansom cab passing. Gerald, still in his morning coat, smiled and touched the brim of his hat. It was only after the cab rumbled on down the street that Corrine was able to find her voice.

"Where did he get a carriage so fast?" she said with hand up to her throat.

"I don't know," Rachel replied shakily. "But what if he had followed us to St. John's?"

"I can't even imagine." She shuddered, looked at Rachel. "That's twice you've saved me from his temper."

"It's all right, missus."

"No, it's not. I've treated you like an imbecile since the first day you came to live with us—when it's your wits that saved me." The driver cleared his throat from the side of the chaise, where he waited with his umbrella. "Oh, we're not getting out," Corrine said over the rain. "You may drive us to the first address I gave you."

Rachel gripped her arm again. "Surely you aren't thinking about—"

"St. John's? Why not? Gerald should be on his way home now."

"You shouldn't risk it."

"But what if Anna won't eat?"

"What if Mr. Moore comes back this way?"

Corrine looked back towards the road. "Anna will think . . ."

"You coaxed her to take food for two days now, missus. If she won't eat today, she won't starve, and you can find a way to see her tomorrow."

"Tomorrow?" Corrine echoed, and sighed. "I suppose so."

~

Joseph Price held his left forefinger on an advertisement for a house to let in the *London Chronicle,* spread out upon the table in his room, while writing the address with his right hand.

*It'll take me a week to check out all of these,* he thought, surveying the stack of last month's newspapers. Not to mention combing the pubs at night. *They knew what they were doing when they chose the biggest city in the world!*

At least he had a description of the man and a name. *Let's hope he feels safe enough to use his real name again.*

He folded the newspaper and reached for another, ignoring the rumbling in his stomach. Food and sleep were necessary, but right now his determination to beat Scotland Yard to catch

Gerald Moore—and Corrine Hammond—took precedence over everything.

~

After the rain forced Adam out of the garden, he sat under the terrace for a while and watched the colors of the garden become muted and yet the greens become sharper under their curtain of rain. When he finally walked into the kitchen to hint for a cup of hot chocolate, Lucy said, "Oh . . . there you are, Lord Burke. Dora's looking for you. You've some visitors in the parlor."

"Who are they?"

"Mrs. Hammond and Rachel."

He accepted the towel from the girl. "Where's your mother?"

"Papa made her go lie down after breakfast was cleared."

"Is it her rheumatism?"

"Yes, sir. The dampness in the air and all."

"Shall I send for Doctor Gilford?"

"She wouldn't allow it. Irene's comin' in here to help me with lunch, and Mummy says she'll be up before it's time to cook supper."

"Tell her she mustn't concern herself with supper. Just some bread and cheese or whatever's cold will do fine."

"Beggin' your pardon, sir, but you know she won't—"

Adam sighed. "Yes, I know. I'll just have to advise your father to lay down the law to her."

The girl nodded, but with doubtful expression. "She doesn't always listen to him . . . not where her kitchen is concerned."

"Then *I'll* go up and speak with her after lunch. Just send word when she's awake."

~

Climbing the steps leading to the rest of the house, Adam was torn between pleasure at the thought of seeing Miss Jones—even with Mrs. Hammond present—and guilt.

*You got carried away yesterday,* he chided himself. *It won't happen again.* It wasn't fair to take advantage of the girl's obvious pity for him. By the time he reached the parlor, he had convinced himself that a restrained politeness was the best way to handle the situation.

*For both of them,* he thought.

During supper last night, he had realized that his instincts about Corrine Hammond's being after his money were still on the mark . . . in spite of her surprising tenderness toward the child at St. John's. Still, there had been a sense of futility about her flirtations which had puzzled him.

Sheets of rain were hammering the parlor windowpanes. "Good morning, ladies," Adam said, pretending not to see Mrs. Hammond's lifted hand as he took a chair facing the sofa. "What brings you out on such a day?"

"How foolish you must think me!" Mrs. Hammond replied. "But we were out for a ride and suddenly realized that a storm was almost upon us."

While still intending to remain aloof, Adam knew that he couldn't very well send them back out into the deluge. "Is your driver taken care of?"

"We asked him to come back for us when the storm blew over," she replied breezily. "So, I'm afraid you're stuck with us. But Rachel's always delighted to visit with Lucy and Bernice, so it's an ill wind which blows no good, yes?"

"But I'm afraid Bernice is lying down," he said as thunder rattled the windows. "And Lucy's quite busy."

"Is something wrong with Bernice, Lord Burke?" Miss Jones asked cautiously, as if having been warned too many times that her mistress was to be given center stage.

He finally allowed himself to look at her. She wore a sea green gown trimmed with jet buttons, which suited her quiet beauty. Anything fancier—such as Mrs. Hammond's coral silk with layers of lace and ruffled skirts—would be gilding the lily. Was she even aware of how fetching she was?

"The weather has made her rheumatism flair," Adam replied. "For Bernice to lie down during the day, it's probably even worse than she's letting on."

"How terrible for her," Mrs. Hammond said with forehead furrowed, and she actually sounded as if she meant it.

Warming toward her just a little, Adam said, "Thank you. I'm going to try to talk her into allowing me to send for the doctor."

Miss Jones nodded. "I'll be happy to help Lucy."

"Yes, Rachel is a very good cook," Mrs. Hammond said right away, sending the girl a meaningful glance which said, very clearly, *Why aren't you on your way to the kitchen?*

The dislike Adam had for Mrs. Hammond returned with a vengeance. Quietly he reminded her, "Miss Jones is my guest, not my servant."

"Well . . . I just . . . ," Mrs. Hammond stammered.

*Chill politeness,* Adam reminded himself as another clap of thunder rattled the windows. He rose from his chair. "The library will be quieter."

This time he did not offer an arm to either woman.

# 17

W ell, I'm certainly glad the rain didn't last long,"
Mrs. Hammond said as the carriage wheels
splashed through puddles, carrying them away
from Lord Burke's lukewarm hospitality. "He didn't even
invite us to stay for lunch."

"Perhaps he felt out of sorts," Rachel said quietly. She
wished her mistress would stop going on about Lord Burke,
for she didn't even want to think about the way he had
received them with such obvious reluctance. While he had not
been actually *rude,* he got the point across that he had more
important things to do than entertain them through a rainstorm.

One good thing came out of his behavior, she realized. She
was absolutely convinced that he was not likely to be beguiled
by Mrs. Hammond's charms. She no longer had to feel guilty
every time she delivered a message to his house or visited with
Bernice and Lucy.

But that brought on a worry of another sort. She glanced at
Mrs. Hammond. For years she had almost hated her mistress.
Now, she worried that her failure was going to put her in an
awful spot with Mr. Moore.

"Why, Miss Jones!" Mr. Solomon beamed two hours later, as the bell tinkled over the door of his shop. "I was going to call upon you tomorrow—now you haff saved an old man the trouble."

"You were?" Rachel set her basket down just inside the door and made her way over to her friend. "Why?"

He pointed to a huge trunk in the back of the gallery. "You see? I must find places to put more paintings." After glancing out the bow window, he lowered his voice. "From the estate of a certain member of Parliament who passed on last year. He did not leave enough money to satisfy his eldest son, who wishes to continue a life of wanton idleness."

His voice rose with indignation. "So the worthless boy wishes to sell paintings that haff been in his family for years. He is selling some of the carpets and furniture, too, I haff heard."

As if suddenly remembering Rachel's question, he said, "I haff some good news for you, Miss Jones. First, would you like some tea? Levi is upstairs making a pot."

"No, thank you." Rachel stifled her impatience to hear Mr. Solomon's news. He would get around to it when he was ready.

"What are you doing, marketing in the afternoon?" he asked. "You haff always before shopped in the mornings."

"I had somewhere to go this morning with my missus. And with the rain . . ."

"Ah yes . . . the rain."

Rachel shifted her feet, smiled. "I'll have to be leaving soon."

"Oh, then you must forgive an old man's chattering! The good news is this. My gifted grandson I told you about—Reuben—is doing well in his studies, and he would like to tutor and inspire other lovers of art while he is trying to make a name for himself." Clasping his hands together at his chest, he exclaimed, "I haff the portrait you made of the young girl here, to frame. I showed it to Reuben, and he would like you to be his first student!"

Her breath caught in her throat. *"Me?"* she said when she could speak.

"I see no one else in here," he quipped.

She smiled. "I'm honored, Mr. Solomon. But I can't afford—"

He waved away her protest. "Afford nothing! There is no charge."

Rachel could not believe her ears. How many times had she stood in front of a painting, following the patterns of brush strokes and looking for any hints on how such a thing was done. "I can't possibly accept such a generous offer."

"But don't you see? Reuben will benefit from this, too. So many artists have not the temperament for teaching others—it is good that my grandson finds out before accepting any money from someone he may have to disappoint." He smiled. "But you will not be disappointed, my dear Miss Jones. He will teach you to use the oils and canvas just like the masters. And who knows? You may be selling your paintings in your old friend's gallery one day."

Tears blurring her eyes, Rachel reached for the man's hands. "My salary is small, but it'll help pay for the paints. This is so overwhelming!"

Mr. Solomon squeezed her hands. "The paints are included,

my young friend." Seeing that Rachel was about to argue, he lifted a finger. "You must respect my age and not argue."

"I . . . I don't know what to say." Remembering that Mrs. Hammond and Mr. Moore were waiting for her to prepare supper, she said, "I'll come back and speak with you more as soon as I can. Thank you so much for your kindness—and please thank Reuben!"

The old man returned Rachel's wave as she started for the door. "I shall do that, Miss Jones."

Rachel lifted her basket. "Sunday afternoons are the only times I have off. Will your grandson mind?"

Mr. Solomon chuckled. "We are Jews, my young friend. He will not mind."

~

*What's wrong with you?* Corrine asked herself, pacing the kitchen. For the second time she lifted the lid to the pastry crock and peered inside, as if she might have overlooked a seedcake or scone. Finding it still empty, she reached on the cupboard shelf above it for a much smaller crock, then took a spoon from the drawer. There was no sound coming from above stairs, but just to make sure, Corrine eased over to the door and listened. Gerald had been napping when she and Rachel returned from Lord Burke's and was apparently still doing so. *I hope he sleeps all day,* she thought darkly. *In fact . . . I hope he never wakes up!*

She opened the sugar crock and plunged the spoon inside. As the sweet white powder melted upon her tongue, she wondered, *How can I tell him we're wasting our time?* She had never failed before, partly because Gerald was a genius at finding just the proper gentleman for her to pursue. What if he decided to leave her? As much as she now wished for such a thing, she knew he would take every last penny with him.

Then what would she do? The only thing of value she owned was her treasured strand of pearls, and now that she realized how selfish Gerald could be, she feared that he might force her to dig them out of their hiding place and hand them over before he left.

*I'd have to get a job,* she mused. But she had become accustomed to the soft life. She doubted that she could still work as hard as she had at the dairy back in Leawick. And the thought of standing in front of a machine in a textile mill or factory for ten to twelve hours every day was a horrid one. Even then, she would not be able to afford this house, but would have to find a flat in some slum.

Another possible profession came to Corrine's mind. She had seen those women, brazenly walking the streets along the river or standing near lampposts, lifting their skirts to reveal their ankles to any man who seemed a likely prospect. She shuddered in revulsion.

She was no fool. There were clear parallels between what those women did for a living and what she had been doing for the past eight years. She had always told herself that it wasn't the same, but deep down she knew that it was.

Taking another spoonful of sugar, she blinked tears from her eyes and leaned against the cupboard. How did her life get to be such a mess?

"Oh, hello, missus."

Even though it was only Rachel's voice, Corrine was wound so tightly that the spoon clattered from her hand.

"Here, I'll get that," Rachel said.

"I have it." Corrine bent to retrieve the spoon, then replaced the sugar crock. She turned to the girl."

"Did you bring . . . ?"

Rachel smiled and handed her a small bakery box. "Macaroons."

"Thank you." As Corrine opened the lid, she wondered why Rachel's cheeks were glowing. And the way she was eyeing her, as if trying to decide whether to say something. "Well, what is it?"

"I beg your pardon?"

Corrine sighed, taking out a macaroon. "Why is your face all lit up like a Christmas candle? Are you going to tell me or keep me standing here guessing?"

The girl bit her lip.

"Well, out with it . . ."

"Oh, Mrs. Hammond, something just happened!" Smiling, Rachel embraced herself. "I've been offered art lessons—free!"

"Art lessons? But you already know how to draw."

"Only with pencils. And there are still many things I don't know. Mr. Solomon's grandson Reuben is going to teach me to work with paints."

"Mr. Solomon?"

"The nice man who owns the art gallery."

"Art gallery?"

Rachel's smiled faded a bit. "I sometimes . . . stop to look at the paintings after I market."

Corrine shook her head wearily and pulled out a chair for herself. "Sit down, Rachel." When they were seated across from each other, she popped the rest of the macaroon into her mouth, chewed, and swallowed. "Now, why would this Mr. Solomon's grandson offer you free lessons?"

"Because he needs to give lessons to help support himself, but he wants to see if he has the temperament first."

*Balderdash!* Corrine pressed her lips together. "Rachel, that doesn't make any sense. You're too naive to realize this, but there are lots of people out there who make a living by cheating others."

*You should know,* said a voice in her head, but she shook the thought from her mind.

Uncertainty washed across Rachel's face for only a fraction of a second. "But how can he cheat me when the lessons are free?"

Corrine thought. "The supplies. He'll have you use plenty of expensive paints and such, then bill you for double or even triple their worth."

"The supplies are included."

"Then the young man hopes to win your affections."

Rachel clamped a hand over a smile. "I'm sorry, missus. It's just that we've never even met."

"What about this Mr. Solomon? Perhaps he wishes to curry favor so you'll be grateful enough to become his mistress."

"Mr. Solomon?" Rachel's eyes grew wide. "But he's very old. And happily married."

"Well, no man is too old to make a fool of himself," Corrine snorted. "I've seen plenty of old men with young mistresses."

Shaking her head, the girl insisted, "Not Mr. Solomon. He's not like that."

Corrine had a strong feeling there was more to this than the obvious, and she was determined to find out what it was. "Then tell me everything he said to you."

"I can't remember every word," Rachel admitted. "I got

flustered when he started talking about the lessons. But he did say he was planning to come here tomorrow and speak with me . . . before I showed up at his shop, that is."

"So you've given him this address?"

Rachel's brows drew together. "Hmm . . . I'm sure I've never done that."

*I knew it!* Corrine thought. "Then how was he going to find his way here?"

"I don't know." Rachel held up a hand. "Wait—Mr. Solomon mentioned Lucy's portrait. Lord Burke must have already asked him to frame it and must have given him this address."

"I beg your pardon?"

"Lord Burke had asked if I knew someone who would do a good job framing it, and I recommended Mr. Solomon."

"I see." Corrine nodded. Now that two macaroons were digesting in her stomach, she felt generous enough to pass the box to Rachel.

"Oh, no thank you, missus. I'm too excited to eat."

Corrine forced herself to close the lid. She might wish to raid the kitchen at midnight, and spoonfuls of sugar were poor substitutes for pastries. "Then Lord Burke has obviously already spoken with the old man. And he has my address."

"But why would he find it necessary to give *this* address to Mr. Solomon?"

*I was right . . . Lord Burke is smitten with her,* Corrine mused. *Even though he put on that ridiculous act this morning.* A bitter smile curled the corners of her mouth. She would have laughed had her conclusion not added to her sense of impending doom. "Lord Burke. He arranged to pay for these lessons."

"But that can't be. Mr. Solomon didn't even mention him."

"Of course he didn't," Corrine sighed. "Rachel, if there is

one thing I'm an expert at, it's plots. Lord Burke is a tediously honorable man who doesn't wish you to feel beholden to him. So he instructed your Mr. Solomon to keep that part quiet."

Rachel shook her head. "Begging your pardon, missus, but why would Mr. Burke do that? Pay for the lessons, I mean."

The bewilderment on the girl's face was genuine, Corrine realized. She felt a twinge of envy at the innocence in those green eyes.

*You'll do all right in this world, Rachel Jones. There's a man out there who is falling in love with you, whether or not he is aware of it.*

"Can't you guess why?" Corrine asked.

"No, missus."

She sighed again. "Because he's in love with you . . . or is close to becoming so."

~

Rachel stared across at her mistress. "That can't be."

"Oh, come now," Mrs. Hammond said. "Surely you've noticed the way he looks at you."

Rachel could not deny that she had occasionally caught glimpses of something in his eyes. "But this morning—"

"This morning he was *just* as obvious by his avoidance of you. No doubt he's in a battle with himself over his feelings. After all, you *are* a servant, and much younger than he is."

"That just can't be possible," Rachel said, shaking her head.

"And the scars," Mrs. Hammond continued. "They may have something to do with it as well. He may be afraid that you find him repulsive."

"Repulsive? Why would he be afraid of that?"

Mrs. Hammond seemed genuinely surprised. "He has mirrors, hasn't he? I know you have this fascination with faces that aren't quite . . . aesthetic, but you can't rightly call him anything but ugly."

Sadly, Rachel shook her head. How could Mrs. Hammond have seen Lord Burke's face so many times and missed the beauty in it? Why, his eyes were the gentlest Rachel had ever seen. She even found the crooked half smile endearing.

*There's no use in even hoping she's right,* Rachel thought. *He's never going to be interested in a servant, no matter how fine a gentleman he is.*

"If Mr. Burke *is* paying for my lessons," she insisted, "then it's only because he is a kind and generous man."

"Whatever you say." Mrs. Hammond opened the lid to the pastry box again. "But I'd wager my last pound that the man's falling in love with you."

Something about the tone of her voice gave Rachel pause. "How can you say it like that?"

"What do you mean?"

"As if you wouldn't mind even if it were true."

"Because I *don't* mind." A nervous smile flitted across her lips. "You deserve the chance to get away from here. And I've come to the realization that Lord Burke is simply not interested in me, so I'm not going to waste any more time grieving over it."

"But Mr. Moore . . ."

Mrs. Hammond glanced toward the door. "Now that's another story. How am I going to tell him?"

Rachel reached across the table to put her hand on her arm. "You mustn't, missus—he'll hurt you again."

"But how long can I pretend that Lord Burke is interested in me?"

"At least long enough to think of something else."

"That's all I've thought about since yesterday," Mrs. Hammond said. "And I'm no closer to a solution."

"Then why don't we ask for help?"

Mrs. Hammond's eyes widened. "Don't even think of such a thing!"

"Why can't we ask Mrs. Morgan? Or even Lord Burke?"

"Because we just can't!" Mrs. Hammond glanced at the door, lowered her voice. "I don't want to go to prison, Rachel."

"Are you sure it would come to that?"

"Yes." Breathing a long sigh, Mrs. Hammond closed her eyes and began rubbing her forehead. "Not that I don't deserve it and not that part of me wouldn't welcome the chance to do penance for the evils I've done. Maybe that would give me some peace of mind. But . . . who would see about little Anna? And when would I ever see my—"

She stopped abruptly, and Rachel looked up to see an expression of utter misery. *She wants to see her daughter again.*

With all her heart she wished she could help Mrs. Hammond—but even if they had the opportunity to leave, they were going to have their hands full just keeping a step ahead of Gerald Moore.

~

"Bernice?" Adam knocked at her bedchamber door.

"Come in, Lord Burke," he heard from the other side.

She sat propped up with pillows at the head of her bed, an open Bible in her lap. Giving him a suspicious look, she said, "First Jack and now you."

Adam pulled the stool from her dressing table close to the bed. "I beg your pardon?"

"Aren't you here to order me to see Doctor Gilford?"

"No, I'm not." He propped an ankle upon his knee. "I'll admit that was my first thought, but you're a grown woman, and I wouldn't presume to run your life for you."

She blew out her cheeks. "Thank you. All he can do is give me laudanum, and I'd rather bear a little pain than drift about with my head in the clouds."

He could understand, having spent days in a laudanum-induced fog after being wounded. "But I am going to order you to stay out of the kitchen for the rest of the day."

"But I'm much better now that the rain's drying up."

"Well, that's good to hear. Just to be sure, though, I want you to take it easy until you can get back on your feet without hurting." With a stern look, he cut short her attempt to protest. "Even if you have to take a few days off. I daresay we won't starve."

She opened her mouth again as if to argue but closed it. "Thank you, Lord Burke. But I just know I'll be back to work in the morning. I can't bear to be away from my kitchen for too long."

"We'll see. Now, is there anything I can send up to you?"

The cook glanced down at the Bible in her lap. "Got all I need right here, sir. Food for the soul."

Adam smiled. "You're a good woman, Bernice."

Waving away the compliment, she changed the subject. "Lucy says Mrs. Hammond and Rachel came by earlier."

"They were caught in the rainstorm."

"Did you have a good visit?"

She was fishing, of course, Adam thought, smiling to himself. But he rather needed a dose of her common-sense counsel, so he said, "I'm afraid I was rude."

"Why?"

"I thought it was a good idea at the time," he admitted, "after my behaving like a lovesick schoolboy yesterday."

"Over Mrs. Hammond?" Bernice said with a little glint in her eyes.

Adam mugged a frown at her. "No."

"I *knew* you had feelings for the girl." The cook smiled. "So you decided to play coy this morning?"

"Only for her sake."

"For her sake or for yours?"

Sometimes Bernice was *too* perceptive, Adam thought. But he was determined to be honest with her. "Very well . . . perhaps for my own sake. What if I were to let my feelings for her to be known and she reciprocates? I'll never know if it's because of pity—or even my money."

"And you think that those are the only reasons a woman would feel affection for you? Pity or greed?"

"Well, it certainly wouldn't be because of this." He touched his cheek. "No woman in her right—"

"No woman in her right mind would want you, is that it?" Bernice shook her head wearily, as if having to reason with a willful child. "Well sir, what if Kathleen had gotten injured and lost her looks. Would you have loved her in spite of it?"

"Of course," Adam answered immediately, but doubt sprang up in his mind just as quickly. Would he have still loved her? Of course he would have done the right thing and married her, but hadn't her beauty been the thing of which he was most proud?

Come to think of it, they had shared little in common besides a mutual admiration of her complexion, her eyes, and her flair for the latest fashions. Had Kathleen's beauty blinded him to her shallowness? *Have I been a shallow fool myself? Expecting everyone else to be as enamored of physical beauty as I once was?*

Bernice was smiling sadly, as if she understood his internal struggle. "Are you all right, m'lord?"

He stroked his leatherlike cheek again. "This certainly has complicated my life."

"Maybe God allowed those scars to happen for a purpose," she said gently.

"A purpose?" He frowned. "I'm not sure what you mean."

"Well, look at Saint Paul. He had some sort of affliction, and he asked the Lord three times to take it away. But God wouldn't do it. Do you know what the Lord told him was the reason why?"

Adam nodded. He had read the account many times, sometimes even wondering why God didn't go ahead and remove the apostle's affliction. "He said that his grace was sufficient."

"God's grace," Bernice echoed, her voice touched with awe. "Our Lord knew that Paul would have to keep depending upon him. Paul's body was only a temporary thing—he ended up dying just like we're all going to do one day. But it was good for his soul to walk close to his Father. It made him an even better person. The soul doesn't die, Lord Burke."

"No, it doesn't." Adam smiled, envying Bernice's ability to find something in the Bible to apply to every situation. "And you think these scars can make me into a better person, Bernice?"

"Yes, sir, if you'll allow them. In fact, I think they already have. You've learned the hard way about where the real worth of a person lies . . . and it's not on the outside. I've got a feeling that Rachel learned that lesson, too, sometime in her life.

I've seen the way the girl looks at you, and it seems to me that it's not your fine brown eyes . . . or your money that she's admiring. It's the Adam Burke that I've known for years that she's longing to get to know better."

Her words made sense and gave him more hope than he had possessed in years. Still, he had been mistaken about someone's feelings for him before. "I'm afraid I'll get hurt again," he admitted in a near whisper.

"You'd take that chance with anybody, m'lord. Do you plan to be a hermit for the rest of your life?"

He shook his head. "No, I don't want that. But how can I know for sure about Miss Jones?"

Bernice glanced down at her Bible. "It says here that our Lord gives us wisdom if we ask for it. Pray for some of that wisdom. And get to know her better—that is, if you didn't frighten her off this morning!"

"You think I should apologize?"

"That might frighten her off, too. Why don't you just invite her for supper tomorrow night with the Morgans?"

Adam snapped his fingers. "I forgot about that! You're not ready to cook for guests. I'll just send . . ."

"Really, sir, please don't spoil my Friday night! It's the only time you allow me to cook as fancy as I like."

"It won't hurt to skip a week, Bernice. I really must insist that you rest."

Bernice shook her head. "I'm feeling much better. And I have Lucy—and the others will help if I need them."

"Are you sure?"

"Positive." She sighed. "I suppose you'll have to ask Mrs. Hammond, too, or she may not allow Rachel to come. I wonder what she thought about your acting like a lovesick schoolboy, as you put it, around her maid last night."

"I'm not sure," Adam mused, rubbing his chin. "Sometimes I think I've got the woman pegged, and then she surprises me. I can't quite figure her out."

"Me, too," Bernice agreed. "At first when she mentioned going to see that little orphan girl, I knew it was just to get your attention. But she really seems to care about the child."

"Perhaps she has a heart after all." Abruptly changing the subject, he said, "Do you really think this is a good idea—inviting Rachel to dinner?"

"Yes, I do, sir." She winked. "But then, I'm just the cook—what do I know?"

"Apparently more than I do," Adam conceded as he got to his feet and pushed the stool back under the dressing table. He smiled at the woman in the bed. "Perhaps I should learn to cook."

# 18

It was morning, that is, it was not yet daylight, but about six o'clock. I woke up in the same arm-chair; my candle had burnt out; everyone was asleep in the captain's room, and there was a stillness all round, rare in our flat.

The words of *David Copperfield* began melding together. Yawning, Rachel marked her place with a rectangle of brown paper and closed the book. Swinging her legs over the side of the bed, she leaned toward her night table and snuffed the candle. *You'll be worn out in the morning.*

Yet, after what seemed an hour later, she was still tossing and turning. Her body cried for sleep, but her mind was restless, jumping from one remarkable incident of the day to another.

Why would Lord Burke arrange her art lessons—if Mrs. Hammond's theory was correct—and order Mr. Solomon not to tell her? It did not make sense. And her mistress *had* to be wrong about Lord Burke's affection for her, as much as she wished it were so. Things like that didn't happen to servant girls.

*Don't they?* another part of her brain argued. *How many servants get to take art lessons?* One day she would be a great portrait artist and make enough money to live on her own. *I'll even take Mrs. Hammond with me if she still wishes to leave.*

With a little shiver she recalled Mr. Moore's threat to fix Mrs. Hammond so that no man would ever look at her. He had said something else, too, just before storming out of the house. She was too concerned with tending to her mistress to allow the words to sink in, but now she remembered the words with unnerving clarity. He had pointed his finger at her and said, "The same goes for you!"

Sleep would not visit any time soon, Rachel realized. She swung her feet around, felt for her slippers, and lit the candle again. *May as well get a start on tomorrow's work,* she thought. Then she remembered that Mr. Moore was staying close to home lately. It wouldn't do to run into him in the dark. She picked up the novel and propped an arm against her pillow. She would read a couple of more pages.

The window was open wide to allow in the cool night air. Charles Street was a quiet vista, without much traffic even in the daytime. But she imagined she heard the creak of carriage wheels just in front of the house, and the slow cadence of iron horseshoes against stones.

~

Adam's original plan was to pass by the house in his one-horse roundabout. No one would be awake, this time of night, and he simply wished to know where Miss Jones lived. When the amber glow appeared in the window, he reined Jupiter to a stop just across the street.

He was certain that was her window. Most attic bedrooms were given to servants. *Is she having trouble sleeping, too?* What would she think if she knew he was outside the house? Would she be frightened? Assume he had some ulterior motive?

Staring up at the window, he felt close to her, as if he could sense some turmoil going on in her mind. Had Mr. Solomon informed her of the lessons? They had only made the arrangements that morning, but the old man had seemed eager to tell her as soon as possible.

Adam tried to imagine the surprise and joy upon Miss Jones' face, envying Mr. Solomon for being able to witness it. He was happy he could give her this opportunity without causing her to feel obliged to him, but another part of him could not help but wish she could know the truth.

It was selfish to think that way, he told himself. The important thing was that she would be able to advance her talent. Still he could not help but harbor a hope that one day, even if it were years from now, she would find out.

When he looked up again, the window was swallowed by the dark facade of the house. *It's just as well,* he said to himself. Decent men did not lurk outside young ladies' windows, and loneliness was no excuse. Adam flicked the reins, clucked softly to Jupiter, and headed for home.

~

The following morning, Rachel jumped slightly at the sound of footsteps outside the kitchen doorway. She was becoming as skittish as a mouse with Mr. Moore underfoot whenever he wasn't asleep. But it was her mistress, clad in nightgown and wrapper, her long hair uncombed.

"What a sight *you* are," Mrs. Hammond said, pulling out a chair at the work table.

*You're no beauty yourself at the moment,* Rachel thought on her way to the stove. She lit the jet beneath the kettle, covered a yawn, then turned again. "I'm sorry, missus."

"Don't tell me . . . you stayed awake all night pining for Lord Burke."

Rachel did not attempt to restrain her frown. "Mrs. Hammond . . ."

Mrs. Hammond smothered a giggle with a cough. "You should see the indignation on your face, Rachel. It's a relief to be able to laugh at *something*."

"I didn't sleep," Rachel admitted sheepishly.

"Nor did I. But I had sense enough to powder the circles under my eyes."

"I don't imagine it matters how I look, missus, as long as I get my work done."

"Ah, but that's where you're wrong." Mrs. Hammond spooned sugar into her cup. "While you were in here banging pots about, one of Lord Burke's servants was at the door with a note."

Rachel poured the tea and attempted not to look too interested as her mistress brought a folded page from the pocket of her wrapper.

"Oh, pour yourself some tea and sit," Mrs. Hammond scolded. "You make me nervous standing there holding your breath."

"Thank you, missus," Rachel said, already on the way to the cupboard for a cup. Seconds later she was seated with the page in her hand. She recognized Mr. Burke's even script. Silently she read:

> *Dear Mrs. Hammond,*
>
> *Will you and Miss Jones be so kind as to have dinner with me this evening? Reverend and Mrs. Morgan will be here as well.*

*Please give your reply to my footman, Hershall. If you desire,*
*I will send a coach for you at six o'clock.*

*Yours very truly,*
*Adam Burke*

~

"As liberal as the man is about the treatment of servants,"
Corrine remarked as Rachel set the letter down on the table,
"he cannot stray too far from the bounds of propriety. That's
why the invitation is in my name. But I'm sure you realize it's
for your sake."

"But why—"

Corrine yawned. "No doubt he grieved all day and night
over practically ignoring you yesterday morning. Men in love
are so predictable!"

When Rachel started to protest, Corrine raised a hand. "We
went over all of this last night, and I'm not in the mood to do
it again. But I do think you should get a nap today so you
won't frighten the man."

"But the floors need polishing."

"Can wait till next week—or even the next. We never have
guests, so what does it matter?"

"Oh, thank you, missus," the girl said with a grateful smile.
"I'll get them done as soon as possible."

"I'll not sit up nights worrying over it," Corrine said, lifting
her cup again. "Now, more tea, if you please. And you had
better start breakfast. I heard Gerald stirring upstairs just before
I came down."

She sighed and lowered her voice. "No doubt he'll be
ecstatic over this invitation."

That gave her an idea. Gerald would have no reason to follow them this time. Not when she had proof of where they were going. And she did not think Lord Burke would be too disappointed if Rachel showed up for dinner alone.

~

"Actually, the house belongs to my husband's sister," Mrs. Graham explained, perched on the edge of her chair in the front parlor of her Park Lane home. "She's spending a year in Italy and asked us to lease it for her."

She patted her white chignon. "This is so exciting—someone unaware that he's inherited a fortune!"

Joseph Price took a sip of his tea and smiled. "That's what I like about my job—surprising people."

"The only thing is, my husband will not be home until quite late tonight. And I'm afraid I don't know the name of the tenant."

"Aren't there any papers you can look through?" Joseph asked. "Rent receipts?"

Mrs. Graham laughed, "My dear Mr. Price, I wouldn't know where to begin to look. And anyway, Charles is quite touchy about his desk and ledgers."

Setting cup and saucer on the tray, Joseph thanked her for the tea and got to his feet. "I have some other landlords to look up in the meantime. May I return in the morning if I don't get any leads?"

"Well, not *too* early. We're usually finished with breakfast by nine."

"Thank you. And by the way, on the off chance that you should hear from this tenant, please don't mention our conversation. It wouldn't do to give people false hopes."

The woman was clearly delighted to be in on a secret. She put a conspiratorial finger up to her lips. "Not a word."

~

Occasionally checking the list of rentals in his pocket, Joseph called upon a dozen other landlords. He was fortunate to find every one of them at home or at his office, save one, but that one had a wife who knew her husband's business matters better than had Mrs. Graham. None had ever heard of Gerald Moore or Corrine Hammond. Even more discouraging, two of the landlords mentioned that an investigator from Scotland Yard had been around earlier, asking about Moore.

The *London Chronicle* had mentioned nothing about the slain woman, but the authorities could not keep news such as this quiet for much longer. Scotland Yard's search would be intense. Unless he found a lead soon, he just might be beaten in the race.

He was under less pressure to capture Corrine Hammond right away because, so far, it did not seem that Scotland Yard even knew of her existence, much less her past activities. Once he had her lover in bounds, he would take them both back to Treybrook and let the squire decide what to do with them.

~

Gerald smiled across the breakfast table at Corrine. "You've done it again, you little temptress. How could I ever have doubted you?"

Smiling back, Corrine was careful not to allow any dislike to seep into her expression. *He only cares for me when he thinks money's on the way,* she told herself. *Why didn't I see that years ago?*

"In fact," he continued as he speared a piece of bacon with

his fork, "I'm going to take a little stroll after breakfast and buy you some bonbons. Just a couple, mind you."

"Bonbons would be lovely," Corrine answered. *Anything to get you out of my sight for a while.*

~

At twenty past six that evening, when the coach Lord Burke had arranged stopped in his carriage drive, Rachel started protesting again. "But it isn't proper for me to call on him alone."

"Now, now, Rachel." Corrine patted her hand as the driver opened the door. "Stop whining and allow the poor man to help you."

She had no qualms about taking over the coach. After all, Lord Burke was interested in the welfare of the orphans he sponsored, and besides, he could afford the fare if she chose to ride down every street in north London this evening.

"I'll be back shortly," she went on. "And besides, the Morgans are here."

"But what if they aren't, yet? May I not go with you?"

"And waste the time I spent arranging those curls of yours? Just be sure to inform Lord Burke that I'm taking the coach on to St. John's. We'll come again for you when I've had a nice long visit."

~

Realizing the futility of arguing the matter, Rachel turned and walked with resigned steps toward Lord Burke's door. *He'll assume I'm part of the scheme,* she told herself. Especially the way she was dressed. She wished she hadn't allowed Mrs. Hammond to talk her into curling her hair and putting on the sea green dress, the one which she said enhanced the emerald color of her eyes.

Marie answered the door. "Why, don't you look lovely, Miss Jones!"

Rachel swallowed. "Thank you."

"But where is Mrs. Hammond?"

"She went on to the orphanage."

"Well, do come in!"

As they walked up the corridor, Rachel could hardly absorb the maid's gay chatter over Lucy's portrait. Lord Burke rose from a parlor sofa and came over.

"Good evening, Miss Jones."

He seemed to be expecting her to extend her hand, so she did so. "Good evening, Lord Burke. Mrs. Hammond asks if you would mind her taking the coach on to St. John's."

Which wasn't the actual truth, she realized after speaking, for her mistress could hardly ask permission when the coach was a mile up the street by now.

"I gather she was concerned over the little girl?"

"She's worried that she might not eat."

"How thoughtful," Mr. Burke said, but not looking too disappointed at her absence. "Perhaps she'll join us later?"

"Yes, sir—I believe she will."

"Well, good! Meantime, do come have a seat, please. If the Morgans arrive soon, perhaps we'll have time for a game of whist before dinner."

"Yes, sir."

~

Adam tried not to allow any amusement to show on his face. The girl sat beside him, gloved hands clasped, only looking up when spoken to. She would no doubt be more comfortable in the kitchen helping to prepare the meal.

249

"Have you had the chance to read any of *David Copperfield* yet?" he asked.

Finally she nodded and smiled. "Yes, thank you. I read until quite late last night."

*So that's why your light was on.*

He couldn't resist saying, "I find that reading is helpful when I have trouble falling asleep, don't you?"

She darted him a quick, questioning glance, then dropped her eyes to her hands again. "Yes, sir. How is Bernice?"

"Much improved," Adam replied. "Or, so she says. I tried to convince her to rest today, but she's, well, a mite stubborn."

That made Miss Jones smile. Marie came into the room again, pausing just inside the door. "Lord Burke, Reverend Morgan sent a note." She brought an envelope over to him and then left the room.

Adam opened the envelope. "I'm afraid the Morgans aren't coming."

"Oh, dear. Is someone ill?"

"Drop-in guests for the evening, it says. I'm afraid some of Robert's family members take him for granted because he's a minister." An unsettling thought entered Adam's mind. He gave Miss Jones a worried look. "I hope you don't think . . ."

"Think what, sir?"

He cleared his throat. "That I planned it this way. This evening, I mean."

~

Rachel could feel her cheeks burning. *He's disappointed I'm the only one here.* If only she had tried harder to get Mrs. Hammond to take her along!

"I'm sorry," she said quietly.

"Sorry?"

"The evening hasn't turned out as you intended."

"It certainly hasn't," Lord Burke said.

He seemed to be making a huge effort to restrain himself from smiling. Annoyed that he should find her discomfort so amusing, Rachel forced herself to look him directly in the eyes and reminded herself, *It's not your fault you're the only one who showed up.*

"If you please, I'll wait with Bernice and Lucy until Mrs. Hammond returns," she said with as much dignity as she could muster. "I'm sure there are things I can help out with in the kitchen."

To her surprise, he looked disappointed. "Is that what you'd rather do?"

"Wouldn't you rather I did?"

"No," he replied. "I'd rather you stayed with me. That is, if you would care to."

A strange tension crept into the room, settling around them. Rachel wondered if she was the only one who sensed it. "But you just said you didn't plan . . ."

"I didn't want you to think I *arranged* for this to happen." His lips quirked into a smile. "But of course that would not enter your mind, would it? After all, how could I know that Mrs. Hammond wasn't planning to stay—or that Robert would cancel?"

"You couldn't," Rachel answered.

"Exactly! So why don't we just enjoy each other's company?"

Suddenly light-headed, Rachel managed a smile. "Yes, sir."

"Would you care to see the conservatory?" he offered suddenly.

"That would be nice."

"Good!"

Rising, he turned to take her hand and help her from the sofa. He tucked her hand into the crook of his arm and led her down the corridor, past dining room and drawing room to a sitting room in the east wing of the house. They walked through a set of French doors, into a room with low brick walls on three sides and windows glazing up to the level of the eaves, allowing in the dimming but still adequate summer sun rays. Murky aromas of soil, damp leaves, and flowers abounded, and Rachel found herself breathing more deeply.

"This is Jack's favorite part of the house. In fact, I'm surprised we didn't come upon him just now." He pointed out exotic plants and ferns, lilies and jasmine, stephanotis and gardenias, arranged with artful chaos in brass and china planters and hanging pots. "Careful," he warned. "The tiles are slick in spots."

"How lovely," Rachel said. She turned her head to ask him the name of a particularly colorful purple flower and banged the top of her forehead against a hanging pot of ivy. "Oh!" she cried, more from surprise than pain.

"Watch out!" Lord Burke warned, too late, and reached up to steady the swinging pot. He turned to her with brow creased. "Are you all right, Miss Jones?"

"Yes, sir," she replied, embarrassed at her clumsiness. Moving her hand from the place above her brow, she nodded. "Really, I am."

He stepped closer and studied her forehead. "I don't see a knot, but perhaps we should let Bernice look at it."

Rachel couldn't help but smile. "Perhaps you should inspect the pot instead. Sometimes a hard head is convenient."

He laughed. "You're the last person I'd consider hard-headed. Let's get into some better light and make certain."

Taking her hand, he led her back through the French doors and into the sitting room. A lamp burned brightly on a corner table. He drew a stool close and bade her sit.

"I thought earlier we would all come in here for whist," he said, frowning studiously as his fingers gently probed her forehead. "I'm glad the lamp was already lit—it's a beast to tamper with."

"My head feels fine."

"That's good. But if you should experience even the slightest nausea or have trouble seeing clearly, you must let me know right away so I can send for the doctor."

"Yes, sir—thank you."

He dropped to one knee beside her. His warm brown eyes met her own. "May I ask a favor, Miss Jones?"

"Sir?"

"Would you stop addressing me as *sir?* In fact, do you think you could possibly manage 'Adam'?"

Rachel's heart pounded against her rib cage. "I don't think I can," she murmured.

"Why can't you?"

"Because I'm . . ."

"Because you're a servant?"

She nodded.

He smiled gently. "But you're not *my* servant."

She thought she heard footsteps coming down the hall . . . or was it her own pulse pounding? Strong was the urge to lower her eyes, but she fought against it.

*It's not fair to pray for courage if you're not willing to put forth at least a little effort,* a little voice seemed to say in her mind.

"It's become such a habit," she explained.

His eyes were crinkling at the corners. "You mean like covering your mouth when you yawn?"

"Yes, sir." Rachel returned his smile. "I mean, yes."

"There you go!"

"But I'm not sure I can stop saying 'Lord Burke'," she confessed.

He laughed. "We'll work on that some other time, if you wish. I can't go expecting too much from an injured lady, can I?"

Both heads turned at the sound of a throat clearing. Lucy stood in the doorway, watching them.

"Yes, Lucy?" Lord Burke said.

The girl's cheeks flamed crimson. "Mum says dinner is ready," she mumbled before disappearing through the doorway.

Lord Burke got to his feet and held out a hand. "Shall we?"

# 19

What do you mean, she's not here?" Corrine said as her eyes scanned the cribs in St. John's nursery.

"Her mum came for her yesterday," Mrs. O'Reilly explained. "Said she had some family in the country willin' to help out, whereas they wouldn't before. You know how—"

"But she had no right!"

Taking Corrine's elbow, the Irish woman gently but firmly guided her away from the children's curious stares, out into the corridor. "She was her *mother,* Mrs. Hammond. You should have seen little Anna's face when she walked in."

Corrine fumbled in her reticule for a handkerchief and blew her nose. Through thickened throat she said, "*I'm* the one who got her to eat."

"You saved her life, in my opinion. You were good to the child when she needed someone. I think little Anna will remember you, somehow."

Helplessly, Corrine raised her hands and allowed them to drop to her sides. "I . . . I don't know what to think."

Mrs. O'Reilly's eyes moistened. "Mrs. Hammond," she began, with a voice full of compassion, "you were only with the child two—no, three times."

"What does that matter?"

The woman hesitated. "Perhaps there's somethin' else that's troubling you? Maybe somethin' that's just too hard to think about?"

In spite of her misery, indignation managed to rise in Corrine's chest. How dare this woman presume to know how she was supposed to feel! She raised her chin and said, tersely, "I certainly appreciate your words of wisdom. I'll let you get back to changing nappies."

She turned for the staircase. By the time her foot touched the top step, she was already feeling remorse for snapping at Mrs. O'Reilly when she was just trying to help. But she was too full of grief and loss to turn around and apologize.

~

After his fifth game of solitaire, Gerald brushed the cards away with the back of his hand—a dozen or more fell to the carpet underneath the Pembroke table, but he made no effort to retrieve them.

*Boring, boring, boring!* He walked from the parlor into the dining room and took another bottle of gin from the sideboard. Not bothering with a glass, he drank several gulps straight from the bottle. The liquor scorched the length of his throat on its way down, but he paid it no mind. He wiped his mouth on the back of his shirt sleeve. The *London Times* lay open on the table. He pointed a wavering finger at the newspaper.

"I'm sick of reading about von Bismark and Western provinces and Mr. Lincoln!"

Gerald started when he realized that it was his own voice filling the room. *Get hold of yourself!* he thought, setting the bottle back on the sideboard. He *had* to get out of the house. It was three days since he had abandoned caution and blathered on about the girl from Lancaster. He could not even recall their faces, the men who had invited him to their table. And they were probably as drunk as he was.

Surely no one had believed him. Surely it was safe for him to go to another pub. And he could always count on finding men ready to lose money—or to take money, depending on how his luck went with the cards.

~

"I asked Bernice to keep the meal simple," Lord Burke said. He nodded toward the spread of buttered prawns, boiled capon and oysters, spinach with croutons, stewed celery *a la creme*, early potatoes, and bread pudding. "She didn't listen, naturally."

"It's all delicious," Rachel said. "But I'm sorry she worked so hard."

"She insists she's fine now. Still, I can see that I'm going to have to keep an eye on her when the weather's damp."

"You treat your servants so well."

"I hope so. They're good to me."

Rachel could hardly believe they were carrying on a conversation like old friends. Lord Burke had a way of making her feel at ease.

"Tell me how it was to grow up in an orphanage," he asked, then quickly amended, "Unless that's too painful for you."

"It's not at all painful," she replied. "It was all I ever knew, and so I didn't pine for anything else. With thirty . . . sometimes as many as fifty girls, I didn't lack for playfellows. And Reverend and Mrs. Stockbridge were kind to us."

"Did you have regular meals?"

"More or less."

"And what exactly does that mean?"

"Well, contributions went up and down depending upon the harvest. There was never a day when we didn't have *something* to eat, if only watered-down porridge. Fortunately, the Lord Mayor's estate was next door. He had a huge orchard, but would allow what apples his family couldn't use to fall and rot."

"But why?" Lord Burke asked.

"Because he'd fought so strenuously against having an institution so close. But the house was donated, and there was no law against us."

"And why was it fortunate to have him next door?" Rachel studied his face. "I'm not boring you, am I?"

He smiled. "I'm fascinated. Do go on."

She drew breath and continued. "It was *fortunate,* because during the fall some of the older girls would slip out nights and scale the wall. They were careful only to pick a couple of dozen apples each time, then would carry them back and leave them in a heap outside the door."

Lord Burke's good eyebrow lifted in mock suspicion. "They?"

She gave him a sheepish look. "Well . . . I eventually became one of the older girls."

When he laughed, she said, "Please don't think I condone that. But I have to believe God doesn't judge hungry children too severely."

"I believe so, too," he said, and his brown eyes grew tender. "Poor Miss Jones."

Rachel shook her head. "Thank you, but you mustn't feel

too sorry for me. We rather relished the adventure of getting away with something."

He smiled again. "I don't quite understand, though. Why leave the apples outside the door? I would have thought you would have brought them inside, shared them."

"This was our way of sharing, you see? We wouldn't have been able to give any to the younger girls for fear of the Stockbridges finding out. And besides, the cook—a Mrs. Wright—made the most delicious apple tarts."

"But were the Stockbridges never suspicious? From where did they think the apples came?"

Rachel nodded. "I'm convinced they believed the lord mayor was leaving them there—that his conscience had gotten the better of him, but that he was too proud for anyone to know it. So they respected his desire for secrecy and never thanked him. But he was always in our evening prayers."

"The old grouch had the better end of that deal after all, didn't he?" Lord Burke said.

"We girls didn't think so at the time."

"Why not?"

"Those *were* delicious tarts."

This time his laugh made her smile. But she was going on about herself, she realized. And she wished to know more about him. "What was your childhood like?" she asked.

He looked embarrassed. "Almost idyllic. Or at least I thought so at the time. My brother and sister and I practically had the run of Gloucester."

"Is that a bad thing?" she asked, relieved to learn that he had had some good years after all.

"I'm not too sure. With almost every whim granted, we felt entitled to more, and didn't learn restraint. That ultimately ruined my sister. And drove a wedge between my brother and me."

"A wedge?" she asked, hoping she was not being too inquisitive.

Lord Burke hesitated. "Well . . . he and my fiancée . . ."

"I'm sorry." Rachel put a hand upon his sleeve, realized what she was doing and withdrew it at once, rather hoping he had not even noticed.

He had, for he glanced down at his sleeve with an expression she could not read, then looked up at her again. "It's *I* who should be sorry, Miss Jones. Here I am, complaining as if trying to cultivate your pity."

"I don't pity you," she said.

The eyebrow raised. "You don't?"

She shook her head and summoned the boldness to say, "I wish you had never been hurt. But it's hard to pity someone as strong as you are."

Surprise washed across his face, followed by obvious pain. "Strong, Miss Jones? Do strong men run away from their problems? Or do weak ones?"

He was referring to the situation back home with the fiancée and brother, Rachel was certain. Quietly she offered, "I should think that would depend on the problem itself, Lord Burke."

"What do you mean?"

Rachel thought for several seconds. "If the problem is that your children are starving, then it would be an act of weakness to run away. But if a situation brings only unhappiness and you aren't hurting anyone by looking for a better life, I think a strong person would move on."

*Would that I had tried harder to do that years ago,* she thought.

But then, she would not be sitting here with Lord Burke.
Dared she even hope Mrs. Hammond was right? If it wasn't
affection shining in those brown eyes regarding her, what was
it?

"Thank you for saying that, Miss Jones," he said with a
voice just a trace more thick.

~

"Please go back to Lord Burke's house for my maid," Corrine
said to the driver as he helped her from the coach.

The man hesitated, clearly taking in her swollen eyes. "Are
you all right, madam?"

"Yes," she lied. "Just lovely."

Listlessly she moved up the front walk. The brandy in her
bedroom was waiting for her, and she intended to numb her
senses and sleep for as long as possible.

Only when she turned the doorknob did she remember that
Gerald had been staying home evenings.

*I don't care!* she told herself, swinging open the door. Yet
she felt immeasurable relief to discover that the house was
empty.

~

Following a trail of gaslights down Wellington Road, Gerald
kicked loose pebbles and cursed his luck, cursed Britain and
Parliament, and cursed the two men who had come into Lazy
Jake's Public House asking around for a Gerald Moore. Just
when he had a straight flush and twenty quid on the table, he
had overheard the man behind the bar repeating a question
asked of him by an older man with a bushy mustache.

Fortunately Lazy Jake, or whatever his name actually was,

was hard of hearing. He had leaned over the bar and barked out, "Scotland Yard, you say? Gerald Moore?"

"Nature calls," Gerald had whispered to his startled partners before slipping away, abandoning his twenty pounds on the table. He couldn't remember what name he had given them when they had started up the game, but he was certain he hadn't used his own. Still, it was unnerving to discover that Scotland Yard was looking for him.

He cursed again at the thought of having to spend additional days at home. But they couldn't find him if he didn't go anywhere.

A worry flitted across his mind. He had used his real name when he leased the house! If they were determined enough to search for him in pubs, perhaps they would eventually think of digging up rental records from several weeks ago. If they weren't already.

"Hey, mister—want to have some fun?" came a careworn voice next to a broken gaslight on the corner near the railway station.

Scowling at the woman, who looked pockmarked and unwashed even in the foggy darkness, Gerald continued walking. He could hear her footsteps fade behind him as she sought a safer corner.

*It's no use!* he told himself, frowning bitterly. It was just a matter of time before he was discovered. He was closer than ever to being flat broke. The thought of the abandoned twenty pounds brought a curse from his lips. Never before had he risked so much on one hand, but being forced to stay away from gambling had made him careless.

*We have to get out of London,* he told himself as he turned up the pavement toward the house. And as soon as possible. But how could they relocate without money? Corrine would just have to move faster with Burke. She could do it—she had done it before.

A table lamp was burning in the sitting room. Gerald assumed he must have left it on earlier. Then a noise drifted down through the ceiling. *Corrine?* He squinted at the mantel clock. What was she doing home at half past nine?

~

Corrine blinked at the image framed by the doorway and took another sip of brandy.

"I didn't hear you come in."

Entering the room to stand before her, Gerald narrowed his eyes and studied her face. "How long have you been home?"

"Hmm." Corrine tilted her head, trying to think. "I'm not—"

"And what happened to you?" he cut in.

The way he was looking at her brought on a surge of fear, which immediately sharpened Corrine's senses. *Why didn't you have sense enough to go back to Lord Burke's?* she silently berated herself.

"Corrine?" Gerald frowned. "Corrine?"

"Lord Burke's cook served oysters," she lied, her mind trying to outpace the growing sluggishness the brandy was inducing.

"You *ate* them?"

"I'm feeling bet—"

"That's just wonderful!" he seethed, the veins in his temples prominent. "You *know* you can't eat oysters! You're supposed to get money from the man, and you allow yourself to become ill!"

She had to pacify him somehow. The oyster story may not have been the best one she could have dredged up on the spur of the moment, but she was stuck with it now. Trying to keep her voice calm, she said, "But, Gerald, before I got sick, he said he loved me."

"What?"

"The Morgans were late, so he asked me to walk with him in the garden. He kissed me."

Gerald smiled and seized her shoulders, causing some of the brandy to slosh from the glass. "I knew you could do it! The money's as good as in our pockets, yes?"

Returning his smile, Corrine handed him the glass to share. The immediate crisis had been taken care of. Perhaps Gerald would leave soon and allow her to sleep. A dreamless state of unconsciousness was what she craved more than anything, with no thought of little Anna. Or little Jenny.

But Gerald wasn't finished. "Do you think tomorrow's too soon to ask him to lend you some money?"

*"Tomorrow?"*

"A couple of detectives from Scotland Yard were asking around for me tonight. I'm afraid we'll need to leave London as soon as possible."

~

After dinner, Lord Burke escorted Rachel to the parlor. "We need four for whist. We can play draughts if you like. But I'd really rather just talk, if you don't mind."

"I'd rather talk," Rachel admitted.

"I'm glad."

He led her to the sofa, and sat a foot away from her on her right side, obviously in order to present his unscarred profile to her. It pained her to think he would assume her so shallow, until it dawned upon her that it was probably a habit.

"What's to be your next art project?" he asked casually.

Just a little too casually.

Rachel smiled to herself. So, the dreams of servants did come true, at times, she thought with wonder. God was good!

"I'll be taking art lessons on Sunday afternoons," she replied just as casually.

"Indeed?"

"Mr. Solomon—the man I mentioned who has the gallery?" she reminded him.

As if he did not know.

"Yes," Lord Burke said. "I seem to recall the name."

"His son has offered to tutor me. For no charge."

"Hmm. Isn't that nice?"

It was all Rachel could do to keep from hugging herself. "It's incredibly generous and wonderful."

At that moment the atmosphere in the room changed, or rather, some inner intuition told her that Lord Burke realized his acting efforts had failed, that she knew his secret. Still, he suddenly devoted his attention to a cuff link which was supposedly loose. "I'm glad for you, Miss Jones."

"Begging your pardon, m'lord, but that driver is back," Marie said from the doorway.

"And Mrs. Hammond?" Lord Burke said.

"He says he dropped her off at the house. And that she looked as if she'd been weeping."

"Thank you, Marie. Please have him wait."

When the maid was gone, Lord Burke turned to Rachel. "Do you think this has to do with the child she was visiting?"

"I'm afraid so." But this was risky, Mrs. Hammond going

home alone, what with Mr. Moore assuming they were both having dinner with Lord Burke. "I should see about her."

She started getting to her feet. Lord Burke rose first and offered his hand.

"I'll go with you," he said.

Panic seized Rachel. Quickly she said, "That's very kind, but Mrs. Hammond prefers to be alone when she's melancholy." Rachel certainly couldn't invite him into the house with Mr. Moore there—not that she wouldn't have minded exposing him and his insidious plot.

But then, Lord Burke would know that she had been dishonest about her personal life. What would he think of her if he knew she had participated in the scheme against him in exchange for the promise of a letter of character and some money?

*He would hate you,* she thought dully. Or at least, lose all respect for her for not trying harder to escape from her employers. She was nineteen years old—twenty next month—and had not the excuse of youth anymore. The affection shining from his brown eyes would fade like morning dew in July.

"Very well then," he said, still holding her hand. "I'll walk you to the coach."

Beneath a star-crusted sky, as the driver held the door, Lord Burke raised Rachel's hand to his lips and brushed a kiss against it. "Good evening, Miss Jones."

"Good evening," Rachel murmured back, wishing she could capture this moment forever, like a photographer's camera. Even through the glove, her hand felt the imprint of that kiss all the way to Charles Street. If only she had the right to that kiss!

Or to the art lessons, she thought, exiting the coach. Tears stung her eyes. *You can't accept them.*

"Thank you," she murmured to the driver.

He touched the brim of his hat. "You're welcome, miss."

She entered the house through the kitchen, as usual, and hurried up to the parlor. A chill coursed through her veins at the sight of Mr. Moore's silk bowler hat upon a chair cushion, his frock coat tossed over an arm. But the fact that no sounds were drifting from the ceiling led her to hope that there had not been a fight.

Still, to be sure, she slipped upstairs and listened outside Mrs. Hammond's bedchamber door.

*Thank you for silence,* she prayed from her own cot minutes later. *And thank you for this evening.*

It was with a stab of bittersweet pain that she prayed the latter, for she doubted if she would have another such evening.

*Please watch over Lord Burke.*

She swallowed, and added, *And please help Mrs. Hammond and me to get away from Mr. Moore.*

# 20

Rachel turned toward the kitchen doorway at the sound of familiar footsteps the following morning. She hesitated, taking in a pair of swollen blue eyes. "Are you all right, missus?"

"Yes," Mrs. Hammond replied, entering the kitchen. "Do you think Gerald heard you come in last night?"

"Why, I don't think so. The house was quiet."

Mrs. Hammond blew out a long breath and pulled out a chair. "No doubt he assumed you returned with me. . . . I didn't think about your coming in later. I have to speak with you before he wakes."

Rachel set a cup of tea before her and took the facing chair. "Shall I make you some breakfast?"

"Later." Corrine took a sip from the cup. "If Gerald asks, you must say that I had supper with Lord Burke last night, then took ill on some oysters."

"Yes, missus." Rachel felt a pang of regret at the possibility of having to add still another lie to the lengthy list which she had started at the age of thirteen. *You'll just have to avoid him as much as possible,* she told herself. Already she was in the habit of listening for his voice outside rooms before entering.

*Just a little while longer,* she thought. She would go to Mr.

Solomon, confess that she realized it was Lord Burke who had offered to pay for the lessons. She would ask him to ask his son to tutor her anyway, with the understanding that, once her paintings were good enough to sell, she would repay him. Surely that was possible, if she studied hard. And she *would* study hard, even if that meant working up in her room for hours after chores.

*Then I'll leave—rent a room somewhere and take Mrs. Hammond with me if she wishes to come. We'll warn Mr. Moore we intend to send for the police if he threatens us.*

"Rachel?"

She snapped back to reality. "Sorry, missus. Would you care for more tea?"

Mrs. Hammond was frowning, while her eyes had a faraway look. "Anna was gone yesterday."

"Oh, dear!" A hand went to Rachel's heart. "You mean she . . ."

"Her mother came for her. I didn't get to say good-bye."

Rachel breathed a sigh of relief. "But at least you know she's all right."

"Yes," Mrs. Hammond said listlessly. "She's all right."

At a loss as to how to console her, Rachel thought of the one thing which had always worked in the past. "I'll butter a scone," she offered, starting to push away from the table.

"They're gone. I couldn't sleep last night, and I finished them off."

"Then I'll make more."

"No. There's no time." She leaned closer, and her voice became a whisper. "Gerald says you're to start packing today. We're to leave London as soon as possible."

Rachel's heart lurched. "Leave London!"

"Sh-h-h!" Mrs. Hammond hissed. "He says Scotland Yard's looking for him."

"Only him?"

"It appears so. Perhaps the family of that girl back in Lancaster decided to press charges."

It was too good to be true after all! Rachel swallowed in spite of a lump in her throat. She knew there was no point in even asking about a letter of character or money for living expenses so that she could stay behind. Even if Mr. Moore *was* telling the truth when he made the promise—which she doubted—he would not want to leave any loose threads behind. Not with Scotland Yard after him.

The idea of turning him in entered her mind, bringing a flutter of hope. But then, was he telling the truth about his father's connections? Would he be out within days, and thirsty for revenge?

That was the trouble with living with a liar. One never knew what to believe. She swallowed, asked, "When are we to leave?"

"As soon as I can . . . borrow some money from Lord Burke."

Rachel looked at her, stunned.

"I *know* the man feels nothing for me. But perhaps his generosity will compel him to lend me some anyway."

"But you *can't* do that to him! I won't allow it."

Mrs. Hammond opened her mouth as if to snap a sharp reply. She closed it again, studied Rachel's face. At length she said, "What happened last night, Rachel?"

"Nothing." Rachel closed her eyes, squeezing out tears. "Everything."

"You love him, don't you?"

"Yes," she whispered.

"Then that's wonderful! It means he'll help you get away from Gerald."

It was so startling to hear Mrs. Hammond speak like that, putting her welfare ahead of Mr. Moore's for a change. But Rachel had to shake her head. "I can't ask him."

"But he obviously cares for you."

"He doesn't *know* me. How I've helped . . ." Rachel's voice trailed to nothing.

"Helped us extort money," Mrs. Hammond filled in sadly, then shook her head. "You'll explain you were under direct orders."

Nonetheless, a chill snaked up Rachel's spine at the thought of going to him with her hand out. She shook her head. "I just can't do it."

"Oh, very well. Be stubborn. I'll just have to write your letter of character."

Rachel's breath caught in her throat. "You will?"

"You'll have to find someplace to hide until we're gone. Perhaps with that Mr. Solomon's family." A sheen covered Mrs. Hammond's eyes. "We'll probably never see each other again."

"You're *still* going with him?"

"I *have* to—don't you see? He won't allow me to leave him alive."

"But if he has to leave London, then all you would have to do is hide until he's gone."

Mrs. Hammond laced her fingers together and pressed them into her chin. "And then what?" she said cautiously. "How would I live?"

"You could find a job."

"A job?" She winced. "I'm not qualified to do anything but play the—"

"That's not so," Rachel cut in. "Didn't you work for a dairy before you met Mr. Moore?"

"Well, yes . . ."

It was as if a clock were ticking in Rachel's mind, warning her that they had precious few seconds to waste. "Mrs. Hammond," she said with gentle firmness. "Do you *really* want to continue supporting Mr. Moore the way you—"

"No!" Tears lustered the blue eyes again. She said thickly, "I'm afraid, Rachel."

"And so am I." Rachel reached across the table, took her mistress's trembling hand. "Remember Reverend Morgan's sermon about Daniel? God can give us the courage to do this."

Mrs. Hammond barked a dry laugh. "He'll give *you* the courage. Why would he give me even the time of day?"

"Because he's good."

"Then ask him, Rachel," Mrs. Hammond whispered, squeezing her hand.

Closing her eyes, Rachel said simply, "Father, we haven't much time. Please give us the courage to get away. . . ."

Her hand was squeezed again, tightly.

"Tell him I'm so sorry for everything," came the throaty whisper. "So sorry . . ."

Rachel looked up. Tears were streaming from Mrs. Hammond's closed eyes.

"I think you just did," Rachel whispered back.

Rachel flinched in her chair when a sound came from upstairs. Both pairs of eyes locked. Mrs. Hammond's looked fearful. And yet hopeful.

"I have a plan," Mrs. Hammond whispered, wiping her

cheeks. She paused thoughtfully. "God must have sent it to me. Does he answer prayers that quickly?"

"Sometimes," Rachel said, flinching at another sound upstairs.

"I'll sell my pearls. You and I can live off the money until we find positions."

"I can't accept—"

Mrs. Hammond raised a silencing hand. "We've underpaid you for years. It's the least I can do."

"Thank you, missus." There was no time to argue. Rachel glanced up at the ceiling. "But how will you get them past him?"

"While we're finishing breakfast, slip upstairs and get the necklace from my felt slippers in the back of my wardrobe. You can put them in your apron pocket. Then take your basket out, like you're going to market, and try to sell them."

"To whom, missus?"

"Your Mr. Solomon can advise you, I'm sure. I would sell them myself, but Gerald's expecting me to go to Lord Burke's—and who knows if he'll follow?"

"You're *still* going to Lord Burke's?" Rachel said uneasily.

Mrs. Hammond gave her a knowing smile. "I give you my word, I'll not ask for a shilling. I'll just pretend it's a social call. But I'll tell Gerald he's sending a cheque over tomorrow. That should give us time to slip away."

Pushing out her chair, Mrs. Hammond came around the table and patted her shoulder. "Thank you for giving me hope, Rachel. Perhaps my life will mean something after all."

~

"And when did you say Mr. Moore answered the advertisement for your sister's house?" Joseph Price asked.

Standing in the spacious foyer of his home, Mr. Eugene Graham kneaded his lined brow. "Middle of February or first of March. It's recorded in my ledger if you require the exact date."

"That won't be necessary," Joseph said. "But thank you for offering. I would be grateful for directions to the house, however. I'm still not familiar with the city."

"My pleasure." Mr. Graham lifted his bushy gray eyebrows. "My wife says Mr. Moore has an inheritance coming?"

"Yes. From a distant cousin he kindly lent assistance to several years ago."

"That's good," the man smiled and nodded. "I like to see people get their due rewards."

Joseph smiled. "My feelings exactly."

~

"I think you should wear the red silk," Gerald said after breakfast, scanning the dresses in Corrine's wardrobe. "It won't hurt to show a little cleavage at this point."

"Yes," Corrine answered absently. For the seventh or eighth time, she glanced at the clock on her mantel and wondered if Rachel was having any success with the pearls.

"How much do you think he'll be willing to lend you?"

Corrine held her brush poised against her shoulder. "How much? I'm not sure. We haven't known each other for very long. Two hundred pounds?"

Gerald frowned. "Don't you think he's good for five hundred?"

"Five hundred? I can certainly ask." She would have agreed to a million, just to keep Gerald happy and unsuspecting for a while longer. "Or more, if you wish."

"No, that may not be wise." Gerald sighed bitterly. "If only you'd slept with the man!"

Corrine winced inwardly, but managed to keep her expression serene.

She was glad for this one last reason to visit Lord Burke. She felt compelled to ask his forgiveness for attempting to deceive him—as well as congratulate him for not being deceived! And while she had his attention, she would inform him how Rachel felt about him, including her shame over having unwillingly participated in her and Gerald's schemes.

It would be humiliating, admitting her past. But she could not allow Rachel to throw away her chance at love with such a good man. It was the least she could do for her.

"Are we really leaving in the morning?" she asked Gerald.

"Sooner, if you come back with money. Did you tell Rachel to pack our clothes?"

"Yes. She'll get on it as soon as she returns from market."

"Why did you send her? We don't need food if we're not going to be here."

"We'll need supper tonight," Corrine reasoned smoothly. "As well as a hamper to take on the train."

Gerald nodded. "Good idea—I didn't think about that." His face paled when a knock sounded from downstairs. "Are you expecting anyone?"

"No."

"Then we won't answer it."

"Very well," Corrine said.

He started pacing the floor. "But then . . . they'll only watch the house, and question Rachel when she returns."

Corrine set her brush down and stood. Her knees felt like water. "What do you—"

"Wait!" Gerald said, and held up a warning finger. "If it's the law asking for me, you'll say I got wind of Scotland Yard and left town in a hurry last night. Got that?"

"Yes," Corrine said, nervously tightening the sash to her dressing gown.

Downstairs, she opened the door with trembling hands. Standing on the porch was Jack Taylor, Lord Burke's gardener.

The big man snatched his cap from his head. "Beggin' your pardon, Mrs. Hammond," his deep voice boomed. "Got a letter here, from Lord Burke for Miss Jones."

Corrine was so relieved that she took the envelope without thanking the man. "Very well," she murmured and pushed the door closed.

That was when she realized her mistake, by not simply saying that Rachel was not here and refusing the envclope. She slipped it into the brass stand, pushing it down past Gerald's umbrella. But when she turned, Gerald was standing at the foot of the stairs with arms folded.

"Why would Lord Burke write to Rachel?"

"You heard him?"

"He didn't exactly whisper, whoever he was." Gerald held out a hand. "Come on, let's see it."

With forced casualness, Corrine said, "I didn't accept it."

Gerald advanced slowly, menacingly. "What sort of simpleton do you take me for, Corrine? Where is it?"

"I don't think we should—" She let out a cry as he grabbed her by the waist and shoved his hands into her pockets, and then down the front of her dressing gown, bruising her skin.

"Where is it!"

"I tell you, I don't have it!" she cried.

He pushed her away and started for the door. Two long steps took him to the umbrella stand, and an instant later he was holding the envelope.

"I'm disappointed at your lack of imagination, Corrine," he said, tearing open the seal.

*Just leave now!* Corrine thought. She could meet up with Rachel somehow, warn her. They would both escape.

And Gerald would simply sit back and allow it! Corrine's newfound courage was evaporating quickly. Her feet felt as if they were nailed to the floor. *Oh God, please help us!*

"Let's see what our snow princess has been up to," Gerald muttered. He obviously sensed the agony Corrine was going through, for he kept his face free of any expression. He delighted in tormenting others, allowing them to believe everything was all right—for a little while. How could she ever have found this sadistic man attractive?

"A most interesting letter," he said at last, holding the page out to her. "Perhaps you'd care to read it?"

Now her feet allowed her to move, but only a step backwards. "I don't think . . ."

"Oh, but I insist." There was an ominous gleam in his pale blue eyes. "Or would you like me to read it to you?"

Her throat dry, Corrine took the letter from his hands. Lord Burke's even script was instantly recognizable.

> *My dear Miss Jones,*
>
> *Hershall delivered some documents to St. John's for me this morning. He returned with the news that the child to whom Mrs. Hammond was so attached is gone and that the good woman was inconsolable when she found out last night. Please give her my condolences. I am ashamed to admit I misjudged her*

*greatly. I pray she will not mind that I took the liberty of sending a message to Penelope Morgan, asking if she would look in on her soon.*

*And as long as I am taking liberties, Miss Jones, may I add that I enjoyed yesterday evening more than I could have thought possible? I do not wish to frighten you away, but would you and Mrs. Hammond consider joining me for dinner again this evening?*

*Sincerely yours,*
*Adam*

With fingers trembling, Corrine lowered the page. "Gerald, I realize this looks—"

The back of Gerald's hand struck her face so forcefully that she stumbled backwards and fell.

"I should have realized all along you were lying!" he raged, standing over her with eyes bulging and fists clenched.

"No!" she cried, trying to rise. Her whole face throbbed with pain, and blood trailed down from her nose to her chin. "Please let me explain!"

"Don't you say a word, you traitorous, deceitful—!" Gerald reached down and grabbed her by the front of her dressing gown, yanking her to her feet. This time he slapped her across the face openhanded, keeping a grip on the gown so that she would not fall.

"Please stop!"

He suddenly let go, and Corrine automatically lifted her arms to protect her face. But his fist slammed into her stomach, and she screamed and doubled over.

# 21

As she turned down Charles Street, Rachel was careful not to swing her basket, for two twenty-pound notes, one ten-pound note, and four half-sovereign coins rested beneath the fruits and cheeses.

The pawnbroker Mr. Solomon had recommended had apologized for not offering more, explaining he had to make a profit as well. But seventy pounds seemed a fortune to Rachel. Surely it would provide Mrs. Hammond and her a decent living in a modest lodging house somewhere while they looked for employment. Even after they found jobs, perhaps they could continue to live together. She had a feeling Mrs. Hammond would need some looking after and encouragement, at least until she became used to honest labor.

*Thank you, Father,* she prayed, approaching the house. In just a matter of hours, hopefully, they would be free of Gerald Moore forever. The dark road which had stretched out before her for years had suddenly veered off into a new, brighter direction where anything was possible.

*Anything but seeing Lord Burke again,* she thought. Before her spirits could descend too deeply into melancholy, she reminded herself that one could not expect to engage in deceptions for years and not suffer any consequences.

~

*Must be the maid,* thought Joseph Price, watching from the window of the hired coach as a fair-haired young woman with a basket on her arm went down the service entrance. According to his sources, Corrine Hammond had dark hair.

He fingered the linen curtain. An identical one hung from the opposite and back windows. They were thick enough not to allow any pedestrian a glimpse of the couple who would shortly join him as passengers. And the driver had been well paid not to question his manner of escorting the two to the coach.

Joseph did not relish the idea of binding and gagging a woman, however evil her crimes. If Mrs. Hammond at least agreed to be quiet and not attempt to untie herself, perhaps he would remove the gag when the city was behind them.

Gerald Moore was a different story. Joseph patted the pistol in his coat pocket. He would bind and truss Mr. Moore with every inch of rope he could spare.

~

Gerald kicked like a madman, snapping out of his frenzy only when his ears caught the sound of movement. He left Corrine huddled on the floor and sprinted downstairs. The kitchen was empty, but the larder door was partly open.

"Rachel!" he called, pushing the door wider.

With a startled cry the girl jumped and turned to face him. Her eyes were wide, frightened, like those of a deer caught in a thicket. *Like a girl poised at the edge of a ravine . . .*

She was drawing back, clutching her market basket close to her body like a shield. Gerald's rage was a coal in his chest. He snatched the basket from her hands and flung it against the shelves. The sound of coins pelting the flagstoned floor drew his attention, and he stopped long enough to gape at the over-turned contents.

"Why, what have we here?" he demanded as he seized her shoulders. "You've got Lord Burke paying for your services? Here I was sending the wrong woman . . ."

Rachel's face went white. "No!"

"And how cleverly you played the chaste maiden, only to go throwing yourself at a freak like him! You should be on the stage, Rachel . . . you're quite the actress!"

"I haven't . . ."

But she let out another cry as her eyes lowered to his disheveled shirt. Automatically Gerald glanced down at the red smears.

"Where's Mrs. Hammond?" the girl demanded weakly.

"Dead for all I care!"

"Dead?"

Rachel attempted to pull away from him, but he grabbed her arm and bent it behind her back. Pushing her toward the stairs, he put his mouth inches from her ear and whispered, "We don't need her anymore, dearest Rachel. You and I are going to be partners starting right this minute—in *everything!*"

~

Corrine was able to raise herself to her knees only by strength of will. Never had she been in so much pain—her whole face ached, and her side throbbed so badly that she had to take shallow breaths to keep from passing out.

Her heart skipped a beat when she became conscious of Gerald's muffled, ranting voice. Was he coming back to do her in? She couldn't take another beating.

Crawling on hands and knees, she made it to the door, grabbed the knob, and pulled herself up. *Can't stop now!* she thought, though the urge to lie back down was almost overwhelming.

~

"Wait here," Joseph said to the driver. But then, the instruction was not necessary, he realized, for the man lay slumped to the side, snoring like a pig in the sun.

He decided to slip down the service entrance, knock at the door pretending to be a tradesman. Surely he could determine, just by chatting up the maid, if Gerald Moore and Corrine Hammond indeed were inside. The element of surprise was crucial in a situation like this.

At the bottom step he paused, catching the sound of a man's loud but unintelligible voice. *Must be Moore,* he thought with pulse jumping. Joseph eased the doorknob—it yielded to the pressure of his hand.

~

Holding her side, Corrine opened the door and fell through the doorway. Then she got to her feet again and staggered to the road.

A young man dressed in the clothes of a laborer was passing by on a horse. He dug his heels into the mount's side and hurried away before Corrine could reach him. Panting and still clutching her side, she tried to wave down a carriage with two startled women passengers, but the driver refused to slow down.

Across the street, a driver was slumped, snoring, at the reins of a coach and team.

"Help me!" she called.

When he did not move, she stumbled to the middle of the road, intent upon waking him. The sounds of hooves and wheels came from the near distance. Corrine wheeled around as fast as her fading strength would allow. A hansom cab was slowing down. Waving an arm, she croaked out, "Help!" and fell to one knee.

"Mrs. Hammond?" A familiar voice called down from the inside of the carriage.

"Mrs. Morgan!"

Corrine crumpled to the road. She heard the minister's wife instruct the driver to help her. Moments later she was propped up in a pair of arms. Pain racked her whole body now, but at least she wasn't going to die in the middle of the street.

"Must get Lord Burke before Rachel comes back!" she whispered.

"Let's get the police," Mrs. Morgan said.

Corrine grabbed her arm. "No police! Get Lord Burke. *Now!*"

~

"No!" Rachel screamed, wrestling with Mr. Moore. Her left arm felt as if daggers were cutting at her nerves, but she determined that she'd rather have him kill her than have his way with her.

"You're going to obey me if I have to beat the stubbornness out of you!" he snarled, dragging her through the kitchen and up the stairs. "Don't think you can get away with—"

"Let her go, Moore!"

Still struggling desperately, Rachel caught a glimpse of a

dark-haired, bearded man. He was holding a pistol pointed in their direction.

"What the—?" Mr. Moore jerked his head to look down at the intruder, easing his grip on Rachel a bit. She seized the chance and pulled away, dashing farther up the stairs, out of his reach.

The next thing she heard was a crash, a shriek, and then silence.

"Mr. Moore?" she heard the stranger say hesitantly.

Rachel held a hand to her racing heart and leaned against the wall, catching her breath. She could see Mr. Moore's red face on the floor at the base of the stairs. His panicked eyes were wide open, eyeballs darting in all directions while his mouth was gaping like a fish on land. And then his face froze.

Slowly, she made her way back downstairs.

The tall stranger put his pistol in his pocket and leaned down to touch Mr. Moore's neck. Straightening again, he turned and met Rachel's eyes.

*He must be from Scotland Yard,* Rachel thought. "Is he dead?" she asked.

The man nodded. "He lost his balance. I think his neck's broken." He looked again at Rachel. "Are you all right?"

"I'm not . . . sure," she breathed. She felt weak, and her teeth had started chattering. "You saved my life. Who are you?"

"Joseph Price is my name." He nodded toward the ceiling. "Is Mrs. Hammond . . . ?"

*"Mrs. Hammond!"* With a strength born of sheer panic, Rachel gathered her skirt and hastened upstairs. Drops of blood were flecked upon one wall of the entrance hall, and smears on the floor led a path to the gaping door. Ignoring the

man's questions as he followed in her wake, she ran outside and peered in every direction.

"She *can't* be dead! Not if she could move! But where did she go?"

"Do you think she went for the police?" Mr. Price asked.

"I don't know!"

~

Joseph glanced over at the waiting coach and frowned. Obviously someone had aided Corrine Hammond. She was probably on her way to hospital now, meaning the police would arrive here at the house any minute.

*At least you've got Moore,* he thought grimly. He had to get the body out of the house before anyone could come along to prevent it.

As for Mrs. Hammond—he wasn't about to kidnap a woman who could be dying. He thought about the blood on the floor. Surely she would have to stay in London for a while as she recovered from whatever wounds Moore had inflicted. He would deliver Gerald Moore's remains to Mr. Nowells and return.

"Will you be all right?" he asked the maid, who was taking sluggish steps back toward the house. There was an unnatural pallor about her face, and he wondered again if she might faint.

"Yes, sir," she answered, worry etched into her features. Still, after a few seconds she managed to add, "Thank you for coming inside when you did."

He turned and joined her. "I'm glad he didn't hurt you," he said truthfully. His concern returned to business. "Don't you have *any* idea where Mrs. Hammond might have gone?"

~

*Lord Burke!* Rachel thought. But a warning sounded faintly in her mind, and she merely gave him a blank look. At length he sighed.

"Perhaps you should see a doctor. If there's a blanket you can spare, I'll get Mr. Moore out of the way for you."

Rachel shuddered. "Please take him."

They went back upstairs. Mr. Price waited at the staircase while she went for a blanket and, mercifully, said he did not require her assistance.

"What's your name, miss?" he asked.

"Rachel Jones."

"Are you Mrs. Hammond's housekeeper?"

"Yes, sir."

The man smiled, nodded. "I'm sure I'll be seeing you again soon, Miss Jones."

~

*Just a few more minutes,* Penelope Morgan said to herself in the swaying carriage. She heard a soft moan, then words, and bent closer to the woman she was holding steady. "Mrs. Hammond?"

"Faster," came the whisper.

Penelope tightened her arms and steeled both herself and the woman against the sharp turn up ahead. "He's going as fast as he can."

The lips moved again. "Taking too long. Get police instead."

"Sh-h-h," Penelope answered, wishing she had insisted on doing that in the first place. "We're almost there now." She lifted a silent prayer for Rachel and wondered if the girl was in

288

the hands of whatever monster had so severely beaten Mrs. Hammond.

Seconds later they stopped in Adam's carriage drive. Jack was tending to some shrubbery on the front lawn. "Get Lord Burke!" she called.

The driver had jumped from his seat and was at the side of the carriage now. "What can I do?" he asked, his eyes wide.

"Can you carry her inside?"

"Right away!"

~

Joseph Price sat beside the now-awake driver atop the north-ward-heading coach. Inside lay the body of Gerald Moore, wrapped like a mummy with blanket and rope. He had done it . . . beaten Scotland Yard's finest detectives! *I'm not too old for this job after all!*

He would eventually alert Scotland Yard to the fact that Gerald Moore was deceased—after he had delivered the evidence to Squire Nowells. Perhaps he was guilty of interfering with a murder investigation. But the authorities would no doubt be glad that a murderous beast like Moore had gotten what he deserved. And once the body was examined, there would be no doubt over the cause of death.

Half his job was done. Wherever Corrine Hammond was now, her maid would no doubt tell her that Moore was dead. That should make her feel safe enough so that she would stay in the city until he could return to find her.

~

*Just don't think about him,* Rachel ordered herself as she returned to the larder. Gingerly she picked Mrs. Hammond's money from the overturned fruit and shards of glass. She went to the sink and washed both bank notes and coins, wrapping them in a towel and hiding them behind other towels in the cupboard drawer.

She would clean the larder in a little while, she decided. The entrance hall was more acutely in need of cleaning, for the blood would stain the wood. A raw ache settled in the back of her throat as she filled a pail with water. She had no idea to where Mrs. Hammond had disappeared, or if she would ever see her again.

Ears alert, for she halfway feared Mr. Moore would somehow return, she shoved some rags from the rag bin into her apron pocket with a cake of soap and went upstairs. She scrubbed the floor with an almost maniacal zeal. She was almost at the door when, with her head lowered, she grazed the coat tree with her shoulder. The tree began to sway, and she automatically reached out a hand to steady it. Mr. Moore's cloak fell from a hook and landed across her shoulder and left arm. It smelled of him. With a cry, Rachel shrugged it away. Then everything grew dark.

~

Adam Burke leaned forward and dug his heels into Jupiter's side. As the Cleveland bay gelding galloped around omnibuses, coaches, and wagons on Wellington Road, he became aware that drivers and pedestrians were staring. Whether it was because of the speed of his horse or the scars on his face, he did not care. Rachel was in trouble.

*Why didn't I grab my army pistol?* he upbraided himself. *Or at least my sword!*

It was too late to do anything about that now. He would

use whatever weapon he could find to protect her, even his hands. He only prayed that it was not too late! He rode Jupiter right up to the steps of the house and jumped from the animal. The front door opened readily, and he almost tripped over Rachel's body. To his horror there was blood on the floor.

~

Vaguely aware that whoever had been speaking in her dream was now pressing fingers gently against her scalp, Rachel blinked her eyes, stared up at the foggy image.

"Lord Burke?"

"Rachel!"

His voice was the most welcome sound her ears had ever heard. As her vision sharpened, she noticed the concern in his expression.

"I don't feel any lumps," he said. "Did you fall? Where are you hurt?"

Her thoughts were still muddled. She had to lie there for a few seconds before she realized that she was all right. "Not hurt," she murmured. "Mrs. Hammond . . ."

"She's at my house." He helped her to her feet, then put his arm around her shoulder and led her into the sitting room.

"Is she all right?"

"I left right after Penelope told me you were in trouble," he said as he eased her into the cushions and sat down beside her, "so I don't know the extent of her injuries, or even what happened. Who did this?"

"Mr. Moore."

"Mr. Moore? Who . . . ?"

"He lived here," she tried to explain. "He beat her, and then he tried . . ."

Lord Burke's expression darkened. He made a move as if to get to his feet. "Where is he?"

"He's dead," Rachel answered flatly. She put a hand upon his sleeve. "Gone."

"Where?"

"I'm not exactly sure. A man named Mr. Price took his body away. He saved my life."

Adam leaned back on the cushions and rubbed his temples. "I don't understand any of this, Rachel."

He looked so confused that Rachel's heart went out to him. She longed to have him say that he did not even want to know what had happened in the past. But that wasn't going to happen. Besides, she owed him a confession. But she first had to know if her mistress was going to live.

"May we first see about Mrs. Hammond?" she asked him. "Then I'll explain."

"Are you strong enough?"

"Yes."

He nodded. "Jack's bringing the wagon. He should be here shortly."

When he turned away and didn't speak for a little while, Rachel thought he was angry. Unsure of what to do, she touched his arm again. He turned his face toward her. Tears were shining in his eyes.

"Lord Burke?"

Hesitating only for a brief moment, he drew her close. The feel of his arms about her, of her head resting against his strong shoulder, made her feel protected, safe, for the first time in years.

"I'm so sorry," she whispered.

"Sorry?" His voice thickened. "I was so afraid I'd lose you right after I found you."

"You were?" she said, hard to believe her ears.

"I was so lonely when you came into my life. I've fallen in love with you, Rachel."

What bittersweet torture to hear those words when she did not deserve them! "You don't mean that, Lord Burke," Rachel said, squeezing her eyes shut against the burning tears.

"Call me Adam, please. And I do, Rachel." Gently he cupped her chin, raised her face to look at him. "Is it . . . possible at all that you feel the same way for me?"

"I—"

She could not say the rest, but something in her expression must have spoken for her, for he gave her an incredulous smile. "Dearest Rachel."

"You won't feel that way after I explain . . . everything."

"I think I need to hear it," he said. "But, Rachel, whatever it is, it won't make me stop loving you."

# 22

L ucy was standing on the porch, wringing her hands. She rushed out to the wagon. "I was afraid you were dead!" she blurted to Rachel, her red-rimmed eyes proof of her state of mind.

"I'm fine." Rachel gave the girl a weak smile and allowed Adam to help her down to the carriage drive. "How is Mrs. Hammond?"

"I'm not sure. Mum and Doctor Gilford are in there with her now. Mrs. Morgan, too."

"How about you make Miss Jones some strong tea?" Jack suggested to his daughter as he approached, holding Jupiter's reins.

"I believe we all could use some, Lucy," Adam said. He turned to Rachel again. "Are you able to walk?"

"I am." They left Jack to tend the horses and went inside. Though concern about the condition of her mistress was uppermost in her mind, Rachel couldn't help but think, *Am I able to walk?* With his strong arm about her like that, she almost felt that she could fly.

~

Doctor Gilford was leaving the guest room.

"How is she?" Adam asked.

"Her ribs are bruised badly, but none appear to be broken," the doctor replied. "I can't say the same for her nose. That was where all the blood came from. She is asleep at the moment. I shall return this evening to see about her."

"You don't think she needs to be in a hospital?"

"That isn't necessary. She'll mend much more quickly right where she is. Complete bed rest for at least three weeks. I've given her some laudanum. I almost had to give her another dose to calm her. She was quite concerned about a young lady. . . ." Looking over his spectacles, Doctor Gilford seemed to notice Rachel for the first time. He gave Adam a questioning look.

"This is Miss Jones," Adam said, "the young lady Mrs. Hammond was worried about. Would you examine her as well?"

"I'm fine," Rachel protested. "I'd like to stay with her so she won't be alone when she wakes."

"Now, now," Doctor Gilford clucked in mild reproof. "That will be hours from now, and there is already a woman with her. Perhaps you are fine, but let me just make certain that you aren't going to faint ten minutes after I'm gone."

They moved into the drawing room, and after Rachel was persuaded to take a seat on a couch, the doctor peered into her eyes with practiced skill. "Your pupils are not dilated." After taking her pulse, he continued to hold her arm. "Your skin still feels warm," he remarked with a smile. "That is a good sign."

"Are you sure?" asked Adam, hovering over them. "She still looks pale to me."

"Some rest would be good for her, but I see no evidence of anything that should alarm us." Straightening, he gathered up his black bag. "I'll be back this evening. Send for me in the meantime if you need me."

Lucy came and served tea. She had just left when Penelope Morgan hurried into the room. The minister's wife sat down beside Rachel. "I was so worried!" she exclaimed, putting an arm around her. "Mrs. Hammond didn't want me to summon the police until it was too late to do so. I've felt wretched since we arrived here. I was afraid that something would happen to you, and it would be my fault."

"Please don't blame yourself," Rachel said. "The police couldn't have gotten there any faster than Mr. Price."

"Mr. Price?" she asked. "Was it he who beat Mrs. Hammond so severely?"

~

Rachel had not had a chance to take a sip of tea yet, but the warmth of the cup in her hands was a comfort. "No. Mr. Price saved my life." She blinked, trying to recall exactly what he had said to her. "He was from Scotland Yard. And he took Mr. Moore's body away."

Mrs. Morgan shook her head. "I'm sorry, I don't understand. Was *Mr. Moore* the man who beat Mrs. Hammond?"

"He fell . . . an accident."

"Why was Scotland Yard after him, Rachel?" Adam asked. "Are you in some kind of trouble?"

Rachel looked up into his grave brown eyes "I'm not sure," she answered in a feeble voice. "I just don't know."

Mrs. Morgan patted her arm and got to her feet. Quietly, she said, "I'm going up to inform Bernice that you're safe, if Lucy hasn't already. Then I must go home. I'm certain that Robert will want to come back here this evening and see about Mrs. Hammond, so we'll visit with you then."

Adam rose as well, walked her to the door, then returned to sit beside Rachel.

"It's time to tell me everything."

"Yes," Rachel murmured.

"But drink your tea first," he said gently.

She did so, and then he took the cup and saucer from her hand. Avoiding his eyes, she gave an account of her part in the extortion of Squire Nowells and half dozen other men. She had to pause and draw a fortifying breath when she reached the part about Mrs. Hammond's most recent target.

"I delivered letters here that I knew were written to ensnare you," she confessed. "It was only a miracle that you weren't duped. You're the first one."

Silence enveloped the room. She sat staring at the hands clutched in her lap and waiting for him to walk out.

But when he finally spoke, it was to say, softly, "Tell me again, Rachel . . . how old were you when Corrine and this man took you from the orphanage?"

"Almost thirteen."

"And you're nineteen now. That makes over six years of being manipulated by a pair of clever criminals. You can't be held responsible for that."

Rachel shook her head. "You're being kind, making excuses for me. But I could have at least left them. At least in the workhouse I wouldn't have had to tell lies and hurt people."

"No, you wouldn't," he agreed. "But it would have been a hard choice to leave the only home you knew, however mistreated you were. I understand that."

"I don't want you just to *understand*. What I want . . ." She drew in a shaky breath. "What I *need* is your forgiveness."

"Very well," Adam replied at once. He gathered her hands up in his own. "I forgive you, Rachel. The past is over, so let's concentrate on the future."

They sat in silent harmony for a little while, Rachel thanking God beneath her breath that the bad years of her life seemed to be over for good. And then Adam gave her a worried look.

"But what should be done about Mrs. Hammond? Shouldn't the police . . ."

"Oh, please don't," Rachel pleaded. "She's changed. You mustn't blame her for this."

"But you don't have to be afraid of her anymore, Rachel."

"I'm not afraid of her. She tried to help me get away from Mr. Moore. In fact, that's probably why he beat her."

He didn't look convinced. "What if she tries to extort money from someone else in the future?"

"She's not going to do that."

"How can you tell?" he probed gently.

"I just know," she answered. "You forgave me. Can't you forgive her?"

He raised her hand and kissed it. "For you, I could forgive Napoleon. In fact, she's welcome to stay here for as long as she needs. And as *long* as she behaves."

"Thank you, Lord Burke."

"Adam," he reminded her.

Rachel smiled. "Adam."

He returned her smile. "Now, what will we do with you? We certainly can't send you back to that house alone." His brow dented in concentration. "And it wouldn't be proper to have you stay here."

"It wouldn't?" she asked before thinking. Not that she

would have *asked* to stay, but she would have thought he would want her to look after Mrs. Hammond, so that she would not be a burden to his servants.

"Not with my feeling for you the way I do," he said, and the warmth in his voice was even more comforting to Rachel than the tea had been. "I'll ask my solicitor to recommend a hotel with a good reputation. . . ."

"I can't afford a hotel, Adam," she said, and held up a hand before he could say what she knew was on his lips. "And I'll not accept charity from you."

"I could lend—"

"No."

He sighed. "Very well then. How much money have you?"

"Well, only four shillings or so," she confessed.

"Four sh—"

"But Mrs. Hammond had me sell her pearls so that we'd have something to live on while we looked for jobs."

She hated the thought of using any of it until Mrs. Hammond could be moved, however, as it was not rightfully hers. An idea struck her. "Do you think the Morgans would hire me for three weeks or so . . . for room and board alone?"

"You mean, as a servant?"

"That's what I am, Adam," she reminded him.

He winced and then blew out a sigh. "You're quite stubborn, aren't you?"

"So I've been told. I could help them with Mrs. Morgan's mother, and with Margaret."

Adam thought it over. At length he said, "Very well. I'll ask. They'll probably be delighted, and I would feel better about your being with them."

"Thank you," Rachel said.

The crooked smile returned to his face. He kissed her gently, then rested her head against his shoulder. "Just please don't get too comfortable over there."

~

Mrs. Hammond lay propped up on several pillows. Her nose was swathed with white bandages and her bruised face was shaded a deep purple. Her eyes were the only part of her that moved, following Rachel from the door to the side of the bed.

"Oh, Mrs. Hammond!" Rachel breathed.

"Rachel," came a hoarse whisper through stiff, barely moving lips.

"Are you hurting terribly?" It was a foolish question; Rachel could see that she was in pain.

"Doesn't matter. You're safe. How . . . you got away?"

"It's a long story. Perhaps I should tell you when you're better."

Mrs. Hammond gave a slight shake of the head, then winced at the effort. "Does he know where we are?"

Rachel lifted a hand from the coverlet. "He's dead. He can't hurt you anymore."

There was no reaction from the woman in the bed, and for a moment Rachel wondered if she had heard. She was just about to repeat herself when Mrs. Hammond asked, "Are you sure?"

"I saw him die."

Mrs. Hammond's eyes began blinking tears. "I should . . . have died, too."

"Oh, no." Gently, Rachel squeezed her hand. "You mustn't say that."

301

"Hurt too many people . . . just like Gerald. Why didn't God let me die?"

A soft knock prevented Rachel's reply. Dr. Gilford, accompanied by Bernice, entered into the room. "I see my patient is awake," the man said as he carried his black bag over to the bed.

Rachel leaned close to murmur, "Maybe God has a good reason for letting you live."

~

A week later, Corrine was sitting up in the bed in Lord Burke's guest room.

"The soup was delicious."

Bernice smiled and moved the tray to a nearby dresser. "Thank you, Mrs. Hammond. Now, let's get you back under the covers."

Corrine winced as the cook helped her slide down from the pillows.

"Are you hurting much?" Bernice asked.

"My ribs still hurt a bit when I move, but I believe I could manage the stairs now. It must be a terrible inconvenience to bring my meals up here."

But Bernice waved away her concern. "It's no bother at all. And let's wait and try the stairs on Sunday . . . that is, if you're still determined to go to the meeting."

"I'd like to go very much." For the first time, the thought occurred to Corrine that Lord Burke probably knew about her past by now. He had not turned her in to the police, no doubt for Rachel's sake, but would he welcome her at his chapel meetings?

She bit her lip and looked up at Bernice. "The only thing is . . ."

"Yes?"

"Do you think I'll be welcome?"

The cook smiled. "You're worried about that? Well, Lord Burke asked me this morning if I thought you would need some help with the stairs, come Sunday."

"He did?"

"Indeed he did. We'll have to get one of your pretty dresses ready, and Dora can style your hair for you."

"It won't help, I don't think." Corrine lifted a hand and gingerly touched her swollen nose. "I've put so much stock in my appearance—it seems somehow fitting that this should happen to me."

"Now, you mustn't say things like that," Bernice scolded as she stood over her. "Doctor Gilford said it'll still take a while for the swelling to go down, but one day it'll be almost as good as new—you'll see. As for its being fitting, you could have died coming here to get help for Rachel, so don't be too hard on yourself."

Corrine gave her a weak smile. "Thank you, Bernice."

The cook smiled back. "Well, I had best return to my kitchen."

"Will I see you at supper time?"

"Try and stop me! You think I trust anyone else around here to see that you get the proper nourishment?"

When Bernice had left, Corrine closed her eyes and waited for sleep. After the first day, the doctor had left some laudanum in case her bruised ribs caused too much pain, but she had refused every time Bernice or one of the maids offered to give her a dose. *I've numbed my thoughts too many times,* she told herself. *It's time to face the things I've done.*

Some of the scenes from her life that replayed in her mind were far more painful than her physical injuries. She wondered what Jenny was doing at this moment. And Thomas, her own husband . . . would he still be terribly bitter that she had left, even after all these years?

She was determined to find out, one way or another. Dr. Gilford had said that, since none of her bones were broken, she could ride in a carriage in about two more weeks. She would go to Leawick and see if it was possible to make amends for the hurt she had caused two innocent people.

# 23

I thought you'd never get here!" Adam greeted Rachel and the Morgans in the hall on Sunday morning.

"Were you missing me, my friend?" Reverend Morgan teased. "Or was it Penelope or little Margaret here that you couldn't wait to see?"

Adam patted Margaret's curls and then reached for Rachel's hand. "Why, I missed all of you equally, of course."

And then he winked at Rachel, causing the minister to chuckle and his wife to smile.

The Morgans had refused to consider hiring Rachel as a maid.

"You're to stay as our guest," Mrs. Morgan had said. Still, Rachel made it a point to lend a helping hand to the house-keeper and entertain Margaret and Mrs. Morgan's invalid mother, an agreeable woman named Mrs. Woodhouse.

Her first art lesson was Wednesday morning past. Now that she had more free time, Reuben Solomon had graciously agreed to change the day and time of the appointment. He was a talented artist and a patient tutor. She was still uncertain when to tell Adam that she was aware that he had arranged the lessons. For now, she would allow him to enjoy his little secret. She would thank him by working hard to become the finest artist she could be.

~

The theme of the sermon was the grace of God. Seated in Lord Burke's comfortable overstuffed armchair, carried into the drawing room just for her, Corrine drank it all in. Marie and Dora had fussed over her, gathering her dark hair in ringlets at the crown of her head.

But they could do nothing for the swollen bridge of her nose. It didn't matter. Corrine was barely aware of her appearance, or of the fact that she was dressed up for the first time in days. Closing her eyes, she drank in the words of Scripture the minister was reading.

"'Where sin abounded, grace did much more abound.'"

~

After the worship service, Mrs. Hammond was positively glowing, but too physically drained to continue sitting. She allowed Hershall and Jack to help her upstairs, first admonishing Bernice not to follow with a tray. "I'd like you to stay and enjoy your lunch," she told the cook. "Besides, I'm more in need of a nap right now than food."

Rachel insisted on escorting them upstairs so that she could turn the covers. After the men had left, she brushed a kiss against her former mistress's forehead. "Sleep well," she whispered.

"Thank you," Mrs. Hammond murmured.

"And I'll come up later and tell you what happened during lunch."

"Oh?" Mrs. Hammond gave her a weak smile. "Some important announcement, perhaps?"

Rachel returned her smile and thought of the walk she and

Adam had taken in the garden two evenings ago when she accompanied the Morgans here for their usual Friday evening.

"You'll be able to entertain yourselves for a bit?" he had asked his old friends after supper.

"We'll try," Reverend Morgan replied with a knowing smile.

Close enough to the pear tree to hear an occasional *peep*, Adam gathered her into his arms.

"I know it's soon to be asking, Rachel," he said. "But I've waited for someone like you all of my life. Will you marry me?"

Rachel had given her reply a heartbeat later.

~

She arranged the coverlet about Mrs. Hammond's shoulders. "You'll find out after your nap."

~

When the sweet course, an excellent rice pudding, was reduced to a few moist grains at the bottoms of dessert dishes, Adam stood at the head of the table.

"If you please, I have an announcement."

A hush fell upon the room. Rachel blushed and smiled at the glances sent her way.

"I'm pleased to announce, in the company of everyone we hold dear, that Rachel has consented to be my wife," he said. "What I would like to ask . . ."

He stopped, smiled at Rachel, and corrected himself. "What *we* would like to ask, is that you attend our wedding as soon as Robert can arrange to marry us."

Congratulations rose up from all corners of the table.

"This is the best day of my life!" Lucy enthused.

Rachel looked about at the expressions of warmth and acceptance, and realized that she had a family at last.

"If *when* you plan to get married is dependent upon me," Reverend Morgan said, "I can marry you in the morning. After all, the chairs are already set up in the drawing room."

"That's probably too soon," Adam replied. "I don't think you could have Saint Andrew's ready by morning."

"You wish to marry in a *church,* m'lord?" Marie asked.

Even Rachel was caught by surprise. She, too, had assumed that the wedding ceremony would be held here in Adam's home.

Adam cocked an innocent eyebrow. "Why, a church is the proper place to have a wedding, is it not?"

"But, Lord Burke," Lucy blurted, "you don't like folks to see—" At the sharp looks from her parents, the girl cut her sentence short.

"It's all right, Lucy. I've hidden away in this house long enough. It's time to see what London looks like in the daylight."

Reverend Morgan was beaming. "I think it's a wonderful idea!"

"What made you come to this decision?" Mrs. Morgan asked.

"I had a little help." Adam sent Bernice a wink. His voice grew husky with emotion. "If this lovely woman can accept me as I am, then I must accept myself as well. Perhaps when people realize I'm not ashamed, they'll see a picture of a man who has found God's grace to be truly sufficient."

Another hush filled the room, broken only by a few sniffles. Adam turned to Rachel, his face lit with the crooked smile she had come to love. "That is, if anyone even notices me. I suspect that all eyes will be on the beautiful woman at my side."

# A Note from the Author

Dear Reader,

You're obviously fond of historical novels. And I obviously am too! Particularly stories set in Victorian England. I love the romance and innovation of the era, and am fascinated by the ironclad rules of convention which governed upper classes and servants alike.

And the dresses! Surely that was when women looked their most feminine. Not that I would wish to spend my days in tight corsets and layers of silk, mind you. Especially down here in south Louisiana!

I do hope you enjoyed *Like a River Glorious*. If you've ever felt trapped by adverse circumstances, have ever been plagued by fear, you may have identified with Rachel Jones. And if you've ever tasted victory (and I hope you have), you know how sweet it was to her when she finally achieved it. I agree with Zig Ziglar, who says, "Happiness is not pleasure; it's victory."

May God bless you with health, faithful friends, and many victories!

Warmly,

Lawana Blackwell

# About the Author

Lawana Blackwell is an accomplished novelist whose books have found a strong following. Her books include *The Widow of Larkspur Inn*, *The Courtship of the Vicar's Daughter*, *The Dowry of Miss Lydia Clark*, and *The Maiden of Mayfair*. She and her husband live in Baton Rouge, Louisiana, and are empty-nesters who love every opportunity to get together with their three recently married sons and their wives. Besides writing, Lawana enjoys Home and Garden Television, vegetarian cooking, and garage sales.

Lawana welcomes letters written to her in care of Tyndale House Author Relations, P.O. Box 80, Wheaton, IL 60187-0080.

Turn the page

for an exciting preview

from Lawana Blackwell's

next HeartQuest book,

*Measures of Grace*

# *Measures of Grace*

t ten o'clock the next morning, a cleaner, much more
presentable Joseph Price knocked on the front door
of the house on Clifton Hill. A maid opened the door
seconds later, an older woman with striking blue eyes. "Yes,
sir?" she said.

"Good morning, madam," Joseph said, smiling and holding
his hat. "My name is Joseph Price. I'm looking for a Miss
Rachel Jones. Would she happen to be here?"

"Miss Rachel?" The maid returned a shy smile. "She's in
Paris, sir—on her honeymoon."

"Her honeymoon? You don't say?"

She nodded. "Got married last week, to Mr. Adam, the
man who owns this house. Would you care to leave her a
message?"

"I don't suppose it's necessary." Joseph shrugged. The look
of discouragement he gave the maid came easy, for he was
beginning to doubt the wisdom of this rash course of action.

"Is there something wrong, sir?" asked the woman at the
door.

"Of course not," he answered right away, then let out a
sigh. "She probably doesn't even remember me anyway."

315

"Are you a relative, Mr. Price?"

"A relative? No, not at all. I just wanted to make certain that the lady is suffering no ill effects from . . ." He stopped and smiled. "But of *course* she's fine now, isn't she? After all, she was well enough to get married."

"Ill effects, sir?" The maid tilted her head. "Are you talkin' about that bad man who . . ." Her voice trailed off, and she watched him with a questioning expression.

*There we are!* Joseph thought. Of course she had heard about the girl's struggle with Mr. Moore. As in other households, it was impossible to keep the goings-on from the servants. Wearing a frown, he offered, "The fellow was a scoundrel, ma'am, not deserving to be called a man."

Her face brightened. "You're the gentleman that helped her get away, aren't you?"

Joseph hung his head modestly. "Any gentleman would have done so, madam. I just happened to be nearby when the lady was in distress." Taking a reluctant step backward, he replaced the hat on his head. "But since she's away, I suppose . . ."

"Wait," she said, opening the door wider. "Mrs. Hammond will be wantin' to meet you, I'm sure."

He stopped short, his heart quickening in his chest. "Mrs. Hammond?"

"Mrs. Burke . . . Rachel, I mean, was her maid. Mrs. Hammond is stayin' here for a while. She's been wondering about the man who helped Miss Rachel get away." Her eyes took on a pleading expression. "Wouldn't you have time to let me tell Mrs. Hammond that you're here?"

Removing his hat again, Joseph clutched it to his chest and smiled. "If you think it's important to your Mrs. Hammond, I've got all the time in the world."

The woman led him down a central hall to a large drawing room, its walls pale green above rich cherry wainscoting. She motioned to a comfortable-looking wingback chair, then asked him to have a seat. "Mrs. Hammond was in the conservatory a little while ago," she said as she started back for the door. "I'll see if she's still there. May I fetch you some tea?"

Joseph was settled into the chair. "Why don't we wait and see if Mrs. Hammond cares to have some?"

With a nod the maid was gone. Joseph listened to the sound of her shoes against the quarry tiles, counting the steps mentally until they faded away. Presently, two sets of footsteps approached.

A stunning woman, petite and shapely with raven black hair, came through the doorway, followed by the maid. Rising from his chair, Joseph opened his mouth to speak but found himself at a loss for words.

"Mr. Price," the woman said, walking toward him with her hand outstretched. Her voice was low, almost husky, but still very feminine. "How good of you to call."

"Thank you," he managed, irritated at himself as he gave a little bow over her hand. He had expected the woman to be beautiful, of course, but he hadn't expected that she would make him feel awkward, like a schoolboy. Her simply cut ecru gown he would have considered plain on any other woman. But the lack of decoration on her garment drew attention to her huge, smoky gray eyes, delicately clefted chin, and flawless complexion.

The only thing that rescued her face from being classically beautiful was a slightly Roman nose. Far from hindering her looks, it gave her face character, something he was not expecting to see.

*Remember all the poor fools she's destroyed,* he reminded himself as he watched her lower herself into the chair facing his. She was waving away the maid's attempts to assist her. "I'm all right, Dora." She smiled up at the woman. "Would you mind bringing some tea?"

"Right away, Mrs. Hammond," said the maid and left the room.

Corrine Hammond was looking his way now. "Dora tells me that you're the one who rescued my former maid, Rachel."

He was disconcerted to feel warmth in his cheeks. "Actually, the scoundrel fell down the stairs. I just surprised him, and it caused him to stumble."

"How fortunate that you came when you did." She studied his face, her gaze direct without seeming bold. "I've thanked God for your intervention, sir, ever since Rachel told me what happened."

*Thanked God?* He was taken aback until he reminded himself that the Corrine Hammond he had heard so much about was an expert at presenting herself as a proper lady. "I'm just glad the girl wasn't hurt," he finally replied. Leaning forward, he looked at her with concern. "But what about you, Mrs. Hammond? I seem to remember the girl worrying that her mistress had been injured."

"I'm fine now." A look of sadness passed over her features, and she murmured, "That was a terrible day."

Joseph could *almost* feel sorry for her. "At least it's in the past now," he said gently.

～

That night Corrine, dressed in her dimity nightgown, pushed aside a pillow on the window seat in her bedroom and sat down, turning toward the glass. She blew out the candle and pressed her forehead against the windowpane. The sky was brilliant tonight, and she squinted her eyes in the direction of a cluster of stars and wondered if she were looking at a constellation. Little Bear, perhaps?

Gerald Moore had taught her many things about the world, but everything she had learned had been for the purpose of getting ahead by using people. There were so many little things that she didn't know, so much knowledge that other people took for granted.

The sense of loneliness she had felt all evening had settled in her chest, causing an actual ache. She wished she could talk with Bernice now, but she had taken enough of the good woman's time away from her family. Lucy needed her mother, and Jack needed his wife.

Besides, she wouldn't want to see the disappointment that would be on the cook's face if she knew. Bernice and the others had been so proud of her when she decided to become a Christian. How could she reveal to any of them that she had failed so soon?

*I was sure that part of my life was gone forever,* she thought, frowning bitterly. How easy it had been to fall back into her old ways, if only for a moment.

As grateful as she had been to that Mr. Price for saving Rachel, she now wished that he had waited just a few more days to visit. Why did such a handsome, charming man have to call when her faith was still so obviously weak?

This morning, as she sat across from him, she had found herself wondering if he had a wife, if he thought her broken nose made her look unattractive—even, for just a moment, how his strong arms would feel around her! A shudder of humiliation racked her. *I'm a married woman!*

She chewed on her knuckle. *What if it happens again? Am I going to have those thoughts every time I talk with a man?*

Bernice had warned her that temptations would come, but Corrine had been too wrapped up in the joy of her salvation, too certain that she would never want to go back to her old ways again, to pay the warning much heed. She had glibly imagined that when temptation came, it would be to commit an act that she wouldn't want to commit anyway, like using bad manners at the table or even killing someone.

*I didn't know it would be something so hard to resist.* What had Bernice told her about that? A picture of the cook's face came into her mind. *"Resist the devil, and he'll flee,"* she had said.

That was what she was going to have to do. If men were still her weakness, she would have to make sure that she didn't get into another situation like the one she was in this morning. And she would pray to God that if the temptation came again, he would give her strength to resist it.

# *Must-Reads!*

**HEART QUEST**

## OVER A MILLION BOOKS SOLD!

**WILD HEATHER**
*Olivia Hewes and Randolph Sherbourne
are drawn toward a forbidden love that will
mean betraying both their families.*

**DANGEROUS SANCTUARY**
*Kent Anderson is committed to making
Camp Hope a sanctuary for his campers.
But when Georgia MacGregor joins his
staff, her troubled past threatens to
endanger them all.*

Visit **www.heartquest.com** today!